DEMON SEED
BY
JASON R. DAVIS

Published by
JASON R. DAVIS
Weston, WI 54476

Please visit us online at http://jasonrdavis.com

Author website
http://jasonrdavis.com

Cover Illustration and Design by
Don Noble

Special Thanks to
The Cameron Family

CHAPTER 1

"Mommy! Daddy!" David sat up in bed, throwing anything he could grab—his pillow, a few toy cars, and a rock—across the room. The rock hit the far wall with a solid crash, bouncing off it just a few inches from the gap into the darkness.

His closet door was open just an inch, but the thing hiding beyond it lay in wait for him. He heard its breathing, the harsh rasps punctuated by a long growl.

When a door opened, David jumped, thinking this was it. The creature would rush across the room and tear him apart like he had seen happen to those other kids. It was there for him, and it was going to get him.

Light ripped through the room, chasing away the darkness. His dad stood in the doorway only a few feet from the closet, but he didn't even look toward it. He was oblivious to the danger as he shuffled across the room. His eyes were only open to slits, his hair a mess, and he wore only a t-shirt and gym shorts.

"Hey ya', buddy. Bad dream?" his dad asked as he sat on the edge of the bed. David already had his legs pulled up to his chest, leaving plenty of room for his dad to sit without the risk of squashing him.

"No, it's real! It's in the closet. It was coming out, and it wanted to get me!" David said in a rush, pointing to the closet.

"Yeah?" His dad stood, the bedsprings creaking.

As he walked to the door, David fought the desire to scream out, *No! Don't do it! Get away from the door and get them out of here. None of them were safe. The creature wanted to kill them all and it wouldn't stop until it had.*

His dad pulled open the door, making an exaggerated action of looking through the contents and studying the clothes hanging there. "Nothing scary in here."

"It comes out when the lights are off and no one else is here."

This wasn't the first time the creature had come. He had been hearing it for the last week, making different noises in the closet. He had called out many times, and each time, his mother came in to check on him. This was the first time his dad had been home since the monster started terrorizing them. It was also the first time the creature actually appeared from the closet, and David knew it was their last night. It would get them all.

"How does it get in?" His dad quietly closed the door to the closet so as not to wake anyone else. His mom must still be asleep in the other room. David's screams were not loud enough to reach her tonight.

"I don't know. He just comes to get me." David had meant to say "us."

"Yeah?"

"Yeah."

"I think you need to stop watching horror films before bed."

David blew out his breath. "I know they're not real, Dad."

"Yeah? Then we're good, right? You know it's all fake, so you shouldn't be having these nightmares."

"Dad?"

"Yeah, bud?"

"It's not a nightmare. I know the difference. I've seen it."

"Yeah?"

"I saw it earlier. It was the monster from your film. It has those glowing red eyes and long nails. It's like an evil, porcupine man-shaped thing. I saw its long nose come out of the closet, those glowing eyes looking at me."

David wanted to say he had seen more, but didn't think his dad would believe it had crept back into the closet when he had started throwing things. He knew he would just point out that a big, scary monster, especially like the ones in his films, wouldn't have hidden away from things thrown at it by a nine-year-old.

"You said it's from my film? How did you see it? The movie, I mean."

"It was on cable tonight," David mumbled, playing with the blanket and avoiding his father's gaze. He knew he wasn't supposed to watch the creature features, but they were fun. Not only that, but the host was funny and had this thing called the "kill counter", which showed how many people had been killed during the movie. His dad's movies never rang too high on the kill counter, but David liked them. How cool was it that his dad directed them? "Though they cut out all the good stuff."

His dad smirked. "The good stuff, eh?"

"Yeah."

"You remember John Winters? He comes to the parties your mom throws every year."

"Yeah. The really tall guy."

"Yeah. Well, he's the one wearing that costume. He plays the porcupine-man, as you call it."

"I know it's just a man in a costume, Dad. But the one in my closet is real. I saw it. He was coming out to get me. He wants to eat me. He wants to get all of us."

"David, come on. You just told me it wasn't real."

"The one on TV isn't."

"Okay, how about this? Tomorrow morning, I will take you to the set with me and you can see the costume. It's not real."

His dad reached out and ruffled his hair, giving him that bright smile. Most times, it reassured David to see it. His dad always exuded confidence with that smile, but now it just let David know he was being ignored. He had to get his dad to listen.

"Yes, it is!"

"Just wait until morning, okay?"

David looked at the closet. The door was closed. It was quiet now that his dad had come into the room. Maybe it would be okay. The monster had left before, letting them live another night.

Maybe his dad had some superpower that scared away monsters. Maybe his movies weren't as fake as he liked to say. Maybe it was because his dad truly was some monster slayer, and now that he was in the room, the beast had gotten scared and ran away.

"Okay."

His dad stood. He bent down to give David a kiss on the forehead and a hug before pulling back and looking into his eyes. "Remember, Davey. I'll show you it's only a movie. Just remember, it's only a movie."

David watched him walk to the door and stop for one last look back, his hand lingering over the light switch. "Get some sleep. I'm sure Tammy would love to see you on set tomorrow. We'll have a fun day of it."

David smiled briefly, thinking of the lead actress in his dad's film, Tammy Sheep. She was really nice and always had a huge smile for David when she saw him.

His dad flipped off the light and closed the door, plunging his room into partial darkness. His Batman nightlight, which his dad had gotten him after they saw the Lego version, lit the room in a faint yellowish glow.

David looked at it, then back at the closet. The door was still closed. Should he put something in front of it, just in case? He had his toy chest. It was heavy and wouldn't be easy to move, but he thought he could push it across his room.

No, that wouldn't work. He remembered he had tried to move it once when his mom was vacuuming, but had to wait for her to help him.

What else did he have that could block the door?

He had himself... He could sit against it, but then how would he sleep? Well, he supposed he could sleep on the floor in front of it.

He pulled himself out of bed and crept across the floor, walking on his tiptoes. For each step he took, he held his breath. He heard his dad in the bathroom, then walking down the hall to their bedroom.

Finally, David made it to the door. He planned on sitting down immediately, but thought since he had made it this far, maybe he should listen first.

He slowly leaned forward...

The door clicked open. He hadn't even touched it yet but had been close enough to see it open a crack, then a little bit more, hearing the unmistakable growl on the other side.

David didn't hesitate. Remembering how the monster had torn through the walls in his dad's movie, he knew holding the door closed would never work. He shouldn't have wasted his time. He should have just snuck out of the room and slept on the couch or on the floor in his parents' room. Although, with his dad home, he probably wouldn't have been allowed to sleep in there tonight. Even if he had, the monster would still get them all, anyway. It was coming after them. It was going to get him.

At least he could warn his parents. His dad, the monster slayer, probably wouldn't be able to save him, but he could save his mom. He had to warn them!

"Dad!" he screamed as he dove into his bed, quickly pulling the covers over his head.

* * * *

David followed his dad as he walked down the hallway. The security guard, a larger, older man, led them through the maze of offices until they reached a door. David's dad unlocked it, then nodded to the guard.

"Thanks for letting us in, Chuck. He just won't go to sleep until I show him."

His dad stepped into the room, flicking on the lights to flood the room with the glow of fluorescents. David's breath caught. He had been on his dad's set a few times, but it was usually with an assistant watching him, and they always stayed on the set. Now he saw where the magic was created.

Wardrobe carts, packed with costumes, filled the room. Most were normal clothes, but as the carts went deeper into the room, David saw various creatures hanging there. At the end of the room was a full porcupine man costume staring right at them, its large size towering over the rest of the wardrobe.

David followed his dad into the room, his mouth hanging open. There was just so much in there. He was sure he saw a costume from the cheesy old movie Flash Gordon. Although, after he walked past it, he guessed it could have just looked like it. It might have just been some knockoff that his dad used in the background of his own movie. Like something a character in the movie was watching on TV.

Anything was possible. After all, it was the movies.

"So, this is where we keep all the monsters," his dad said, running his fingers along some of the costumes hanging from the rack. He pointed to the porcupine man at the end.

"Wow. Is this where you work?"

His dad chuckled as he bent down, picking his son up. "Yep, this is where daddy works." His dad looked at the security guard as he approached.

"David, your dad here..." Chuck nodded toward David's dad as he joined them, "runs the whole shebang. He makes all those scary horror films that I hear are keeping you up at night."

David's dad laughed as he lowered him back to the floor. They were near the end of the row now, stepping closer to the darkness of the room. The light just caught the hard surface of the hideous monstrosity before them.

"Well, me and my producing partner, Cody, but yeah."

"I'm not afraid of the movies. What I saw was real." He was certain of it. David hadn't seen all of it, but he'd heard it, and he had seen the claws. They were just like the ones a few feet away from him, and now that he could see them, they were longer than his hand, each one looking sharp enough to tear through flesh and bone.

His dad turned to the guard. "He saw Stickler coming out of his closet."

Chuck grinned and bent down, looking past his dad to talk directly to David.

"So, you saw the Stickler, huh? Yeah, he's a creepy one. I hate to come in here at night on my rounds because he scares the hell outta me." He looked back at his dad as Chuck straightened, holding his back, which made an audible pop. "That's the current sequel you're doin', isn't it?"

"Yeah, that's what we're filming. Hey, did you hear why Celeste has Frankie here..." He nodded to the large monster positioned at the end, "out like this? She's usually much better about closing up shop."

"I thought I saw her leaving with that new P.A. just as I was coming onto the lot. Not really sure."

David inched toward the large creature. The light from above cast a shadow over him, but he wanted to see. He needed to see the eyes. In his room, the eyes had been red, but they were always black pits in the movies.

Throughout the room, the lights started to flicker. David jumped back to grab his dad's leg, making Chuck laugh.

"David. Come on." His dad reached out and lifted the large claw of the costume so David could look at it. "It's fake. A piece of silicone and latex."

David reached out and slowly touched the outstretched claw. It was cool and smooth, like plastic. It almost felt like his toys. He recalled playing with a toy knife. It had those same hard edges that looked like they would be sharp, but when he stabbed his friends, it didn't hurt them.

He brought it up to his nose and sniffed it. It stank, the acrid stench smelling almost like one of his dad's farts. The ones his dad always blamed on random toads hiding in their house.

"It stinks."

"It's latex and foam. You would have to talk to the FX guys. They could give you the details. But it's not alive, and it's not real. Okay?"

David looked over the glove, turning it over in his hand and studying its long nails and the fake porcupine quills. They bent as he pushed them. He couldn't control the laugh, realizing he was playing with this horrific monster and that it was harmless. Man, what he would give to wear it. Sure, it was much too large for him, but if he had one his own size, he could wear it to school. How would Jimmy like that? He wouldn't tease David anymore. Not after he chased him down wearing this bad boy.

His dad reached over him and tugged on the hanger the costume hung on. David watched him, realizing his dad wasn't trying to get the costume off. With a tug, he pulled the monster's head away from the body.

The lights flickered around them, then winked off, leaving them in darkness. Only a red glow from the far end of the room illuminated the still shapes of the costumes around them. David tightened his grip on his dad's leg, holding his breath as he tried to look everywhere at once. The glow...

It was the eyes. It had to be. The beast was there, and it was going to get them.

"Shoot it!" David cried out, pointing at the red glow.

The lights flickered back on, but continued to flash intermittently.

"David, cool it." But David kept hold of his leg and wouldn't look away from the door. Above it was the large EXIT light. "Hey, Chuck, in the morning, give maintenance a call. Get someone in here to get this damn light fixed."

"I'll have them get right on it."

David's dad turned around to face him, the mask still in his hand. It was black with a long nose and quills sleeked back on the top and around the sides. The eyes were deep pits of darkness, left open for special lenses to be inserted.

David couldn't stop the shiver that ran through him as he took a step back. Even in his father's hand, the beast looked hungry and ready to tear into him.

"See, it's fake. The monster is only a creature in the movie. Okay?"

David stood there, afraid to move, just staring into where the eyes should be.

"David, come on. Touch it. Feel it. It's silicone and plastic."

David slowly reached out, his heart pounding in his chest. He felt every painful breath as he touched the mask. He ran his finger over it and pushed down on the point of one of the quills, bending it.

"It's like rubber."

"That's kinda what it is. It's foam rubber."

David moved closer to the mask. "That's cool."

"Yeah, it is."

"Your dad's pretty cool. He came up with all this," Chuck said, smiling warmly at David.

His dad put the mask back with the costume.

"Thanks, man." His dad nodded to Chuck before turning back to David.

He knew his dad was trying to calm him down, but he just didn't get it. David already knew movie monsters weren't real. When would his dad listen and believe there was a real one in his closet?

"Hey, buddy, you know what? Tomorrow's Saturday. Why don't you come to the set with me and watch us shoot a couple scenes?" He smirked. "I think Tina's getting killed tomorrow. It should be a lot of fun. You can meet Mike. I'm sure he'll let you play with some of her intestines."

"Really?"

Sure, David had been on set a few times, but never during a killing scene. Most times, he got stuck hanging out with actors and actresses, so he stayed out of the way. He wasn't sure but guessed it had more to do with no one to watch him at home, so he had his own version of babysitters...also known as actors.

"Yeah. You're getting old enough now. Just remember, you will have to be quiet and stay out the way. Okay?"

His dad and Chuck stepped away, walking down the aisle. David could just barely hear them as he turned, checking out the monster costume. He was finally going to see it tear someone apart. How cool was that?!

"Thanks for letting us in tonight, Chuck," David heard his dad say just as a low growl emanated from the costume.

He quickly stepped back, looking at it. What was that? This wasn't the real monster. There was no way it could be making noise. It must have some kind of sound effects built into it that he had just triggered. Or maybe his dad had. Maybe he had some remote and was just messing with him.

David turned to look at his dad, who was still turned away, talking to Chuck.

"No problem. You pay the bills, right?"

His dad wasn't paying any attention to him. If he were messing with him, wouldn't his dad be watching, seeing if he'd react? Was this some kind of an elaborate joke on him? Had Chuck rigged everything before he had gotten there?

"After all, it's your studio. You can come by anytime."

David backed away from the costume, watching as the eyes started to glow red. Its shape filled out as it hung there, getting taller. David's jaw dropped. He couldn't look away, but he also couldn't say anything. His mouth wasn't working. He wanted to scream and warn his dad as there was no way this was a joke, this thing was real, but no words escaped him.

"Yeah, but I just don't like to interrupt in the middle of the night like this."

When David backed into his dad, he looked over his shoulder at him. "David!"

"Dad!" His mouth finally formed the words just as the lights went out again. The last thing David saw before everything fell away to the red glow of the EXIT light was a lingering claw as the monster slipped behind the wardrobe.

David stumbled in the darkness, not able to control himself from jerking back. He tripped on his dad's leg and felt himself fall. It was an odd sensation of having no control, seeming to be in slow motion. Then he was in the costumes and felt something digging into him.

"David, don't be making a mess. People have to clean that up in the morning. Get out of there."

He tried to yell, but he couldn't. The thoughts screamed through him. *'Don't scream at me about the mess. Your monster, the one you told me wasn't real, just came to life and is now stalking us! And when you designed it, you made it with black eyes and a thousand needles on its back, then gave it large fangs and claws so it could rip you apart! Yes, that thing is alive, and we are now all its food, but don't worry. I'll try not to make too much of a mess getting away from it!'*

David wanted to scream at his father, but his mouth struggled to form coherent sounds into words. He got out the occasional "dad", but his mind fumbled with the rest. It didn't help that he had fallen into a heap of clothes that kept tangling around him. The more he tried to unwrap himself, the more it seemed they reached out to grab him. It was like the clothes had found a life of their own and were trying to subdue him.

"It's just the lights. Come on, bud. You're not afraid of the dark."

David wanted to cry. Sure, he wasn't afraid of the dark, but what was in the dark. His dad never realized all the creepy and evil things hiding there. How would he ever get him to understand? He had to keep fighting. He had to get free. The monster was on the loose, and David must warn them. They hadn't seen it. They didn't know it was coming for them.

And where was the monster? David tried to look toward the costumes on the other side, but it was hard in the dim light. From what he could see, it looked like all the clothes surrounding them kept shifting, dancing in the shadows.

There had to be more of the monsters. There were more costumes, right? What if they had all come alive? He had to get free and warn his dad.

He wiggled his way down, feeling his shirt slip up as he did, finally able to free himself from the mess of clothes. He looked up at the shape highlighted in the gloom of the red emergency light, hoping it was his dad.

"The costume came to life, Dad! It's alive!"

"David!" The shape scowled.

That was when David saw the Stickler's glowing red eyes. It was next to them on the other side of the aisle, just beyond the next row of costumes.

"Dad, look!"

David pushed on his dad, urging him to turn around. He didn't turn to where David pointed. Instead, his gaze lingered on where the costume should be, but the space was now empty. When the creature's eyes moved, it must have caught his dad's attention because he turned, seeing the red orbs slipping into the darkness beyond the other costumes.

"It's just a trick of the light, David. Hey, Chuck, there isn't anyone in maintenance that would be here this time of night, is there?"

Another low growl emanated from the dark. This time, it was loud enough that they all heard it. David watched as his dad stiffened, his eyes focused on where he had seen the red eyes.

"What was that?"

His dad looked at where the costume had been and started taking a step back, keeping his arm protectively in front of David.

That's right. He is the daddy monster in his own right, and anything coming after his little guy is going to have to go through him first.

David looked up at him in admiration, remembering when he was younger, before his dad was gone all the time to make movies. His dad would come home from work, throw open the front door, and roar, loudly proclaiming that the daddy monster had arrived, and he smelled a little one.

That same man would be the one to take him to bed later that night and kneel to say their prayers. Then David would climb into bed and his dad would lean down to kiss him on the forehead, whispering the daddy promise to always protect him.

His dad took another step back, this one making David move with him. He barely heard his dad as he whispered, "Where's the costume?"

A loud roar shook the rack next to them. David saw the clothes shifting. That was when he saw the large claw rise above them, the red glow making it look like blood dripped down its long talons.

Then the claw came down. David felt the warm spray as his dad cried out.

His dad tried to back away quickly, but he had forgotten David was behind him. He stumbled and fell back, blood gushing from his chest. David felt it soaking him. They landed on the cold cement, his dad holding his arm tightly to his chest. He rolled back and forth on the floor, cursing as the pain coursed through him.

"Wes! Wes! Come in, Wes!" Chuck screamed into his walkie-talkie. David looked over at him and saw him backing toward the far door.

"Roger, Chuck. How's the tour going?" the voice hissed from the radio.

The costumes rustled again. David turned back toward them, then started pulling himself away. His dad lay still on the floor, losing a lot of blood. They needed to do something, get him to a doctor.

The red eyes appeared again, staring at him through the clothes. David stopped, transfixed by those large, red orbs.

"David! Run to the door!" his dad screamed. He fought to get back to his knees, blocking David's view of the approaching creature.

"Call 9-1-1, Wes! Now. We need an ambulance here ASAP. Mr. Carey is hurt."

"Damn. What the hell is going on down there?!"

David's dad pushed himself the rest of the way up, swaying back and forth. Still, he moved, taking little steps backward. David watched him as he rushed to the door, but he couldn't just leave his dad. He tried to think of anything they could do. What did they do in the movies?

Well, the girl the creature chased usually went into some random cabin and found a flamethrower. Yeah, like they were going to find one of those around...

Wait, this is a film studio.

If it was in the movies, would it be with the wardrobe? Probably not. It would probably be with the special effects equipment.

"I don't know. You best get the police here as well." Chuck yelled into his walkie-talkie with one hand, fumbling to remove his gun with the other. David knew Chuck was not some rookie security guard, but didn't think he had ever seen anything like this before. "Holy shit."

David made it past him and turned to look back for his dad. The Stickler loomed over him. That large snout emitted deep growls each time David's dad took another step back.

"Dad!"

Finally, Chuck got the gun free and pointed it at the creature. "I don't know who the hell you are or what you think you are doing, but get away from Mr. Carey now. Then come out from there and put the costume on the floor."

David backed up until he was in the safety of the hallway, crying, when he heard the scream. It wasn't even recognizable as his father, but knew it was. Then the sound quieted, turning into a gurgle before stopping. The silence stretched on before he heard something fall to the floor. David turned away. He couldn't watch anymore. He knew what had just happened. His father was dead.

The tears were starting to wet his cheeks, and he wasn't sure what to do. He looked around at the hallway, the light in the long grey corridor still on, but flickering like what had happened in the other room.

Still in the room, Chuck turned to look at the boy. He saw David was just standing there, terrified and crying. "David."

David turned to meet his eyes.

"Get to the security office! Police are on the way."

There was a loud growl as one of the racks behind Chuck was thrown towards him. It missed but hit the doorframe with costumes falling off of it, scattering into the hallway.

A head from another one of his father's film monsters rolled to David's feet. This monster was some kind of large insect monster with large eyes, but instead of mandibles had long fangs.

David didn't want to even think of that monster coming to life as he turned and ran like he had never run before. What was he going to do? He had to find the prop room. Where was it? It wasn't like the rooms were labeled. Most people working on the set knew where everything was, but what about somebody new? How would they ever find anything in the maze of hallways?

He had hoped he'd be far enough away when the gunshots started, but he wasn't. He heard them. First, it was one, then another. Then a series of them came in rapid succession that ended in a scream, followed by a thud. David knew Chuck had just crashed into the wall. He didn't turn to look. He just kept running.

It was no use looking for the prop room. He was just a kid. What was he going to do, anyway? He'd only seen flamethrowers in the movies where it seemed like everyone had them lying around and anyone could figure out how to use them. While that may be true of adults, David had no clue.

It had just killed his dad. He had tried to warn him, but his dad hadn't believed him. He was dead.

David had to push away the memories of him because if he didn't, he would start crying. David didn't think he'd stop once he started. He would end up like his mom on one of her bad days when she barely got out of bed, instead just lying there all day. If he started that, then he would be a crying mess, waiting to be eaten.

I ain't no crybaby.

Somewhere down the long hallway behind him, he heard an earsplitting howl that shook the walls and brought him to his knees, but he didn't let it slow his momentum. Keep going, keep going, keep going. He knew he had to, but the thing must be getting closer, the hallway allowing it to move more freely.

Dang it, just how big is this place?

He wasn't sure of the answer. The few times he'd been in the building, he'd never gotten the full tour, but he knew his dad had gotten the space really cheap. It was some kind of abandoned warehouse. They had converted it and used a lot of the unfinished areas as sets. The offices, including the security office, were toward the front of the building.

But what if he was going the wrong way? He could end up on one of the sets, which would be perfect. What better area to be chased to by a horror movie monster than a horror movie film set? If the creature didn't kill him, he felt like his young heart was going to explode. He already felt the wetness down his leg, knowing that he'd wet himself. When did that happen? Must have been when he fell as he ran away.

He saw the door up ahead marked EXIT, but that didn't seem right. When they got there, he knew they hadn't come from that way. Near it was a turn in the hallway. He could have sworn that was the direction they had come. So which way should he go?

Exit... Go for the exit. Get out of here.

David wasn't sure why he didn't listen to himself as he turned down the hallway, running into something tall and hard. Grunting, he bounced back, landing on the floor with a thump, his tailbone screaming in pain.

"What's going on?" a deep voice asked.

He looked up to see a tall, dark-skinned man standing over him. David could barely stammer a response. He had no idea how he looked, vaguely remembering his father's blood on him.

"Creature... Alive... Killed them," he gasped.

"Get in there," the man ordered, nodding to a room.

David saw the security uniform and guessed this must be Wes, the man Chuck had contacted on the radio. David looked past him, seeing a brightly lit room, a bank of security monitors sitting there. The monster was on one of them. No wonder Wes had already been coming down the hallway. When it neared the camera, its massive shape reared up to look at it. No, it was looking at him. David didn't know how, but he knew it was. It wanted him. It was after him...

It stood there; the red eyes having gone dark to become black soulless orbs. Those dark, dead eyes looking through the lens of the security camera and straight into his own. He was why it was killing. It was killing to get to him. It was tearing these people apart. His father was ripped into pieces because of him. Those eyes that were nothing but wells of blackness drew him in. He could feel the connection, the bond growing as he allowed it to push that fog into him. He could feel a presence growing inside his head, a voice just out of reach, trying to growl something at him.

The guard pushed David, and David felt the connection snap away, and there was a tugging at his head like a band was trying to pull him back.

"Get in the room, it's coming!" Wes said again, and David stumbled, taking a step, his own feet working against him, remembering how to walk. He took a few more stumbling steps toward the room, then looked back up at the security monitors.

The monster was still there. It turned away from the camera and looked down the hall that met with the one they were in, the area David had just come from. Then, with a swipe of its large claw, the camera signal went dead.

David heard the roar from the distant hallway, and his legs remembered how to work. So did his bladder, as he could feel the fresh, warm stream wetting the front of his pants as he ran into the room and looked back, waiting for the security guard to join him. Wes didn't. He just stood there, looking scared in the dim light from the room. With a hard swallow, the man looked at the now dead security camera and then back at him.

"Shut the door."

David nodded and closed the door. Then he locked it.

He waited, his heart pounding in his ears. He heard the gunshots. Then he heard the screaming. David didn't know what was worse, the sounds of those screams, or the silence when they stopped.

CHAPTER 2

Officer Ellis heard a scream and looked around to find its source. He was in a hallway and surrounded by what was left of a security guard. He had been trying to move as gingerly as he could, the same as other officers as they canvassed through the gore, trying to be careful as to not destroy evidence. Though really, with blood everywhere, still dripping from where it soaked into the ceiling tiles overhead, Ellis wasn't sure how he should proceed. There was just no way of moving without blood or body parts getting in the way of walking through the building. His uniform was probably done after this, as it had to be covered in evidence. It was already getting soaked from the amount of blood dripping down.

"Hello," He called out.

He didn't like just how much it felt like he had been walking onto the set of a horror movie. He assumed this warehouse was a studio that produced them from the number of costumes one officer had already found in what must have been their wardrobe storage, but it wasn't just the freaky costumes they found that made this seem like another slasher movie. No, it was because in all his years as an officer patrolling the streets, he had never come across anything like this nightmare that was around him. A nightmare that would haunt him for many sleepless nights going forward. For that, he was sure.

It didn't help as he worked to find the next spot where there was no blood, that the overhead dangling fluorescent lights flickered randomly as he tried to move down the corridor. Mostly, he was finding his way by flashlight, but occasionally the light above would flash on, and he would see another well-lit glance at what was left of the decapitated head at the end of the hall. Next to the head,

17

there was the door he had been working towards, and where he was sure the yelling had come from.

He stepped over what was left of the torso of a dead security officer, having to use the flashlight to not get tangled in the spaghetti of intestines that had been ripped free when the two halves had been separated. Bile bit at the back of his throat and with each shifting of his foot as he tried to not step into any of the blood that was still very wet in pools on the floor. As he was watching those intestines, he was waiting for them to come alive, to reach out and grab him, pull him deeper into this macabre around him.

That's what happened, right? In horror movies, there would be a jump scare, then something you wouldn't expect as the next victim walked slowly down a hallway. The slower they moved, the more the tension built until it reached a crescendo with the sudden loud music and the jump scare as something shot out towards the screen, making anyone watching the damned thing nearly shit their pants. They would laugh it off and turn to their significant other and deny they were afraid just moments later.

Damn this place.

The scream came again. It again tore through the darkness, and he could sense the terror that echoed off the walls.

He took another step, this time feeling something squish between his work boots and the cement floor. He had finally done it. Evidence was destroyed. He knew once the detectives arrived and took over the investigation, they would interrogate him about his screw up.

He couldn't let it stop him or slow him down. The scream had gone quiet again. He was left with the silence of the hallway.

Why was it so quiet in there? There were at least three other officers searching other parts of the warehouse. He should be able to hear them as they moved from room to room, searching for any idea of whatever happened there or caused this. The security guard that Officer Ellis, or Tommy as he liked to be called when he wasn't wearing the uniform, was the third body they had found in there already. They had no idea how much of the studio occupied the warehouse, or just how many people had died in there. The killer could still be there, or they were alone, in which case they needed to maintain evidence and find clues.

Not that he was worried too much about the evidence as he focused on the door and whoever was screaming from inside.

He couldn't get caught up in thinking about the silence that was surrounding him whenever the screaming stopped. If he did, it allowed himself to get caught up in those fears. The fear of what lies waiting deeper in this madhouse. The fear of what was around him now as he tried to walk. Childhood nightmares with his own terrors were beginning to threaten and show their ugly heads.

Focus on the door, take another step.

There were no more steps to take as the last remaining feet before he made it to the door were wet with dark crimson. This was it. He had to take that step, no matter how much his career suffered. He eased forward, being careful so that he didn't slip.

He reached the door, and he wanted to nudge the separated head aside. The one remaining eye stared at him, lifeless, as it watched him reach out. The other eye looked as though it had exploded from the socket, the white jelly dried after having oozed down the cheek.

The door was right there. Why was he waiting to turn the knob and go in? He was right there; nothing was stopping him. He just needed to open the door, confirm nothing was waiting for him on the other side. Then he could put this nightmare behind him, because he was not going any further into this place unless the sun was shining high in the sky.

He turned the knob or tried to. It wouldn't twist. The door was locked.

His fear was getting the better of him and he pounded hard on the door. On the other side, the screaming started again.

Office Ellis stopped pounding on the door and once the screaming stopped, he called out to the other side. "Hello, open up! I'm Officer Ellis. I'm with the police. I'm here to help."

He listened for a response on the other side of the door.

More silence. It felt like the air was getting sucked out of there. The place was getting hotter, like a fire had erupted somewhere else in the building. He didn't see any smoke, but the heat was building through the halls. Sweat started to roll off of him, and he had to wipe it away or let it get it into his eyes.

It was crazy considering the cool night outside. He would have expected the warehouse to be cooler than it was.

He put his ear to the door, hoping to hear something on the other side. Was there breathing? He wasn't sure, but thought he heard frantic, panicked breaths, short gasps of something scared and crying.

His own inner child wanted to find a corner and cry too.

"I need you to open the door. I can hear you in there. I'm here to help."

Ellis pulled back. The fluorescent light fluttered briefly to light again and in that brief second, he caught a glimpse of something shiny out of the corner of his eye. He flashed his flashlight at the corner to reveal the security camera. He switched from flashing the light into it and turned it upon himself, so his features were visible. He tried to keep from making himself become something out of a horror movie, so instead of aiming it from below him, he held it out so it shined directly at him. The light was bright and annoying, but he hoped he looked less threatening.

You know what could be on the other side of that door might have done this? Right? This could be the killer you're trying to get out of there...

"Hey, whoever is on the other side of this door, if you can see the security cameras, I'm right here. I'm here to help you. I am here for you. Look, I know you're scared, and I have no idea what you saw here, but I'm a cop. I'm with the police. My name is Officer Ellis, you can call me Tommy. I'm here to get you out of here. I just need you to unlock the door. Okay. I'm here to help."

He spoke in as calm and as smooth of a voice as he could muster, trying to put all his years of being a father to good use.

His heart skipped a beat when he heard the little click of the door and knew it had been unlocked, but they didn't open the door. They had only unlocked it.

Tommy opened the door, and his heart twisted as he saw a terrified little boy backing quickly away. The boy was shivering, his eyes wide open, his face wet with tears that had run down through the blood that splattered and dried there. The boy moved to hide himself under the security desk.

Office Ellis took a step into the room, slowly, cautiously, and watched as the boy took a quick step of his own backward, trying to get farther into the table that housed all the security feeds. So, whatever this boy had lived through, for however long he had survived to lock himself into this room, he'd had a front-row seat for whatever horror had torn apart this warehouse. This boy could have seen it all.

Ellis looked back at the boy; he wanted to take another step towards him but could see just how terrified the child was. One more step and the boy would probably be scrambling to hide deeper under the table. Just inside the door was the closest Ellis was going to get.

"I'm here. I'm here to keep you safe. I'm a police officer. We save people. Just take a deep breath. It's all going to be okay. You're going to be safe. We just need to get you outside. We need to get you out of here. You okay with that? Getting out of here?" Ellis spoke softly and slowly, trying to coax the boy into relaxing and building up that trust to get him to move closer.

Officer Ellis looked up at the security monitors and noticed for the first time how nothing was moving. He couldn't see any of the other officers as they moved through the warehouse. While it was dark, he should still be able to see the light from their flashlights.

Maybe there just weren't any cameras where they were...

But there were a lot of cameras and there was a lot of still darkness.

Come on, Tommy, you gotta get the kid out of there.

He looked back at the terrified child. What was he going to do to get this boy to trust him, to come with him?

For starters, he realized that having the door open behind him was not helping. When that light did kick on out there, having a view of all that carnage was not good.

So, he closed the door. Then he sat in front of him, quickly regretting that decision, as he could feel the blood that had flowed into the room, seeping into his uniform. He tried not to grimace, feeling the wetness of blood between his buttocks as he looked back at the boy. He was now below eye level in what he hoped was the least intimidating position he could be in.

"Will you tell me your name?" Ellis said, trying to ooze as much calm he could into his facial expression and voice. It didn't work as the boy vigorously shook his head 'no'.

"Okay. Well, my name's Office Ellis, but you can call me Tommy. Is that okay? Do you want to call me Tommy?

The boy just stared at him.

"Can I call your parents? Anyone I can call?"

Another shake of the head. Nothing else. Asking the boy questions was not helping, and he was not getting him anywhere.

"I can't imagine what you saw here tonight. I figure whatever it was, it was something you don't want to think about, or that you can't help but think about. I get that. While I don't think I've ever seen anything like this before, I did have a pretty rough time as a kid.

"See, when I was growing up, my parents were never around. They were always off getting drunk and high. It made it hard for me, being someone they always forgot about, or seemed like an afterthought. It almost made me go down a very different path. I hadn't wanted to be a cop. Hell, from where I was from, cops were the bad guys, the ones always getting in the way of making bread or just trying to survive. They harassed you, bullied you. I've known some back in the day that used to pin stuff on kids on the street that were just like me. It was scary.

"Not something I like to think about, really. I try to forget it. But you know, I loved to play hoops. It was my way of getting away from all that stuff. Hell, there really wasn't much else to do. I wasn't a gamer, and well, the gangs didn't even notice me, so I really was just that loner kid. I'd go to the court and shoot the ball around. Never with the other kids, of course. I wasn't any good. I was there. I liked to throw the ball around, but as I said, I wasn't very good.

"Well, see, when others came, I would often get pushed to the side so they could play.

"Sometimes, these boys that would push me around, they weren't that mean about it. Some of them were actually nice, and I'd stay to watch them play.

"Man, I'm not really good at this, am I?" Ellis said, wiping away fresh tears as he remembered when he was a kid. He thought back to that time in his life that changed who he was, and how it pushed him to become who he was now.

He realized it didn't really matter as the boy had moved a little away from the counter towards him.

"Hey, I'm going to get you out of here. Okay? Like what someone once did for me. Do you want to get out of here?"

This time, the boy nodded and rushed over to hug the unsuspecting officer. The officer hesitated for a moment, then hugged the boy back. As he did, he looked up at the bank of security monitors and noticed the flashing lights as more squad cars were pulled into the parking lot outside. Officers quickly got out of their cars and rushed into the building.

Officer Ellis wanted to grab his radio and warn them of what they were coming into, but with the boy held tight in his arm, he shifted and reached down, turning off the radio before their chaotic chatter plastered the small room with noise.

"You're going to get through this, okay? We're going to get you out of here. You're going to be safe. Okay. You're going to be safe. Help is here now. We're all going to be safe." He said, as he watched the screen, hoping that whatever had gotten everyone else didn't get those other officers. He hoped against all hope that the words he said to the child would be true, and that they truly were safe. After all, if you say it enough times, you may just will it to be true.

He hoped it worked that way. So, he just kept repeating it, over and over again to the boy, wishing it all to be true. That they were all going to be safe.

CHAPTER 3

Lights flashed around him, through him, erupting with every pulse of blood circulating around his skull. David felt like the world was not real. He wasn't real. Nothing... there was just nothing.

There were people talking. They were saying words and talking to him, but he had trouble focusing on what they were saying. Occasionally, a word would slip through, but none of them made sense. Dad, his dad, were they talking to him about his dad?

Dad, dad, dad... No, his dad. They needed to save his dad. They needed to go back in there.

In where?

No, don't think about it. Don't think, don't remember. No, no, no.

Just sit there and listen to the music. Let the music flow, the discordant notes that rambled through his head. It was like dark blindness. Music layered upon cacophonic layer while darkness tinged the outer layer of his vision only to be replaced by bright whiteness and then the black came. Both were endless cycles, while he couldn't focus on anything around him. White, black, blue, red, repeat. They all just danced, and he wanted them to stop.

But no, don't stop. Stopping would be thinking about one thought, and he didn't want it. No, stay away from that one thought. Stay away!

Monsters. Stay away!

David screamed, stopping the madness around him.

＊ ＊ ＊ ＊

It felt like the oxygen was suddenly sucked out from the air around him. Then Officer Ellis heard the scream and recognized it,

25

having saved it once already that night. He looked around. Everyone was looking around, but he had an idea as to where to look.

He looked through the flashing lights and people and saw the boy from earlier. He had learned in the time since he had pulled the boy from the warehouse that one of the owners of the place was his father and that the boy's name was David. Officer Ellis could see that the boy was terrified again, surrounded by one trauma specialist and two paramedics that had been called to the scene. A female paramedic was shining a light into the boy's eyes, and the boy was screaming at her, swatting at her arms as he tried to push and kick her away.

Ellis rushed over, holding his hands up as he approached.

"David, hey David. It's me. It's Tommy. I'm here to help. Okay. I'm here to help." Ellis said as he approached the boy. The boy didn't wait. As soon as he heard Ellis' voice, he jumped down from the back of the ambulance, where he had been sitting, and rushed the officer. Ellis wrapped his arms around the boy.

Ellis noticed that Detective Price had been standing there as well and was looking disappointed with the patrolman. Office Ellis figured he knew why. He had already made his statement to one of the detectives and they had made it clear how unhappy they were about his disturbing the crime scene.

"Officer Ellis, have you had any luck with getting the boy to talk? He seems to have a thing for you."

"No, I've been more concerned with making sure he was okay." Ellis finished, then turned to look at the boy. He lowered himself so that he was eye level. "How are you doing?"

Ellis could see the terror in the boy's eyes, but that was all he knew. And why shouldn't the boy be terrified? From what Ellis saw in there, he was scared, too.

"I think we need to take him to the hospital. I'm concerned with what he has seen. They may need to admit him." The trauma officer said, looking from the boy to Price.

"When can I talk to him?" Price said, his tone heavy with disapproval at not being able to grill the boy for information.

Ellis looked up from the boy to the detective. The other officer was obviously frustrated with the detective, who stood there like he wished none of them were intruding on his crime scene or with his witness. Ellis had never dealt with the man before, but had heard rumors about how Price worked, how he was known for bullying others in the department as well as witnesses.

"I can take him if you'd like." Ellis said, trying to break the tension between the pair. "I can make sure they get him looked at."

Price looked like he wanted to tell Ellis to get the hell out of there. The trauma officer looked relieved for the assistance.

"I can take him, but I would appreciate it if you came along. I think he could use a friend, and right now, you seem to be the closest he's got," she said. David was gripping Ellis's uniform tighter, trying to pull him harder into a hug.

"Hey buddy, are you okay if we take a car ride with her? She's got somewhere to take us. Somewhere that's going to help."

The boy looked terrified at her and then back at Ellis.

"It's going to be okay. We're going somewhere safe. It's going to be safe and away from here. It's all going to be okay. We just have to go."

Ellis started to stand. He couldn't at first, as David was refusing to let go, continuing to hold on to the officer as hard as he could. Ellis looked into the boy's eyes, and they were pleading with him, begging him not to go anywhere.

"Hey, I'm going to go with, okay? I'll sit in the back seat with you and everything. You're going to be okay. I'm going to make sure of it, all right? We just need to take a ride in the car. She's going to take us there."

"Hey David, you want to go with me in my car? Officer-" The trauma officer crouched down so she could be eye level with the boy just as Ellis had. David looked at her, but Ellis could sense that the boy was still skeptical of her. Though he had eased his grip from Ellis' uniform, so that was some progress.

Ellis caught the other officer looking at him, and it took him a moment to realize that she had been asking him his name.

"Officer Ellis, Tommy," he said, nodding his head towards her.

"Tommy here. He's going to come with us. Do you remember my name?" the trauma officer asked as she held out her hand. David shied away from her as though he was going to hide behind Tommy. David shook his head in response.

"My name's Nancy. We only want to make sure you're okay. We're just going to take a car ride."

Ellis looked back and forth from Nancy to David.

"Where are we going, Nancy? If you want to walk us to your car, I'm sure will want to come with us. Right?"

Nancy nodded to him and started walking away from the parked vehicles and their flashing lights to a car on the edge of the parking lot. It was like the other squad cars, but Ellis could see even from the distance that there was no mesh between the back seat and front. He started to follow her, pausing briefly to hold out his hand to David. David was quick to grab it and walk alongside him. They moved slowly. David wasn't ready to rush into anything, but Ellis kept pace, making sure not to rush him and to pause whenever the boy stopped to confirm they should go with her.

"Your mom is going to meet us at the hospital. An officer has already picked her up, and she is on her way. She's worried about you. Everyone just wants to make sure you're all right. We're going to go and get you checked out. Everything is going to be fine." Nancy said as she opened the passenger's side back door of her car. She looked up at Officer Ellis, who was shaking his head no, and realized she had made a mistake. She hid it from her face but hoped that what she had said would soon become true and that she hadn't just broken any trust with the boy by lying.

David hesitated getting into the back seat. Inside, the light disappeared into darkness. The streetlights above couldn't seem to move around the car's ceiling, leaving the interior a black void, darker than it should have been.

David's breath grew shallow, and he took a step back to move away. It was like the darkness wanted to reach out and grab him.

Ellis felt the boy's grip tighten around his own and he looked where the boy was staring. He didn't see anything wrong. There was the back seat, and nothing else.

But did the light move just a little? Was the darkness shifting? Was that a tentacle sneaking out?

Ellis blinked away the strange vision he thought he saw and grabbed his flashlight from his belt, flicking its illumination into the dark interior.

And there was nothing there...

"It's okay, we're just taking you somewhere safe." Nancy said.

Ellis looked back at the boy as David studied the seat now engulfed in the light from the flashlight. Slowly, he moved forward and eased himself into the car. Once he did, he continued to slide forward, allowing room for Tommy to sit next to him. The boy wasn't going to let Tommy out of his sight, not even to go around to the other side of the car to get in.

Ellis slid into the back seat, then made sure they were both buckled in.

"Everything's going to be okay." Nancy said again in her calm, soothing voice, though as Tommy heard it, and sat there in the back seat with the boy, he had a sinking feeling in his stomach, that it was not going to be okay.

He looked back at the flashing lights, and the other officers working in a frenzy to go over the scene. Everything was bathed in blue and red, but all he saw was the red blood as it had puddled in the corridor.

He turned to look at the boy, and for a moment, wasn't sure if he was here to protect the boy, or if he was trapped in there with him. The boy looked so sad, so afraid, but something inside Tommy was screaming at him, telling him to get out of there, get out of there now, or he was not going to live through the night.

He fought through the feeling as Nancy got behind the wheel. She looked back at the two of them, and in the flash of the light, her smile opened wide with rows of teeth stretching beyond the edge of her mouth, her teeth suddenly elongated into fangs dripping with blood and her eyes green and shaped like a cat, piercing into him as a predator ready to tear into its prey...

CHAPTER 4

Jenny felt the darkness as it began to press in around her. At first, she felt it like a warm blanket, and she reached out to wrap it around her. She pulled herself deeper into its depths, enjoying the security she felt in its embrace. It completely encompassed her.

Then she felt the first stinging as it pricked her skin. First on her bare breast, then another needle stabbed in her groin. More started to cascade down her leg, and she felt the warmth as warm liquid flowed from the tiny wounds. More of them pierced her as she felt the darkness around her shift.

In her mind's eye, she felt like she could see the darkness shifting and watched as a long black centipede swirled around her, encasing her. That as it moved, its legs were all tearing into her, ripping her apart.

She tried to scream, but it was caught in her throat. She opened her mouth, but no sound escaped her, only moans, scratching along her throat as they dug their way free.

Twisting, she tried to free herself from the giant insect that surrounded her. She fought, pushing and pulling, trying to get away.

Light suddenly broke through, but somehow it still had its ever-tightening stranglehold. She tried to wrench herself free, slamming all her weight into it to escape, but a strong force slammed into her, pressing her back against...

Against what? What was she pressed against? She was caught as she tried to turn and see what had her when a voice boomed above her, breaking her free...

* * * *

"Jennifer! Jen, wake up!"

Jenny opened her eyes to find her room brightly lit and her mother leaning over her, shaking her vigorously to wake her up. Her blankets were wrapped around her to the point that she had twisted herself in them, cocooning herself in the soft fabric.

"What, wha...what?" Jen said, trying to shake awake the last remnants of slumber as well as her mother. The nightmare was still there at the edge of her memory, as she remembered the fear, but not the details of why she had been afraid. Her heart was still racing, and it was impossible to calm it with her mother shaking her.

Her mom stopped and immediately went to Jen's dresser, pulling clothes out and tossing them over to her.

"Mom, stop! What the hell do you think you're doing? Get out of my room."

Jen was getting covered in clothes as first her mom threw over a shirt, bra, and then with a slam, her mom was going through her pants drawer. Within seconds, a pair of jeans came flying at her and she had to dodge to keep from getting hit with it.

She tossed the clothes onto the floor.

"What the hell!"

But that was when she felt it. She hadn't noticed it before, but there was something wrong in the house. The air felt different, warmer. She'd had the nightmare that was growing common lately. But once she'd woken, she didn't feel it; that unease she had grown accustomed to when she was at home. It was like a there had been a pressure inside her head that had grown slowly over time to where she hadn't noticed the pain intensifying... and now it was gone.

She didn't have time to think about it as a pair of socks were thrown at her.

"Come on, get dressed. We have to get to the hospital." Her mom said, stopping for the first time since Jen had been shaken awake.

Jen saw her mom's eyes, the red puffy eyes that were threatening more tears. The hair that was never seen out in public without being anything less than perfect, now in complete disarray while her mom stood there with last night's shirt, no bra, leggings, yet she was wearing shoes. Her mom looked like she was going somewhere, but like that?

Something had to be wrong.

Jen started grabbing the clothes she had tossed off the bed, studying her mom some more as the tears that had been on the horizon earlier were now in full stream. With the release of the tears, something else must have broken in the woman as she dropped to the foot of Jen's bed and shook, the sobbing intensifying.

Jen pulled on the shirt her mom had thrown at her and moved up behind her, putting her arms around her mother.

"What's wrong? Where's dad? Do I need to wake up Davey?" Jen said, resting her head on her mother's petite shoulder. She had to crane her neck a little, and it was uncomfortable due to how much shorter her mom was. Where her dad was a very large man, one that could fill a doorway with his size as well as his love, her mother was his complete opposite. She was nearly half his size and while her dad was a well-built man, full of muscle from hard work as he always did so much himself on his films, her mother was thin, almost a toothpick of a person. She was not only short but also paper thin to a level that sometimes Jen worried about her.

Her parents were such an odd couple and family photos when they would go on traveling vacations often showed just how different the two looked. Then there was her and David, of course. David, still too early to tell who he took after, though it appeared for now to be more their mother as he was a little on the short side in his class. Jen, on the other hand, there was no doubt she took after their dad. Already she was the tallest in her class, with the broadest shoulders that many of the boys joked with her about. Yes, it hurt her how they would make fun of her, saying she looked like a boy, but what did they know? She was her dad's daughter, and there was no way she would ever be ashamed of that.

Her mom tried to say something, but it was too quiet for Jen to hear her. Jen tightened her grip. "Hey, it's going to be okay. Did something happen to grandma? Grandpa? What's wrong?"

Her mom shook her head, then tried to say something. It was lost to the sobbing; the words garbled beyond comprehension. Then she turned and buried her head on Jen's shoulder. Jen held her, not saying anything because she wasn't sure what to say. She was sixteen, barely old enough to drive, and had no idea what to say to her mom.

She wanted to leave her mom there, go into her parents' room to find her mom's cell phone and see if there were any answers there as to what was going on. If there was any information to get. Her mom barely used the phone. She was still using the landline for most calls. How would Jen figure that out? Then how was she supposed to look at the call history if there was none to go through?

Jen remembered when her dad bought her mom the cell phone. It had taken years to convince her mom just to have one, and then when they had gotten it for her (not as a Christmas present as she didn't want the damn thing to begin with) she never turned it on. Only when she wanted to call someone did she turn it on, and then if she didn't get through, she would turn it off again. How could anyone even call her back if the phone was off? Then, of course, the voicemail wasn't set up so no one could even leave her messages.

Jen heard a sniffle as her mom pulled away from her. As soon as she released, her mom was bringing a well-used tissue she had been hiding in the palm of her hand and blew into it. Jen winced, disgusted by how wet the Kleenex looked.

Her mom closed her eyes and took a deep breath. It was obvious she was struggling to hold in more tears, and the deep breaths were a way she was trying to push out some of the tension. Jen noted that her mother didn't open her eyes right away, instead reaching out to her and tightly gripped her shirt where it pulled it tight on her arm.

"Your dad." was all her mom could get out before she got up and was crying again as she rushed out of the room.

"What the fuck?" Jen whispered to herself before getting up to follow her. She paused for a second and grabbed her pants, quickly pulling them on before leaving to find her.

"What about dad? What's going on? Mom!?"

Jen was in the hallway outside her room, about to go into the bathroom, guessing that was where her mom had gone to. A loud crash from the other end told her that her mom had gone back to their bedroom at the end.

She rushed into the room, worried she was going to find her mom, or possibly even her dad, lying on the floor. Instead, she found her mom at the dresser, a photo frame of them as a family she had kept there was on the floor across the room. Her mom was crying again, leaning over the dresser for support, but the strength had faded from her, and she was slowly slipping to the floor.

Jen rushed to her, quick to grab her and drag her back to the bed so she could lie there. Her mom pulled herself higher on the mattress, and then pulled in her legs, balling herself up.

Jen looked at her, knowing that she should want to comfort her mother, but also angry at how she was just shutting down. This was her mother, the one who gave her life and was supposed to be protecting her, taking care of her, sheltering her... So why was it that Jen felt she had to take care of her right now?

"Mom, where's dad?"

Her mom let out a wail and grabbed one of the pillows.

That was when it felt like something hit her in the gut, and the air was pulled from her lungs. Her own eyes were getting wet, and she was beginning to understand.

NO, you are not her. You are not going to break down like her. No, you are better than that.

Jen clenched her teeth to keep from losing her own shit. Then she forced herself to take a deep, long breath.

"Mom, what happened to dad?"

From under the pillow, she could barely hear her mother's muffled reply. "He's dead. He's dead and your brother killed him."

CHAPTER 5

The trip to the hospital was mostly uneventful. After that brief flash where Ellis thought he was losing his mind, after all, how could he think this beautiful young woman was a monster? The rest of the way, there was nothing. David had nestled close to Tommy, and eventually fell asleep across his lap, much like his son used to do. It had made Ellis' chest hurt as he watched the little boy with his eyes closed, sleeping. The boy kept fidgeting, and Ellis couldn't imagine the nightmares that were playing out behind those eyelids.

Tommy pushed the thoughts away, trying not to focus on seeing his son's own face lying there. He couldn't allow himself to, because at the end of the day, the boy needed to feel safe. Ellis needed to do his best to make sure he was. Besides, the boy needed some rest. A little sleep would probably do him some good.

The car pulled up to the E.R. entrance of the hospital and was suddenly bathed in light. The boy stayed asleep, and Ellis looked up from the sleeping child to Nancy, who was looking back at him.

"You have a way with kids. You should be doing my job."

"I don't know. Just said what I thought would help."

"Well, it worked. I'll get with your sergeant; you'll probably need to stay here tonight to keep him calm so we can evaluate him. Has he said anything to you?"

"As far as I know, nothing. To me or anyone else. I'm thinking he may be non-verbal."

"Autistic?"

"Yeah. My neighbor has a daughter on the spectrum. You don't think so?"

"I don't know. It's hard to say until the parents get here."

"Mother. Father was killed tonight."

"Right. She should be on the way."

"You want to grab a wheelchair? We can roll him inside. Or should I carry him?"

"Probably best if you carried him. That close contact should help keep him calm. Once we get him in there and he wakes up, we can see if he wants a wheelchair. I've already called ahead. They have a room ready for him. We just need to check in at the desk and they'll direct us. Hope you have your walking shoes on. The psych ward is on the other side of the hospital, but to get in after-hours, you have to go through here."

"Yeah, we'll need to get that wheelchair, then. I'm not carrying him all the way."

"We'll see what he wants. He likes you. You may have to."

David woke briefly as Ellis lifted him from the car, but as soon as he pulled him close, the boy fell back asleep.

"Yeah, good luck getting him into a wheelchair." Nancy whispered. "I'm guessing you don't have kids of your own."

Tyler...

The name, the words caught in his throat. He had to take a deep breath that Nancy missed as she was leading the way. He was finally able to speak softly, muttering, "Nope."

"Yeah, could tell. Otherwise, you'd be used to this."

There was a whoosh of air as they heard the fans as soon as the automatic door slid open. Then they were inside, and Nancy was talking to the night nurse. The tall, well-built man behind the desk looked exhausted, as though he was ready to slip off to sleep. Ellis could understand why, as the lobby was quiet, though not empty.

There were two couples that he could see, one man by himself holding his arm and then a family sitting in the far corner. The mother was on her phone while a little boy, probably around 5 years old, was bundled in a light-covered soft-looking blanket asleep on the tired-looking father. The father was rocking the boy back and forth, singing to him as they waited for a room.

There was a loud buzz and Ellis turned back around to see that the nurse had buzzed a door, and Nancy was pushing it open, giving them access to the further depths of the hospital.

"So, now, about the wheelchair," Nancy said, chuckling as he walked past her into the next hallway.

* * * *

Ellis lowered David onto a gurney in what appeared to be a plain hospital room. As they had walked through the hospital, he had a chance to see many variations as they went through the different floors and wings of the building. Of all the ones he had seen, this was surprisingly bland. Removed were the lavishes of many of the rooms. That could be due to the area of the hospital they were now in, how they had to go through additional security just to get access to the area. There was no hiding now, not in this part of the hospital where everyone had to be cautious as to what was in their possession and what was left for someone to grab. Unlike the other parts of the hospital, this nursing station was a room with a locked door, and patients could only speak to them through plexiglass.

This room didn't have the large televisions he had seen on their walk through the building, or monitors heeled around on poles. That was because unlike the other areas, this wasn't a place to heal the body, here the doctors treated the mind. Though the mind wasn't something that could be healed as easily, these wounds were not visible to the eye or diagnosed by machine.

A tired-looking woman in scrubs, with a white coat over them, came into the room.

"I'm Dr. Marsh. What do we have here?" the doctor whispered. She walked up to them where they stood over the sleeping boy.

"Boy witnessed a massacre, hasn't said anything since." Nancy said, also keeping her voice low.

"And what's with tall, dark and sexy over here?" the doctor said, nodding towards Ellis.

"Boy seems to trust him. Wouldn't come without him."

Dr. Marsh seemed to take that into consideration, then looked at her watch and then back at the boy. It took her only a few seconds before she seemed to have come to a conclusion. Then nodding to herself, she motioned with her head that they all leave the room.

Once they were out in the hall, she closed the door and approached the two of them.

"Okay, officer, you should be good to go. He should be okay, and I'm sure you have a patrol to get back to."

"Sure thing."

"Dr. Marsh, are you sure? So far, Officer Ellis here is the only one who has been able to earn the boy's trust. We may need him when he wakes up."

"The mother should be here soon. With any luck, the boy will sleep until then."

"And if he doesn't?"

Dr. Marsh looked at the two of them, then back to the door.

"Well, it doesn't hurt to have you stick around, but you may want to hit the washroom and get yourself cleaned up. You're covered in God knows what and smell like you've been in a dumpster all night. When the family gets here, they may want to speak with you."

"And where would be the closest bathroom?" Officer Ellis said, looking down in both directions of the hallway and not seeing anything obvious.

"Follow me." Dr. Marsh said, then took off quickly down the hall. He had to rush to follow her.

* * * *

Jen pulled the car into the well-lit hospital parking lot. She had already gone to the wrong entrance twice and had to call the hospital's phone number to find out that she needed to go to the emergency room entrance to get into the building. It would be another half hour before the other entrances were opened. Part of her wanted to wait, but that could have been the fear of going in rearing its ugly head again. Another fear, like that of getting into a car accident or finding out her father had just died.

She had been terrified they were going to die on the way. Her mother had been a wreck, and it had been a struggle to calm her down enough to tell Jen what the police had told her. Not that the police had known much at that point. Her mom didn't know more about what happened to her dad or Davey, or if she did, she wasn't telling Jen. She had deteriorated into a sobbing mess of incoherent flesh, and whatever she tried to say was garbled nonsense. God, demons, hell and angels filled curses that came from a woman who had not once stepped foot into a church for as long as Jen could remember.

Jen had been so frustrated after questioning her mom, to suddenly being terrified when the landline sent its loud shilling shriek of noise through the bedroom. Jen, after convincing her heart that it was okay to get out of her throat, grabbed the handset before it went to the answering machine downstairs.

"Hello?"

"Yeah, can I speak to a Mrs. Carey, please?" The grumbly deep voice barked at her through the headset.

"She's not available. Who is this?" Jen said and looked over at her mother, who stayed with her head buried under the pillow. It almost looked like her mother was trying to strangle the life out of herself as she continued to hold the pillow to her face.

"Detective Price. I need to get in touch with her to talk about her husband and to get her consent to question her son."

"David? He's okay?" Jen could barely contain her excitement after hearing there was a chance her brother might be alright.

"Yes, they're taking him to the hospital to be evaluated. He wasn't talking, but we really need to know what he saw. We need consent to talk to him. We know there's no way he could be involved here, but we still need to know what he's seen."

Jen couldn't imagine what her brother had seen. No one was telling her anything, but she knew she didn't want her little brother to have to relive it. He already had night terrors. There was no way she was going to allow him to suffer through any more trauma.

"We'll be at the hospital soon. You do not have our consent to talk to my brother. We're coming to get him. You stay away from him." Jen said and slammed the handset down on the receiver, before turning to her mother.

It had taken Jen another fifteen minutes to get her to the car. There had been frequent pauses as her mother didn't want to leave the house and had at one point slid down a wall to cry on the floor. Jen had to pull her up to keep her walking.

Once they were in the car, Jen didn't even try to get her mother to drive. There was no way she had the capacity to handle it, so Jen eased her into the passenger seat before getting in on the driver's side.

Now that they had made it safely to the hospital, and she had found the right door, all they had to do was go in. The drive must have done something to her mother, as she sat in the passenger seat with no new tears, looking apprehensively at the building.

"Okay, we need to go get Davey." Jen said, pushing open her door.

"I know."

"You up for going in there?"

"Of course. I'm your mother. No matter what, I'm your mother." Her mom said. Jen had to look back at her as the deep voice she heard behind her was strange and alien. She saw her mom there, still looking at the hospital, half her face hidden in the darkness of shadow. The rest of her face was washed in the red light of the emergency sign high above. Even with the light on half her face, Jen couldn't see her eyes, her face stoic, like a statue as she stared ahead.

Her mother blinked, then looked over at her, nodded, then pushed open the passenger door. Jen pushed the odd sensation that nagged at her thoughts as she finished getting out. It was time to go see her brother and bring him home before the damn cops put him through more hell.

CHAPTER 6

The room reeked of human stench. All around, it could smell their filth as it permeated off every object that filled the room. All the clothing, the textures, the walls, the scent of their essence, it was enough for it to crave shifting back into non-existence.

Thankfully, there was the metallic odor of blood that filled the darkness where it hid. It was a perfume in which It wished to bathe. It had enjoyed the bliss of slicing through the soft flesh of the meat bags that had been available when it had first awakened earlier that night. Its only disappointment was when there had been so few of them, but now It felt more around It. It could feel the hunger again.

* * * *

"Detective!" Office Renn was staring at the bank of security monitors. He had been tasked with trying to figure out how to work the software, since none of the other officers had a clue. They were a small department that didn't have a budget for computer techs that might be able to work the system. Renn wasn't sure how bigger cities did or what they did. They probably had a team that could go through the computer system, but there in Cronenberg he was what they had.

It had taken him some time to figure out the software that ran the cameras. There were some out there that were more intuitive, but this system was not user friendly. He was finally able to find the recorded footage and had gone back in time to just before the massacre began when he stopped and called for the detective.

"What you got?" Hill said as she stepped into the small room. She grimaced at the blood that dripped from her shoes. They were all doing a terrible job of tracking it around the warehouse, but there was so much of it that it was impossible not to. It had pushed them into making the hard decision to prioritize finding out what happened over preserving the evidence. Her bet was on a drug deal gone bad and someone sending a message. It fit a narrative and would explain how someone could open a film studio in such a small city. It wasn't like they were in Chicago or St. Louis, somewhere that could justify the place. They were in Cronenburg, a population of 40,000 and just a blip on the scale when compared to some places. Yes, they did get some of the spillover crime of their neighboring larger city, Peoria, but nothing to justify this massacre they had walked into.

"I was able to finally find the recorded footage. It wasn't easy. This system does not explain itself and looks like this was some secondhand system from the dark ages. Definitely something my parents would have had put into their mom and pop and not what I would have expected if this is some big fancy film studio."

"Officer." Detective Hill said flatly, stopping the kid before he went into some spiel that only served one purpose, to make her feel old and out of touch with these damn computers. She still remembered the day when video systems were on recording loops using VHS. Not that she ever had much use for any of them, but she had two VCRs and knew how to record movies from one to another. If she remembered correctly, it had been a similar system on old security systems and was a much simpler time.

"Yes, Detective?" Officer Renn said, stopping himself and looking at the older woman who hovered over him as he sat there. She was short, but he was still seated at the desk, making him need to look up to meet her glare.

"What have you found?"

"Well, I haven't watched it yet. But I have it back to when they first arrived here."

"Who?"

"Them." Office Renn said, nodding to the gore out in the hallway.

"What time did they arrive?"

"Well, from the security log, we know they arrived around one, so once I was able to look up the footage by timestamp, I was able to-"

"Okay, so this is when?"

"One forty-seven."

"And you see them?"

Officer Renn pointed to the upper right monitor, and Hill could see a man getting out of his car. She could just begin to see the back door opening, and she assumed the boy was starting to get out. The footage was paused, blurry from it being dark outside and the crappy system showing gray grain to try to capture as much as possible in the poor lighting.

"Okay, let's see what happened.

$$* * * *$$

It sensed the pull; conscious minds were becoming aware of its existence and its master... it could not feel the presence that had called it forth. It was alone, free to devour and harvest. It was starving. It only knew one thing, and that was hunger.

"Look, right here, they are going into the special effects room." Voices spoke below, and it could smell the corruption. It wanted to pull them in, rip apart their limbs to the depths of their soul and satisfy its own cravings.

The barrier between them was thinning. It could feel them pulling it closer.

Drops of crimson were dripping as drool mixed with the blood of its previous morsels. A fresh puddle was forming beneath it. It could see the two fleshies standing there... They were watching away from it, not noticing as it drew closer.

"Is there a camera in there? No, but- what the hell was that?" The other morsel said.

The one moved away from it to get closer to the moving images, and the other moved back to give her room. The fleshie must have smelled something off as it turned to look at the pool forming on the ground. The drops of drool were moving closer to them, and the first of it landed on one who was turned away.

"What the-" the fleshie said and turned. The other one was already slowly looking up, and now stared at the ceiling, at the shifting darkness that was there...

$$* * * *$$

Renn felt a hot blast of air pummel against him with a stench of sulfur and sewage culminating together into a destruction of his olfactory senses. The odor was so strong that he winced as an intense pain shot through him as he looked up into the darkness in the corner of the room. There was a maze of pipes up there as the security room was located right next to the boiler room, or so Renn assumed, and since there were no ceiling tiles in the corner of the room, it allowed him to see the exposed metal...

A thought was pushing itself forward. He was looking into the darkness, watching as shapes shifted behind the pipes and something was nagging at him. It was something that was obvious. He just couldn't place it.

He had watched where the blood had dripped from; he had followed it up. When he first heard it, he thought maybe one of the pipes had started leaking. *That was a rational thought, right? It made sense. This was an old warehouse converted into whatever they were doing there. Of course, the pipes were old. It made sense that something would start leaking.*

His mind wouldn't let him grasp that what was coalescing into a fresh pool on the floor was thicker than water, that the drops dripping down were large and gooey, reminiscent of dog drool. Nor did he allow himself to focus on the color, the red drops as they fell to the floor.

He just continued looking up at the ceiling and to the space beyond the pipes. He watched as the darkness started shifting. The pipes continued, disappearing into ceiling tiles throughout the rest of the room and matched the tiles in the hallway. There were tiles along the hallway and throughout the rest of this room. So, why were there two tiles missing in the corner? What was different about that spot?

"Holy shit." Hill said, but she was watching the footage. She had pushed him out of the way so she could watch. He was watching the wall below the darkness, noticing for the first time the scratches that ran up the wall. They looked like claw marks, slashing their way, almost like what you would expect to see if you saw the marks left behind by a bear as they climbed up a tree.

Renn saw more of the drool came down on the back of Hill's coat as she was bent forward, watching the footage. He looked at the ceiling as she was turning around to look at him. She thought he had done something. She didn't see it. She hadn't seen the darkness that spun. She thought he was the only thing in the room with them.

Renn knew better as he looked up and saw that more ceiling tiles had disappeared overhead. Now, in the light of the computer monitors he could see more clearly into that darkness, and saw the elongated snout, the long-pointed incisors, the burning red eyes that were glaring at him. That was all he could see. Then it moved, and he was suddenly being sprayed with blood, pushed back with incredible force as the thing tore into the woman he had just been standing next to.

He tried to catch himself but slammed too hard against the wall. Off balance, he slid to the floor, not able to take his eyes off the creature as it tore into the detective. At first, all Renn could see was a shower of blood as it rained down on him. Then the creature pulled back, ripping Hill's head from her shoulders as it was engulfed by the large jaw.

Once free from the body, the monster started chewing. The snapping of the skull as it shattered against the tremendous force was like a shotgun blast. There was more crunching as it continued to shatter the skull, slurping the brains as it fed. Renn tried to push away the image of eating lobster, but the sound of the shattering crunch then chew was so eerily similar that he couldn't stop the vomit from escaping him.

He turned to the side, but much of it already covered his uniform. His stomach was painfully working to eject its contents onto the floor as he convulsed with the tide. His whole body shook as he tried to push the mental image of someone tearing through a lobster, hearing the shell snap as others sat at the table eating. Another round of nausea tore through him, and even though he was sure there was nothing left, he continued to heave, trying to expel as much as he could.

Hill's arm landed in his pool of vomit with a splash, and Renn looked back to see it was watching him, her corpse held up by claws that protruded through her body, dangling there like on a shish kabob on the long talons.

Renn couldn't see much of it, only the outline of its dark body as it stood in front of the monitors. What he could see was there were a lot of needle-like appendages that flared out from its back, flaring up, then easing back to being a part of its back, then flaring again. It was rhythmic as its needles would rise, then fall.

But those red eyes. They glowed with a burning intensity as they were fixed on him. Renn could hear it snarling at him, watching him, debating if it was going to discard its current dinner to take him.

Renn's legs grew warm, and he could feel the puddle beneath him. The odor of his urine mixed with the surrounding stench, and then he started crying.

"Please don't kill me. Please. Please, don't kill me. Oh Lord, help me, please."

The creature made a sound deep in its throat and he thought he could hear what sounded like the monster throatily laughing at him as it turned back to Hill.

A long tendril emerged from the creature's throat, and it took Renn a moment to realize it had to be a tongue. At least, that was what he had assumed it was, but as it reached Hill's lifeless body, it separated into four limbs, each with short, sharp-looking razor-like teeth running along them, then tipped with a long two-inch fang that rose from the tongue-like flesh.

The four limbs tore into her flesh, ripping from the neck down to her chest, tearing away the flesh and slicing through the bone, pulling the pieces into its jaw. Once the opening was large enough, the long threads stopped tearing into the flesh and submerged themselves into her insides, tearing apart her exposed ribs and then gorging on the organs beneath.

Drool dripped to the floor in large rivulets, mixing with the fresh blood as it continued to splash out of the mutilation this creature was doing to Hill's corpse. It was clear it was growing impatient as its motions grew more frantic, until suddenly it withdrew its tongue and used its massive jaw to start tearing away flesh. Each bite ripped away large portions of her body, muscle and bone being crushed together. Then it would lift up its snout and let the pieces slide down its throat, before furiously ripping at more.

Within minutes, her upper body was gone, and Renn was working to pull himself back to his senses. A part of his brain was screaming at him that he had to get out of there, but that part of himself felt so distant. It was worlds away from the carnage that was happening in front of him.

He tried to pull himself up. He didn't make it far and as soon as he tried to use his foot to support himself, he felt a sting on his leg, and fell back to sitting against the cool cement wall behind him.

That was when he noticed what looked like a thin strand of pulsating thread running from where it was wrapped around his ankle to the creature.

His head lolled forward. He tried to keep it up, but it was getting to be too heavy. The world around him was fading. He had one last chance, or it would get him, too. He had to do something.

He remembered the metal object attached to his waist. He struggled to remember what it was called, but he didn't need to remember the name. There had been plenty of training with it, plenty of time on shooting ranges and through academy courses.

Though now, as he tried to pull it free, he struggled. No matter how hard he pulled, he couldn't remove it from the holster. It was trapped; he was trapped. He was never going to get it free. The thing would come for him next...

* * * *

Darkness surrounded him, enclosing him, and he could feel the fear of everything that surrounded him. It sucked to him and pulled the air out of the surrounding room. It was suffocating him. He couldn't breathe. It welled up inside of him. David could feel it growing, building in his chest.

There was something there. David could sense something moving through the sea of black that moved around him.

Then he saw the burning red eyes, and he screamed.

* * * *

Dr. Marsh was talking to Nancy Sheeran, the trauma officer who had brought in the boy whom she had worked with several times over the past few years. They were talking about the boy, and the officer that had brought him in. It was obvious Nancy had been flirting with the officer, which normally Marsh would have disapproved of, but the boy had been out the whole time. This was one of the few times in their career that a little flirtation wasn't going to hurt anyone, especially the traumatized.

So instead, she had been laughing with her about him, admitting that had she been maybe ten years younger, she wouldn't mind tapping that herself. They had been laughing when the scream pierced through the hall, and with it, the lights flashed around them.

Dr. Marsh ignored the failing power grid as it wasn't the first time the electricity had been on the fritz in the old hospital, but was quick to run to the door and unlock it. The orderly was rushing from the locked nurses' station to follow Marsh into the room.

The boy was sitting up in bed, staring at them, screaming as loud as he could. His face was red from the exertion and his eyes were wide with terror. Given what the boy had gone through, she didn't hesitate.

"Get me the sedative." She said to the orderly as she rushed over to the bed. She grabbed the boy and tried to push him back onto the bed. He fought her, twisting out of her grip. Nancy stepped into the room and stood by the door, unsure what to do.

"It's going to be okay. It's okay David. You're safe. Everything's okay." Dr. Marsh said in a calming voice. Then she turned to Nancy by the door. "Find that officer. We may need him."

The orderly quickly appeared at the door and rushed to the bed, moving behind it, out of view of David. David hadn't paid him any attention. He kept his eyes locked straight forward on the other side of the room, never turning away from the darkness that was over there.

Dr. Marsh nodded to the orderly, who in turn was quick to stick the needle she had brought with her into David's shoulder.

It didn't take long before she felt the boy stop fighting her. Then she eased him back into the bed. He was asleep. This time, he would stay that way well into the morning. This time, it would be a dreamless sleep, free of nightmares, of the memories of this tragic night.

CHAPTER 7

"Doctor, the mother is here." The orderly said as they closed the door to the room.

"Okay, is she in the lobby, or on her way back?" Dr. Marsh said, trying desperately to hide the yawn that escaped her, her hand covering her mouth. It was of no use, and she found herself yawning for an extended time, the exhaustion of a long night shift catching up on her.

She looked over to see the orderly following up with a yawn of his own. He was trying to talk to her as he did, and she had to try to make out what he was saying as it was a drawn-out garbled mess, "on... way back. Denise just came on and... bringing... back."

"Talk about timing." They stepped into the little room that served as the nurse's station. As it was more enclosed in the psych ward, Dr. Marsh thought of it more as a guard station, though she knew the dangers of thinking of it in such a poor light. Yes, this was a more secure ward due to the nature of the patients there, but it was not good for the therapists to start seeing everyone as criminals that needed to be watched.

The smell of freshly brewed coffee wafted up from the coffeepot in the corner, and she was drawn to having another cup even though she knew it was not a good idea. They had brewed it to be ready for the next shift, as it had long been routine to have a fresh pot on for their arrival. 'Start the day right, and bright with a cup of joe' or something like that had been their department head's motto since he'd started, and it had been one of his little things.

She needed to avoid it. She'd be on her way home soon, and another cup would only make it that much harder for her to get to sleep once there.

"Have you started a chart on him?" Marsh said, turning from the pot. The orderly grabbed a metal clipboard from the desk in front of her and handed it over. There was a pen at the top, and Marsh reviewed the notes there before adding her own. She was just finishing her writing when she heard a noise in the hall and looked up to see a shorter woman being accompanied by a taller, younger one. Behind them was her relief, Dr. King, who was talking to them as they walked over to the little room. The door was already swooshing shut behind them and locking them into the ward.

"Doctor," Marsh said as she went out into the hallway.

"Doctor. Sounds like we have someone new with us this morning. I was just having Jenny and Cynthia here tell me a little about our newest temporary resident. He sounds like a charming young boy. Hopefully, we'll be able to get him home soon."

Dr. King stood between the two that had just arrived and when she spoke, she made sure to look at them both, keeping that optimistic smile that warmed many hearts and calmed many of those in anger as she spoke. When it came to therapy, there was much to be said with not just what you said to someone, but how you said it. Dr. King was one of their best at soothing the angriest with a smile and a few words.

"That would be nice." The older woman said, as she stood there, holding her arms across her chest, warily studying her surroundings. Her voice was soft, and her gaze never stopped moving. Her dancing eyes kept returning to the locked door behind them, and Marsh could faintly see the shake of the woman's hands. Marsh was sure those tremors would be a lot more visible had the woman not been hugging herself so intently.

"What's wrong with him? Why can't we take him home now?" The younger one said. Dr. King turned towards Marsh, and she stepped closer, handing the clipboard to King as she did.

"As far as we know, there is nothing wrong. He has had a traumatic night, and he has been non-verbal up to this point. For now, we have him resting. Keeping him here, at least for the time being, is in his best interest. He needs time to heal from what he saw."

"What did he see?" Jenny asked. She ignored her mother, who was shut down again, agitated and stepping from foot to foot.

"We don't know. The detective will want to ask him when he's ready. Right now, he's our only witness." Ellis said as he approached them. Cynthia's eyes grew wide, and she wrinkled her nose at the appearance of the officer as he came to a stop near them. His uniform was covered in blood and gore, pieces of flesh he hadn't noticed in the darkness of the warehouse but were now patches of disgusting over the dark blue cloth.

It looked like Jenny and her mother both could see it... all of it.

"Hello, I'm Officer Sheeran. First name's Nancy, and I am the trauma officer for the county. I come out whenever there's someone at a scene that may need a more delicate touch than what a normal officer is trained for. I spent time with your son, and he is very upset about what happened tonight. Officer Ellis here, I think he's trying to get my job. I don't think we would have calmed him enough to get him here without his assistance "

"Thank you, officer," Cynthia said and reached out a small, delicate hand and allowed the man to give it a weak shake.

"Should they be questioning him? He's nine years old. He shouldn't have to go through that again," Jenny said as her mom released the officer's hand then moused away.

"We don't know," Dr. Marsh said. "Until David is talking, we don't know his mental state, but the detective can't talk to him without your consent or without his therapist stating it is okay. Right now, I firmly believe it is not in David's best interest to do-"

Officer Ellis's radio crackled to life.

"Shots fired; shots fired. We have an officer dead on scene, another down." A loud voice came through the speaker.

"What's that?"

The group of people that had been standing there in the hallway turned to see a boy in his teens, one of the temporary visitors there. Behind him were a few other children and another orderly.

"Where did it go? Where is it?" the voice on the radio called out again. Ellis was quickly fumbling with where the radio was attached to his belt, as he was trying to mute it. Another voice, one that sounded near hysterical tears, called out, "It came from the darkness, and in the darkness it has returned."

Ellis looked at the group of scared faces. Some of the children that were gathered around him were already crying. The last thing he heard as he was finally able to turn the radio off was a cackling laugh as that voice screamed, "It's coming. The darkness is coming."

The radio snapped off.

Dr. Marsh was glaring at Officer Ellis, her face red. Dr. King was already rushing over to the group of children, working to get them together and calming them down, speaking soothingly to them.

"Do you realize where you are? You get out of here, now. You're done. David is here. His family are here. You can go. Get out of here, and if you ever come back here again, that radio better be off. You got me?" She said to him, walking quickly to the door. She scanned her card to the pad on the wall, and the door opened. She motioned for him to leave.

He nodded and, with his head held low, he quickly left the ward.

Dr. Marsh turned to Nancy.

"You've had a long night, too. You should probably get out of here, get some rest. If we need any information later, we'll call."

Nancy nodded and followed the officer, who was already turning his radio back on, adjusting it to where he could barely make out what was going on.

"I want to take my son home."

Dr. Marsh turned her attention back to Cynthia and felt for the woman. If she had to guess, Mrs. Carey had seen the inside of a facility not too different from this one. Dr. Marsh wasn't going to try to guess the circumstances, as uninformed assumptions could kill in medicine, whether it was physical or mental. Especially when it was pertinent to the current situation.

"I'm going to recommend against it. We should keep him here. At least until he wakes up, but possibly even a couple days."

"I want to take him home. I'm his parent. Is there any legal reason why I can't take him home?"

"No, not legally, but you would have to sign some paperwork stating that you are removing him from care against doctor's recommendations."

"Mrs. Carey," Dr. King called out, walking up to them. The children that had come out earlier were now walking towards a common area, the morning orderly leading the way. "Your son is currently sleeping, but you can see him. Then, after that, we can show you around and you can see how we might be able to really help him here.

Cynthia looked at them both skeptically, then reluctantly nodded, letting them lead her to a closed door nearby.

* * * *

Officer Ellis kept the volume down on his radio so that he could barely hear it as he rushed out of the hospital. He didn't go through the building back the way he came in. It was obvious by the people coming in through one of the side entrance doors that the rest of the hospital was now open, waking up with the rising sun like so many other people out there.

By the time he made it outside and turned the volume up on the radio so he could hear it clearly, whatever had been happening must have calmed down. He was surprised earlier when that had been broadcasted on an open channel. That wasn't normal, but at the same time it didn't sound like whatever was happening was normal.

There was a nagging part of him that wanted to call in and ask what he had missed. That would require him to explain breaking protocol by turning down the radio.

So, he stood there at the east side entrance, enjoying the cool breeze that bristled with the chill of an early fall. The sun was rising, the orange rays stretching across the sky, burning away the remnants of the night.

God, he could use a smoke. His lungs burned with the desire, and he felt like he'd sell his soul right then and there for a cigarette. Three weeks and he was still craving the damn things. He knew they were addictive, but thought by now the pull wouldn't be as strong. If anything, it was stronger now than when he was smoking a pack a day.

"Got a ride?"

He turned and saw Nancy had followed him out.

"Shit. Forgot I rode with you. I'm going to need you to take me back there if you're okay with it."

He saw the look of horror that flashed in her eyes.

"Yeah, have thought of that. We have to go back. Have you heard any more of what they found? Everyone okay? It sounded like some crime movie in there."

"Not yet."

"Not curious or ignorance is bliss?"

"Ignorance. Full of it right now."

"Yeah?"

"Yeah."

"Well, don't worry that you upset any of the kids back there. There is nothing those two can't handle. Unfortunately, I've had to be here too often. It's never a good time."

"Is it only children?"

"There are other wards. It's not good to have children with the adults. Not with those that could be a danger to themselves or others."

"Makes sense."

"Come on, I'll get you back so you can check in."

"Thanks."

They were walking back to the E.R. as that was where Nancy had parked. As they passed through the emergency room treatment area, an ambulance pulled up to the side entrance. EMTs rushed out, and they were quickly lowering a gurney. On it was a uniformed officer that Ellis recognized but couldn't recall his name. The officer was thrashing on the gurney, fighting against the restraints that bound him, screaming as loud as he could.

A doctor rushed past them to hurry to the gurney.

"Why haven't you sedated him?" The doctor barked at him.

"He is sedated. We've given him all we could without killing him. He's not calming down."

The doctor was checking the officer's vitals as Nancy and Ellis found their way to the exit.

"Darkness. It went back to the dark. IT WENT BACK."

Ellis felt a twinge of guilt as the door closed behind them, muffling the screaming.

CHAPTER 8

Jen sat with her mom in the lobby of the hospital. They had been there for the last hour, and she wasn't sure why they were still there other than her mom was too tired and too emotionally exhausted to face the drive home.

Jen couldn't fault her for that. She shared much of the same exhaustion and, having watched her mother go multiple rounds with the doctors on whether to keep her brother there another day, had grown tiresome.

She should get her mother home before she got her second wind. While Jen wasn't keen on the idea of leaving her brother there, she heard what the doctors had been saying and realized that staying there may be the best thing for him. What would taking him home do for him? He's been suffering from night terrors repeatedly for the last few weeks and they had only been getting worse. If something didn't change soon, he would be celebrating his tenth birthday and still wetting the bed with demons chasing him in his dreams.

Maybe there at the hospital he could get one good night of sleep. Maybe more. Maybe he should stay there.

Jen had to fight to keep the tear from working its way free. She was not going to think about it and she was not going to lose her brother. Maybe she was too much like her mom in that regard, but she was going to make sure her brother would come home. Today wasn't the day, sure, but he was coming home.

They just needed to make sure and make it a place worth coming home, too. That was going to be hard now that...

She broke off the train of thought as she looked around the room. The hospital had a nice main lobby, with much of the decor reminiscent of a modern business office. There was a lot of glass and high-end lighting, even a water fountain at the entrance that

Jen had regularly seen mothers fighting with their children to keep them from splashing in.

As she watched, one mother was having to nearly physically drag her son away from the fountain. He was kicking and screaming, fighting to get back to it.

That's it. She had to get out of there.

"Come on, mom, we need to get home."

"What, no? We can't leave. We have to get David."

"David's staying here for now. We can come back later and check on him. I'll call and make sure they know to call us the moment he wakes up, but he needs to rest, okay? We need to get home. I'm sure there are things that need to be taken care of and I need to let school know I'm not going today."

"You're not going?" Her mother said, seemingly shocked by the revelation.

"No, I'm not."

"You have to go. You have class."

"Yeah, classes are what they have in school." Jen said as she worked to pull her mom up so that she was standing next to her. "But I'm in no shape for class and you are in no shape to be alone."

"But we need to check on your father."

That stopped Jen, and she had to fight the sudden knife twisting in her chest and the urge to scream in a bout of anger. She nearly bit her tongue as she fought to keep it all under control, the madness that was swirling up inside her, wanting to release on the shorter woman next to her. She tried her best to rein in the emotion.

How could she just not get it?

"Mom, you told me about dad."

"What? We don't know for sure. They didn't know for sure. Maybe they found him? Maybe he's okay?"

"Let's get home. I'll call the police on the way. Do you have the detective's number?"

"I think so. It should be on my nightstand next to the phone."

"Okay. We'll go home and I'll call as soon as we get there, okay?"

* * * *

Officer Ellis climbed out of the passenger seat of Nancy's car with the certainty that she wanted to give him her number, and the awkwardness of trying to get out of there before she forced it on him. She seemed nice, but crime scenes and massacres, many of which were his fellow brothers in blue, was not something where he wanted to be setting up first dates. It made him wonder just how messed up she was to be doing so. What was it they always said, the most messed up people go into psychology?

Nancy may not have been a psychotherapist, but being a trauma officer and receiving that form of special training, she may have her own set of baggage that drew her to the job.

Not that he didn't have his own weight to bear. Was he even ready to get back out there? It felt too soon.

"Well, until next time." Nancy said.

"Later," he said, closing the door and wondered if she realized what she just said. Next time, was she expecting another massacre? One with a child involved?

He shook it from his thoughts as he looked around the taped off area. While the scene no longer reflected that of a horror film, it was definitely reminiscent of a drug bust gone bad. There were still plenty of squad cars that were outside the perimeter and farther back, an SUV that had a local news station logo wrapped around it.

There were a lot of squad cars, but Officer Ellis didn't see a lot of other officers. It was quiet in the warehouse parking area, with little more than the sound of a reporter giving a recap of what happened. That there had been some brutal murders but that the police weren't releasing much information yet.

Ellis turned away from the reporter and was heading toward the entrance when he saw the detective from earlier. Ellis struggled to remember the man's name. He wasn't one Ellis was used to seeing around, and was an asshole to anyone still in uniform, so Ellis had tried to stay out of the man's circle. Today, for whatever reason, it just seemed like they couldn't get away from one another.

The detective saw him and nodded, changing direction to walk over.

"Anything from the boy? Is he talking yet?"

"Not yet. Have we found his father?"

"Only pieces, nothing identifiable." The detective said as he pulled a small device from his coat pocket and within seconds, a puff of smoke escaped it as he vaped in from the cursed machine. Ellis grimaced, smelling the sweet fragrance, again feeling that maddening desire for a real cigarette.

"This is a mess. I've never seen anything like it. I've never heard of anything like it. I mean- you know what I keep going back to."

Ellis shook his head; not sure what Detective Price was thinking. The man was a prick who could smoke over a corpse while talking about football or some other mindless topic. He was a schmoozer more than a detective and was completely tone deaf when it came to seeing emotions in others. He didn't have an ounce of empathy in him, and for that, the brass seemed to love him.

Why the hell was it that it always seemed like those who had the littlest of clues, and no sense of others, always rose to lead? It's like narcissism attracted narcissism and they promoted one another.

"I keep going back to the eighties. They had all those drug wars or what have you down in Florida. I heard it got pretty messy down there. Killers, enforcers doing shit to send messages. I keep thinking this is a message."

"So, you think drugs?" Ellis, thinking back to just moments ago, when he was thinking those same thoughts, though he was thinking more of the movies. Ellis doubted Price's experience was any more firsthand himself, but really, what else could it be?

Damn, he hated agreeing with this asshole.

"You don't?"

"I do, but my gut says no," Ellis said, realizing for the first time that it was true. Every time he had thought that it was drug related, it had been more of a rationalization than what he truly felt. Drugs was the easy answer.

"Oh, so your gut is a detective now."

"Nope."

"Good. You know…" Detective Price made an effort to look at Ellis's nameplate on his uniform before looking back at him, "Officer Ellis, maybe take some remedial classes on procedure and how to secure a crime scene. Can't have you contaminating them anymore. You're lucky I don't make a bigger deal about it. Put you on report."

"I saved a child."

"You destroyed evidence. We would have gotten to the child as soon as we could."

"Sure. I'll do that next time." Ellis said, his voice dripping with sarcasm. He had to physically control his breathing to keep his anger from boiling over to where he said something he shouldn't. He didn't think Price had anything that would hold up in reporting him, but Price was also their golden boy.

"You do that." Price said, ignoring Ellis's tone. He wasn't walking away. The two stood there as though they were waiting for something. Ellis started to realize that Price was waiting. He kept looking towards the road, then back at the scene around him.

"What's the latest?"

"What?" Price looked back at him as though forgetting that he was still there.

"I had heard some chatter earlier. Something happen?"

"Yeah. The killer's still in there somewhere, or he was. Took out Detective Hill while you were on babysitter duty. According to Officer Renn, the psycho must be some kind of acrobatic bodybuilder going about in a Halloween costume. Guy leapt down from the ceiling in the security room, took out Hill with some kind of claw type weapon and a whip, then left Renn sitting in his own piss. Now, the state boys are getting involved, so their forensic team is on their way.

"We look like a bunch of fucking keystone cops not able to do our damn jobs and now the staties will show up, pull their dicks out and show us how much bigger they are. We're about to get fucked, and I doubt they're going to be lubing us up first."

Officer Ellis couldn't help but look at the door Price had come out of when he had returned to the scene. It was the same door he had gone into hours ago, when it was still dark out, with only their flashlights to guide them. The perp had been in there all that time. Ellis remembered how he felt, the nagging sense that something was there and was watching. He felt that it was hungry and just wanted him to take the wrong step, go to the wrong place. Then it would have him, and it would have been his body ripped to shreds…

Ripped to shreds. The bodies had to be torn apart, and quickly, too. Too quick for one person to be doing it. How was a whole team of cartel enforcers hiding in there and tearing cops apart? Where were their vehicles? What was their way out?

And where were his brothers and sisters in blue? It was too quiet out there, and there were a lot of squad cars still there, their flashing lights not quite as blinding in the morning sun.

"Where is everyone?"

"Not dead, if that's what you're thinking. Now, I have most of them around the security room and checking the surrounding area. We focused everything on that part of the building. You know we flashed our lights up to where Renn said the guy disappeared too, expecting some kind of hole up there, something to climb through, or some way out. We still haven't found anything.

"Renn's useless. Fucking rookie. It all got to him and we had to send him to the hospital. He lost it when he saw Hill get taken. He's babbling some nonsense about monsters coming out of the dark. He swears the guy in the costume was some monster.

"Whole thing's a fucking shit show. The security room's a mess now, too. That was probably what the guy went back for. Must have had some kind of blade, completely sliced through all the screens and the computer with the footage. All of it, the whole desk is torn apart. Everything is lost. Staties are going to love that. We had two officers in there and one man tore it all to hell right in front of them."

Detective Price shook his head, obviously frustrated with everything. Ellis had the sense, though, that Price wasn't frustrated with the loss of a fellow officer. He seemed more hung up on how he was going to look when the state police showed up.

Ellis' stomach twisted with just what this man would put people through without batting an eye. He would have to remember that in the future if he was ever put in a situation of working directly under him.

"What do you need me to do?" Ellis said, dreading just what the detective would say.

"Find some bodies. We've gone through the building, searched it as much as we could, and still not a single body. Pieces here and there, scraps of flesh, things that would traumatize war zone marines, and blood... So much blood. Still haven't found a single identifiable part of a body. Just scraps." The detective's voice trailed off, then he blinked and looked back at Ellis.

"You go home. Get back to the station and punch out. You've done enough for one night. Go home and give that wife and son a kiss. Try to not take this home with you."

A truck pulled up to the taped barrier, and the detective started walking towards it. He didn't see the pained grimace at the mention of Ellis's wife and son. Detective Price was a narcissistic dick who didn't care about anyone other than his self. Still, even though they were not close, not in one another's circles on a bad day, such a selfless asshole should still have known about his family. They had been gone for over a year. It had been a major tragedy. The news had rocked through the precinct, and he had received condolences from everyone. Even Price had expressed them… So, what did it say about the asshole that he couldn't remember it from a year ago?

"Fuck you too," Ellis said under his breath, holding it in. Like always, he had to hold it all in. The anger, the frustration, all of it building inside. His chest tightened, his heart pounding as he closed his eyes and gritted his teeth. Some day he would release his anger. Some day he would express his rage at God and the world. He was mad at all of them, as they were all guilty of stealing so much from him.

But for now, he just continued… holding it all in.

CHAPTER 9

"Hey Davey, time to wakey. Let's shake that booty and get ready for school."

David heard his father's voice, and slowly felt himself being pulled from some other world, no matter how hard the other world worked to keep him. Not all of him was there yet. Part of him still clung to that other world, so as he opened his eyes, a fog clouded his mind. It was hard to think, and he was still trying to adjust to where he was.

"Dad?" He said, his eyes fluttering open. He could feel the brightness of the room and its comforting glow. Dad. He had heard his dad and that meant all of it had been another nightmare. It had been one of his worst and had been terribly realistic. He'd have to tell his dad all about it. Maybe he'd even make it into one of his movies.

"Yeah bud, I'm here. Come on, time to get up. We gotta get going. We have so many more people to kill."

David pulled himself up from the bed, nearly jumping out of it as he ran across his room just as his room dissolved around him. His toys, the walls, everything melting, the colors swirling around him as they turned to liquid and drained through the floor.

Only white walls remained, and David spun around to see a window dimmed by thickness and metal.

Dad wasn't there. No one was in the room with him, and the weight hit him that it had been a dream, and he was not fully awake. He looked back to the bed and saw himself lying there. He was so still and peaceful.

He didn't look right, neither did he feel right. Something was wrong, missing. Some part of him felt disconnected and that the child that slept in that bed was a shell.

What was he now? Was he a ghost? Why could he watch himself sleeping like that? Was he dreaming? He had heard his dad. Was that part of the dream?

Dad…

Daddy. Where was his dad? Why was thinking about dad making him so sad?

He took a step back towards his body. He didn't want to; something was dark there, and he wasn't sure he wanted to go back to it. Still, he took another step, unable to stop him.

It felt like there were invisible hands on his back that were easing him back there. They were rough hands, not the soft hand of his dad, when his dad used to guide him places or get ready to pick him up and toss him around. These hands were rough, sharp. He could feel large nails as they pushed into his resistant skin.

He took another step, and David felt like he could see the darkness, like smoke drifting up from beneath his clothes. It was faint, dissipating in the air. As he took another step towards his body, he could smell eggs. Bad eggs, like when his mom had left them in the car one time, and they hadn't found them until the next morning. The whole car smelled like that smoke he saw moving towards him, reaching out to him.

David started to cry and tried to turn around, to run away from the body on the bed. He knew it was his body, but he didn't want to get close to it. There was something wrong with it. There was something wrong with him and he needed to get out of there. He needed to find Jenny. His sister would know what to do.

The hand that had been pushing him towards his dark body grabbed him and spun him back around, and again, he took another step. He was hovering near his own body now, standing close enough that he could touch himself.

"Dad!" David cried out, yelling as loud as he could.

"Yes son. I am here." David heard the voice, but it wasn't his dad's voice. The deep rumbling voice was loud and shook everything, but was quiet as well. It was like the voice had spoken with the barest of a whisper, but the power behind it resonated and tore at David, making him want to collapse and run away from it.

That was when the boy in the bed opened his eyes and screamed. He screamed, and then he was back in his body. He screamed and screamed with everything he had. It tore at his throat; the power behind it burning as he screamed louder and with more fear than he had ever felt before. He screamed, and outside his room everyone came running. He screamed, because he was sure that whatever had just spoken to him had been the thing that had killed his dad and now it was after him.

* * * *

"Check him, check his vitals." Dr. King yelled as she rushed into the room. She was rushing over to David, reaching out to ease him back into bed. Behind her, two orderlies rushed in. Juan was a large man who was used to working with kids, though these were always the times he hated. He was quick to get to one side of the bed, reaching for the boy's wrist. Denise was right behind him; an average sized woman who went to the other side of the bed. She helped Dr. King calm David down, easing him back.

Between the three of them, they knew they could overpower the boy, but that wasn't their goal. They needed to ease him, to relax him. The goal was to make sure he wasn't hurting anyone, especially himself. Getting him to lie back on the bed was secondary to just calming the terrified child.

"What's the time? How long has it been?" Dr. King called out, struggling to yell loud enough over the screaming. She was surprised as both she and Denise were struggling to get the boy back. Even with them trying to do it gently, they shouldn't have had such a fight. It was like the boy was fighting them with every bit of strength he had.

"It's just after two. So little over seven hours."

"Okay. Get a shot of Midazolam ready. 4 milligrams."

"BP is 160 over 90. Erratic."

"Get the shot."

"Dr. King?" came a voice from the doorway. A group of kids stood there, some of them with their hands over their ears.

"It's going to be okay. Everyone, out to the common room. Please." Dr. King looked at Denise and nodded at her, then motioned to the door. The older woman understood the signal and quickly made her way over to them, holding her arms wide and shooing the children. Once she had them out, she followed them, closing the door and leaving Dr. King to try to ease David down.

Juan came back a moment later, having left to prepare the sedative.

David stopped screaming as they prepared to stick the needle into his shoulder. Dr. King and Juan looked at one another, then took a step back.

"David. Do you like to be called David? Do you prefer Dave or David." Dr. King said, speaking slowly. David didn't respond or even acknowledge that she was there. He continued to stare straight forward, locked into the plain white wall in front of him. "You can talk to me, David. I'm here to listen. You're in a safe space. We are here to help you."

Dr. King watched David, seeing if there was any reaction. She couldn't see the tornado of thoughts that were racing through him. She had no way of knowing how lost he was in that storm with so many feelings and words swirling around so viciously that the outside world had drifted away. He was sad. He knew he was sad, but the reason why was lost in there somewhere, mixed with pain, fear, and misery. There was a wetness that wanted to escape from the corner of his eye, a tightness to his chest, but the reason for them was distant and out of his grasp.

"David. My friend here, his name is Juan. He's really good with kids. He loves to listen, just like I do, so if there is ever anything you want to say to him, he's right here. We both are. We're here for you."

David did turn and look at Juan, who was staring at the boy. That smile was warm and genuine, and everything Dr. King had said about him was true. He was excellent with kids. They all loved to play with them when it was allowed. It's hard to tell what will get through to the kids sometimes, but Juan exceeded at getting many of them out of their rooms for some physical activity, at least.

Maybe Juan would have better luck. David responded to the officer earlier. Maybe David was more comfortable talking to men. It wasn't unheard of.

Dr. King noticed that David had stopped looking up at Juan and turned his attention to the needle still visible in his hand.

"David. Juan is going to give you some medicine. He's just going to give you a little shot to make you feel better. Okay. Is it okay for Juan to do this? Are you okay with needles?" Dr. King asked gently, looking back and forth between the needle and the boy. As she spoke, she saw David's eyes getting wider and could see the fear filling them.

"It's just a quick shot. David. Look at me. It's just a little poke and he'll be done. Okay? Just a little poke."

David looked at her briefly and then back to the needle. He was backing up in bed, pulling the thin blanket up to him as he worked his way back. Then he started to kick at Juan. They were wild kicks, and Juan quickly backed away before any of them could connect.

"David, David, David. It's going to be okay." Dr. King said, again reaching out for his shoulders as he started to thrash around. "David, we need to give you the medicine and we don't want to have to hold you down, but we will if we have to. Please, let us give you the shot. It's just a poke. You're going to be okay." She said, forcefully pushing David back so that he was lying on the bed. She got his shoulders down, then looked up at Juan. They made eye contact, and she nodded.

In one quick, well-practiced motion, he reached down, put one hand on the boy's shoulder and steadied it. Then, with the other, he quickly stuck the needle into the shoulder and pushed home the plunger. In less than a second, he pulled the needle back and stepped away from David.

Dr. King watched him back away and then looked down at the boy, who had begun screaming again as soon as he felt the needle break skin.

The ground shook, and the fluorescent light above them flickered. It grew brighter, then the bulbs shattered in their frames. The room darkened as only sunlight filtered through thick coated glass windows lit the room.

"Damn earthquakes. I got out of California to get away from the damn things." Dr. King said, unfazed as the room settled.

Juan didn't say anything at first as he studied the broken light above them, then the boy, then finally the corner where he swore it appeared as though the shadows were growing towards them.

"We don't normally get earthquakes in Illinois."

"No? Happens all the damn time out there. "

"Last time I remember there being one, I was twelve."

"So, what, yesterday?" Dr. King said. She looked back at David, whose eyes were already beginning to gloss over, the fight having gone out of them. He turned to her, though, and for the first time, those eyes locked onto hers.

"It's coming for you now. It's coming to kill all of you." David said, his voice a rasp, almost unearthly, as the words were forced through gritted teeth.

His eyes rolled back to the whites, before he slumped back and faded into sleep.

"It's going to be okay, David. We're going to keep working with you. You spoke. I don't care what you said, you spoke. That's progress. We'll get you home soon, to your family. I bet your mom and sister are ready for you to be there. You just need to talk to us, then we'll get you home to them." Dr. King said, stroking his hair back as she spoke.

Juan was already at the door, waiting for her. She finally left David's side and followed him out of the room. She had other children who were waiting for her. Kids that she was much further along on their journey of helping them. She hoped that soon she would be able to get David along on that journey as well.

CHAPTER 10

"Get your shoes on. We need to go get your brother."

Jen looked up at her mother, who was rushing around the living room, frantically looking at the end table, picking up the magazines that were thrown about haphazardly, before moving on to looking under the couch cushions.

"Come on, grab your shoes. We're going."

"Did they call?" Jen asked, closing her laptop. She was confused. She hadn't heard the phone ringing and was surprised that her brother would be feeling better so soon, though she was worried about him. She had just been journaling about her feelings, as there were so many of them struggling to work their way to the surface. She couldn't just be one thing. She'd love to just focus on being worried about Davey, but her dad was dead. Her rock was not there any longer. All that was left was the shell of her mom and her brother. Who did she have to talk to? There was Clara, but Jen just didn't have the energy to be dealing with people's sympathy.

"No, but we need to go. I don't trust what they are doing to him there. Those places are bad places. They just fill you with drugs and lies and pray for your insecurity. David was fine. Of course, he was fine. He's just overly dramatic. He always wants attention. He likes everyone trying to take care of him. We just need to get him home. He's better here."

"Mom, the doctors would not have kept him there if there wasn't a reason for it."

"They don't know what they are talking about. I know my son." Her mother said, slamming down the last cushion. "Have you seen my keys?"

Jen looked at her, not wanting to answer the question. She did know where the keys were as she had driven them home, but she didn't trust her mom with them. At least, not in her mom's current manic state. Jen just hoped that her mom didn't think too much about who was the last one who drove the car. Then she might just remember where Jen normally put the keys, and then there would be no stopping her from going.

You should just take her. You want to see your brother? Now would be a good time to go, get there before it is too late in the afternoon, and hey, maybe they did have some breakthrough with him.

She would love to see him and give him a hug. She really, really needed to give him a hug. She was worried about him. She knew how she was feeling, mostly. Some of it was still raw and hard to tell just what she felt. How was he feeling? How was this getting into his mind?

A lot harder, obviously, if he wasn't talking.

Jen was about to tell her mom that she would take her to the hospital when the doorbell rang, followed by an impatient pounding on the front door.

"Mrs. Carey?" a demanding voice boomed from the other side of the door.

Jen looked at her mom, who was already backing away from the door, her hands on her chest. New tears could already be seen on the horizon as her puffy eyes grew glossy. Before Jen could even move, her mom was whimpering and reaching for the closest chair to sit down in.

"It's okay, I'll get it," Jen said to her mom, speaking as gently as she could before turning to go down their front hallway. She reached it, already pulling out her phone and checking their outside video to see who was there.

Outside stood a man she hadn't seen before, wearing an ill-fitted suit that seemed out of place. She watched as the man moved back and forth, looking at the front of the house and then back to the door.

Jen didn't like how edgy he seemed. It reminded her too much of how her mother had just been, and she debated not opening the door. With the video doorbell, she could just as easily go back to the living room and talk to him through the little silver box attached to the door frame.

Going against her instinct, she opened the door, looking at the man standing there and biting back how much she wanted to tell him off for disturbing them today, of all days.

"Your mother home?" Was the first thing out of the man's mouth and Jen realized just how much she already did not like the man.

"She's not seeing anyone right now. Why don't you try back next week?" Jen said, already closing the door.

"Hey. I need to speak with her. I'm Detective Price. I'm investigating your dad's mur- disappearance last night."

"And how is my mom supposed to help you? She wasn't there." Jen said, not opening the door back up, but holding it open just enough so she could talk to the tall man looking down at her. He must really have been tall, as Jen wasn't used to having to look up at people.

"Well, she could give us some background on your dad. Known associates. You wouldn't know of anyone that would want to hurt your dad? Any shady characters hanging around?"

"No, my dad is never around. He's always off shooting movies and when he is home, he's in the studio working day and night with his crew." Jen said, again preparing to close the door.

"We're just trying to find the people who did this. We need to talk to your brother and find out what he knows. I'm heading over to the hospital and need your mom's authorization to talk to him. I really need to talk to your mom."

Before Jen could even respond, the door was pulled open, roughly forcing Jen back and nearly falling against the wall behind her. It surprised Jen. She didn't think her mom was that strong and hadn't realized her mom had moved behind her.

"You have no right talking to my son. You stay the hell away from him."

"Mrs. Carey, we're trying to find out what happened to-"

"I know what you're trying to do, but do it without David. He has seen too much, and he doesn't need more vultures like you pecking away at him. You're just as bad as reporters, always making up your little stories. You keep the hell away from him."

"The sedatives should be worn off from him soon. Please, before they pump him full of more meds. I'd like to see what he knows."

"What sedatives? I never approved of them giving him sedatives. Doctors with all your cures and vaccines. No, my David should never have been given any shots or anything else. I did not approve."

"Ma'am, I had already checked with the doctor from this morning. They had to give him a sedative to calm him down and get some sleep. He should be coming out of it soon and with your permission, I just want to ask him a few questions. You are more than welcome to be there too; in fact, I would encourage it."

"All of you, stay away from my son." Cynthia was stepping back, and Jen made sure she was out of the way for the door to be closed.

"Where did your husband get his money? What was he really doing in that warehouse?" The detective said, just as Cynthia Carey slammed the door shut.

Jen watched as her mother fell against the door and the anger that she had shown toward the detective was already giving way to more tears. She was lowering herself to the floor.

On her phone, Jen watched as the detective continued to stand there on their porch. It was clear he wasn't used to doors being slammed in his face and wasn't sure how to proceed.

"Fucking bastard can choke on his own dick." Jen said. She took a deep breath, waiting for the verbal assault from her mom, admonishing her for her language. When it never came, she realized just how lost her mom was. When she looked down at the smaller woman, her mother looked as though she had aged a decade overnight. She was so frail sitting there on the floor. "I'll get the keys. Let's go see David, see how he's doing."

* * * *

Tommy Ellis was cursing just about everything in his life. His job, assholes that he worked with at his job, the night shift, the damned sun, which made it so hard to sleep during the day. Hell, he was even cursing a little kid that had done nothing to him, but since he'd been there and saved the boy that morning, he couldn't get him out of his mind. He was worried about the boy; about what he saw that made him so terrified.

Ellis had his own concern that the boy may still be in danger. If the boy saw who killed his father, then not only was he going to be messed up for the rest of his life, but the killer was still out there. The boy could still be at risk, and that prick of a detective was more worried about getting another case solved than keeping anyone safe. Who cares who gets hurt, just as long as everything looks great on paper? At least, that was the reputation Ellis had heard.

His phone rang, the shrilling ring tone loud in the small bedroom. He hadn't slept in the main bedroom since the accident, as he found it impossible to sleep in there and not think about her. Thoughts of her led to thoughts of them both and the runaway train of emotions about how much he missed them.

It didn't take much to get him to think about them. He thought he was getting better, but he was only kidding himself. After last night and helping David, he realized just how deluded he was as the wound was fresh again, and his heart was bleeding their tears.

Slowly, he made his way across the room, sidestepping random piles of debris on his way to the dresser, where his phone was glowing. He just made it before it went to voicemail, but didn't recognize the number. He set the phone back down, getting ready to just go back to bed and spend a few more hours not sleeping, but his bladder decided it needed to be emptied.

The house never used to look this way. In the darkness of day, with the curtains pulled, the house somehow felt emptier with him in it than it ever did before. Tatiana would have joked with him, calling him a vampire for how he now lived and maybe it fit. He had chosen to switch to night shift because he had started to hate the people he was around on days. But overnight meant sleeping during the day, which led to always having the curtains drawn. So maybe he was a vampire, cursing all those still living.

He came back to the guest room, his room now, and saw the light dimming on his phone. He picked it up to see two more missed calls, a voicemail and a text saying to call him back, though Tom still had no idea who "him" was.

Fuck, he thought to himself as he listened to the voicemail. "Him" was that prick of a detective, and he was obviously pissed.

"Officer Ellis, I need you to contact David Carey's mother. I reached out, and they slammed the door in my face. We need to interview the kid, get him talking. The kid likes you, so I'm told. Get down to the hospital and see if you can get him talking."

Ellis stared at his phone in disbelief. How do assholes like that get promoted? Seriously, was that part of the detective exam? How big of an uncaring asshole you can you be? And what was it? Did the detective want him to go to the house or to the hospital? Damn asshat doesn't even know what he wants.

Ellis tossed the phone onto his bed and grabbed a shirt from one of the floor piles, then grabbed a pair of jeans. He didn't worry about the jeans, but the shirt he checked, made sure it didn't smell and didn't have anything inappropriate printed on it. He wasn't on duty and had no intention of putting in any overtime for that prick. So, if he wasn't on duty, it wouldn't hurt for him to stop by the hospital and check up on the kid. Not like he was going there as Officer Ellis, but as Tommy, the guy who found him and was worried.

It was a damn thin line he was walking, but he was comfortable with it because in his heart, he actually believed it. He didn't give two shits what that detective wanted. He couldn't sleep and he was worried about the kid. Stopping by the hospital may ease his mind a little, enough so that maybe he could come back and get a few hours of sleep.

He checked his phone. It was after three. With fall approaching, it would be dark in a few hours. He debated about grabbing his coat and opted for a sweat jacket instead. The nights were growing cooler.

CHAPTER 11

Dr. King heard the shouting. She was in session with Louise. A teenager who had run away from her latest foster home and was once again relegated to their facility for a brief interview before falling back into the system. She was another in the revolving door that Dr. King dealt with. Sometimes she questioned just how much of an impact she made, though how could she really, with how the system worked? Most of the children that came there barely received any treatment for the barrage of traumas they suffered before they were shuffled on to the next foster home, or worse, a shelter.

She hated cutting time short with any of them. They all needed more time, not less, but the shouting in the hallway grew louder, to where it reached a point that it could not be ignored.

"I'm sorry Louise, I'll be back. I'm so sorry."

Louise, who had once been Luis until she had transitioned, broke down into more tears. Dr. King was furious with herself and whatever was going on outside, but she reined in that fury, gritting her teeth as she refused to show any of it in front of the girl. The last thing Louise needed right now was to think that her doctor was deprioritizing her feelings. Too many have dismissed her feelings in the past. This girl needed her.

Dr. King looked back at her one last time before opening the door, allowing the bedlam of noise from the hallway to intrude on the safe space of her office.

"What is going on out here?" Dr. King called, making it a demand for an answer as she eased the door shut behind her.

"You!" screamed an angry voice at her. "You had no right to drug my son. I never would have agreed to leave him here if I knew you were going to poison him. I never agreed to that. How dare you? We have kept him clean for so long, kept your foolery out of his vines. How dare you?"

Dr. King was taken aback at seeing the red-faced shorter woman who was now inches in front her.

"Mrs. Carey, it's part of the process. Your son has faced severe trauma. He is trapped-"

"He's trapped because you damn frauds have kidnapped him. I'm here for my baby. I'm here to take him home."

"Please, quiet down." Dr. King said, then took a deep breath and studied the group that was quickly forming around them. She recognized the daughter, standing back, with her head down. She looked embarrassed by her mother's outburst. Down the hall, she could see counselors and children standing in open classrooms doors, and Juan was escorting a gentleman who must have just passed through security. They were heading towards her as well.

"There are other children here and you're going to upset them. If you would like to talk about this, I can meet you in a few minutes. I'm in a session. Let me finish and we can talk."

"I'm not talking. I'm here for my son."

"Your son is sleeping."

"Why is he still sleeping? He shouldn't be sleeping. I want to see him."

"He was just given another sedative, and he's rest-"

"Another sedative? Are you trying to kill him? Get him addicted? That's all you do here, get people hooked on drugs, so then they're dependent on you the rest their lives. You're all a bunch of scam artists, giving out candy to babies so they can keep coming back for more. You're all nothing but a bunch of drug dealers. You know that. Drug dealers!"

"Mrs. Carey, please. If you don't calm down, I'll have to call security and have you forcefully removed from the premises."

"What, now you're going to threaten to call CPS? You can't take away my son. You're monsters. You know that. You're all monsters. No one is taking away David."

"Please. No one has said anything about calling child protective services. Now, if you give me just five minutes, we can talk. Please." Dr. King said. She looked at all the children around her, the ones that CPS had taken from homes, put into foster care where it didn't take. All the failures of the system that kept coming back there. Some of them were new faces, but many were not.

"Like hell. Where is my son?"

Dr. King knew there was no point. This woman was beyond seeing any reason. It hurt. Not only was it a failure on her for not calming her down, but there was a child in her office that she had just been talking to. That was a child who was used to being pushed aside, and it only deepened her invisible wounds. Dr. King hated that she was going to have to put her to the side, even if only briefly.

What was the alternative? Calling security? How was that going to help anyone? How was that going to do any good for David? He needed his parents...parent. He needed to have people who loved and cared, especially this much, around him. Love was most often the best form of healing if applied properly.

Dr. King wasn't sure she could trust this woman to be the love David needed, but she also knew there was not much she could do.

"Juan, can you please let Louise know that I have a situation that needs to be dealt with and that I will be back as soon as I can?"

"Of course. Officer Ellis is also here to check on the boy."

Dr. King turned to face the man Juan had been leading to her. She had thought he had looked familiar, but hadn't been able to place him without the uniform. He looked handsome in his jeans and t-shirt; Cubs jacket loosely open. He did look tired, but that would be expected as he probably hadn't had a good chance to sleep that day.

"What can I do for you, officer?"

"I was hoping to check on David. I've been worried about him, and just thought-"

"Thought what?" Mrs. Carey said, quickly turning her fury onto the officer. "You think you can question my son, too? I already told that prick not to come near my David. Why are you here?"

"What?" Dr. King said, caught off guard by the accusation.

"That detective called, said he wanted to question David and now this officer shows up. What do you think?"

"Yeah, he called me. Not sure what he's expecting. Asked me to talk to you about talking to your son. Me, I fully expect you to tell him to 'go to hell.' That's not why I'm-." Ellis said.

"Let me make this damn clear to both of you. I don't want you, or any damn officer near my son," Mrs. Carey said, pointing at the officer. Then she turned and pointed to the doctor.

"And you are releasing my son. I don't approve of your 'science' bullshit. You kill enough people with your drugs and vaccines. We don't want any part of it, and I want my son out of here."

"If that's what you want. You will need to sign a waiver stating that you are taking him from care against the wishes of the doctor, and I can't promise that someone won't escalate so that he would be brought back here. If it is deemed that he is a danger to himself or anyone else, they could get a court order to have him brought back here."

"I will advise my lawyer that you threatened to take away my son." Mrs. Carey said, "Now, where is he?"

"Ma'am, that's not what I said." Dr. King tried to protest.

"Where is my son?" Mrs. Carey yelled.

The hallway shook and Mrs. Carey reached out, catching her balance before crashing into the wall.

"What the hell" Ellis said as he stood there struggling to keep his own balance as the shaking stopped.

"Just another shake." Dr. King said. "Probably an aftershock from earlier."

"Earlier?" Jen was visibly scared by the tremor.

"Yeah, didn't you feel it earlier? That's like the second or third one today."

"Feel what?" Mrs. Carey asked.

"The earthquakes. There's been a couple of them today."

"I haven't felt anything though I've been trying to sleep." Ellis said.

"Illinois doesn't have earthquakes." Jen said.

"Well, there was the one about ten years ago, but no, they're not normal for the region." Ellis said.

"Why are you still here? I told you to go," Mrs. Carey said, quickly forgetting about the ground shaking and focusing on him.

"Mom?" The little voice was tired, hard to hear over the shouting, but Jen saw her little brother standing in the door frame of one of the rooms down the hall.

Dr. King was surprised to see that the boy was awake. With the sedative they'd given him, he should have been unconscious for a few more hours. Juan must not have been able to give him the full amount. She understood. It's hard when they are thrashing around like that to make sure. That only made it harder on David, though, as they couldn't risk giving him anymore. That was going to hurt his recovery.

"Baby!" Mrs. Carey said, as she rushed down the hallway.

"Mrs. Carey, he needs his rest. We really should continue our discussion as to his treatment."

Mrs. Carey lowered herself and pulled him into a tight hug.

"What treatment? He was here because he wasn't talking. He's talking now. Didn't you hear him?" Mrs. Carey said over her shoulder, then turned back to her son and gave him a kiss on his cheek. "Right baby. You're coming home where you are safe."

Dr. King looked at the rest of them, visibly confused.

"Mrs. Carey. He hasn't said anything. I understand that you want to believe he did, but I didn't hear anything." Dr. King looked around for confirmation. Jen wasn't sure. She had thought she had heard him, but realized with how quietly she had heard it, there was no way she could have heard him down the hallway, not from this distance. She looked at the officer and he was also shaking his head in the negative.

"Get whatever forms you need signed. I'm getting him away from you abusive assholes. He doesn't need any of your damn mind games. He's a normal boy. He's just upset."

Mrs. Carey had pulled David into such a tight hug, his face resting on her shoulder, and she never saw his body go limp as he fell asleep in her arms.

Dr. King noticed and wondered if maybe the sedative had finally kicked in. At least there was that. That should help him rest today, and the lingering effects may even give him one night without nightmares. She had read in his file that he suffered from night terrors. Maybe one night of peace would go a long way to him getting better.

"I'll get the forms." She said, and went down the hall to the nurses' station, leaving Jen and Ellis to watch the mother and son.

Jen nodded to him, realizing she was left alone with the officer and right then, she just wanted to be with her brother, to give him a hug of her own.

Ellis, however, stood there for a time, watching him. He noticed that the boy had fallen asleep while being held in his mother's arms, but he also noticed what was in the boy's hand. It was something he recognized and had no place in the hospital. It made no sense being there, gripped even as the boy was no longer conscious; the grip so tight that it still hadn't fallen from his hand.

It was 'Cuddles'. Cuddles had been his son's purple octopus, his favorite toy. It had gone everywhere with him, was in bed with him every night, getting kisses just like he gave kisses to Tatiana. Every night, both of them, kisses and a good night prayer before going to bed.

The toy went everywhere with him outside of school, and it had been in the car the night of the accident. He hadn't seen it since. He assumed it had been destroyed in the accident. It had to have been.

Yet, the boy had it. It was identical, those furry stuffed tentacles. More tentacles meant more arms for hugs. It was why he called him cuddles, because it had all the arms and all the cuddles to give.

Cuddles...

Ellis could feel his breath coming in short gasps and knew he was hyperventilating. He had to get out of there. He needed air. The hallways suddenly felt too small and contracting, getting smaller around him. Was there another earthquake? Was the room shaking, swaying around him, or was it just him and he was losing it?

He rushed to get out of there, having to struggle not to pound on the exit door when it didn't open, forgetting about the additional security of the ward. When they buzzed open, he burst through them, and hurried to find the closest door to the outside world that he could find.

* * * *

Ellis made it outside and started patting down his pockets, searching for a pack of cigarettes. Coming up empty, he was reminded that he had quit, and as much as he wanted to give into the craving, he had none available.

He was left bending over, hands on knees, as he struggled to catch his breath. The tears were on the horizon, but he wasn't going to give in. He hadn't before; he wasn't going to now. Deep breaths, he just needed to stick with concentrating on his breathing and he would be fine. Everything would be okay. He just needed to keep telling himself that. It would all be okay. Everything was alright. Just keep thinking of all the ways you can lie to yourself.

His phone rang. He accepted the call without looking at the caller ID, putting the call on speakerphone as he made his way over to the bench. He hadn't gone out of the main exit, but as he looked around, it looked like it was a spot surrounded by gardens and walls; the hospital forming a castle around this hidden area. It was probably meant for smokers to find an escape. He was in the right spot, just had the wrong tools.

"Ellis." He said, still struggling to control his breathing.

"Detective Price. I just got a phone call that one of my officers was harassing the family and showed up at the hospital."

"Isn't that what you told me to do?"

"Yeah, I don't give a shit about that. They told me to reprimand you. So, there, done. Now, did you get anything out of the boy?"

Officer Ellis had to fight to control his anger and not throw his cell phone against the far wall. He came there, and sure, the detective asked him too, but that wasn't why he had been there. The family only sees him as a cop, there to harass them. The detective thought he had followed orders and was there on his behalf. The only one that knew the truth was Ellis, and no one cared about why he came. Fuck 'em. If the detective thought he was there for him, so be it.

"Nothing. He's been knocked out on drugs. Probably going to be out the rest of the night."

"Has the boy said anything yet? Anything that can tell us what happened? We have more officers missing. Feds are starting to nose around because of the possible drug connection. I need something before they take this away from us."

"What do you want me to do? Try to wake the boy up? That's not happening. His mother is here."

"Yeah, that's who called. Look, do what you can. Keep me updated."

Ellis heard the connection end and looked at his phone to see the detective had hung up on him. He shook his head and set his phone down on the bench beside him.

"Did you really come here for my brother?"

Ellis looked up from where he had buried his head in his hands to see the sister standing over him. She was so much taller than her mother. The father must have been a big man. He made a mental note of that, that whoever took down the father had to have been one hell of a powerhouse or fighter.

"I didn't come for that As- jerk." Ellis said as he nodded toward the phone.

"So, why are you here?"

"I don't know. Worried about your brother, I guess. How I found him just has me thinking about my son, I guess. Worried about him, and you guys."

"Worried about us?"

"Little bit. Do you know what your dad did for money?" Ellis realized as soon as he asked that he wasn't sure how old the sister was, but didn't think she was eighteen. As soon as the words left his mouth, he already regretted it and now he could be facing a reprimand.

"My dad made films. You know, bad, cheesy horror films."

"Really, nothing else? Because we're not L.A."

"No, my dad did the L.A. thing and hated it. He said it felt like he was having to sell his soul to get his movies made. After Davey was born, he'd had enough, and he moved us here. He grew up near here. Small town, boring name. Normal, or straight, no..."

"Yeah, we're not far from Bloomington-Normal."

"That's close, but- I think it started with an S. I don't know."

"And that's where he gets good money?"

"Yeah, they like to show his movies on late night. He does a lot of monster movies. Or did, I guess," Jen said, stopping to look down at her hands. He followed her gaze and saw the chewed down nails and cuticles.

"I'm sure your brother is going to be okay."

"I hope so."

"You better get back to your mom. She probably needs you."

"Okay. Thank you."

"For what?"

"I don't know. Listening. Being there for Davey. I'm not sure. I just wanted to say thank you."

"Then you're welcome."

He watched as she went back inside, thinking about what she had said. If she was right, that changed everything about the investigation. Though if drugs weren't involved, then what was?

CHAPTER 12

"When is the funeral?"

"Tomorrow."

"What do you need me to do?"

"I don't know. I don't know. Someone's helping handle it. I think Simone is. She's around here somewhere, or maybe she ran to the store. I think she said something about going to the store earlier. I don't know."

"I understand. We're here for you, sis. I'm sorry it took me so long to get here. I got stuck waiting for a connecting flight. I'm so sorry. I just, I am so sorry."

"Yeah."

David heard the two women talking from the other room. One, his mother, was nearly silent. He could barely hear what she said, some words were lost to the silence of the house; her voice too soft to carry to him as he sat in their three-season room. The other was his Aunt Jodie, who lived further away from them. David wasn't sure where, just that it was out west.

She didn't visit them much, and they never visited them. His dad-

David wiped at his cheek, the wetness from fresh tears lingered and his nose ran. Thinking about his dad hurt. It didn't take more than just a passing thought about him and his chest burned, his eyes watered, and more tears that he couldn't stop.

His dad, his hero...

His dad wasn't home a lot. When he was, he was all there for his little demon slayer, as his dad called him, but his dad made movies. Scary movies that often meant his dad would be gone for a month shooting at some location, or if he was filming in his studio, he would be there for long hours, only home long enough to sleep and return.

In between films, though, his dad would be home for months at a time, and his little demon slayer had his full attention. Weeks of play time where they would build forts, go on hunts in the backyard with nerf guns, or just splash around in the pool, his dad throwing him high in the air and splashing his mom when David landed.

Every night, when his dad was home, there was always a story before bedtime, or a song to sing to him to sleep. There were many nights that David fell asleep listening to his dad read, "The Napping House" or "Row, Row, Row Your Boat." Then, if David didn't fall asleep to the story, his dad would pull out his hideaway bed and lie in there until he did.

His dad, his hero, his protector, wouldn't be there at night anymore. Now he only had her to tuck him in and if she remembered, read him a story. She wasn't the most reliable when it came to bedtime. There were many times she would already be asleep herself, leaving Jenny. Jenny would sometimes do it, and when she did, she would always remember to read him a story like dad had. She would even try to do the voices.

But his dad would never be there to read him a story, ever again. His dad would never be there for him for anything ever again.

And that hurt. That monster had taken his dad away from him, and it was still out there. David knew it was. It hadn't been caught. David never saw the monster leave. All the other cameras were working. He had stayed locked in that room because he had been sure it would be the one to open the door.

"How is...he... handling it?" Aunt Jodie asked. David didn't turn in the direction of the kitchen where they sat at the table. He couldn't see them as he was at the other end of the house and there were two open doorways between them, but he could see his mom. She had a collection of used tissues in front of her, making a little fortress of sadness that surrounded her steaming coffee cup. She was using a fresh one, wiping away the current wave of tears. She looked at him briefly, then tried to look back outside.

"Everyone says he hasn't said a word since it happened."

"He'll bounce back. Kids are resilient. They bounce back. Is he going to therapy?"

"More quacks? No. We don't need any of those people filling his head with nonsense."

"Kay Kay, I love you with all my heart. I know you've had your issues, but you have to think about your son. He is going to need someone to talk to."

"He's not talking. He's not talking to anyone and when he does, I'll be right here. He already talked to me once in the hospital. He will again."

"Sure. Have they said any more about what happened?" David heard the pause but didn't look to see if they were watching him. They probably were. It seemed like his mom was always watching him whenever he looked up, but there was a long pause where nothing was said. Then, as though his aunt just couldn't take the silence anymore, she asked, "Where's Jenny?"

"She's with her friend right now. I think she was taking her to a movie or something. She's been locked up in her room crying for the last day. I had to nearly force her to get out of here. She needs to be around her friends."

"Probably a good idea. I take it they stayed home from school the last couple of days."

David didn't hear the answer, which meant his mom probably just nodded her reply. He closed his eyes and put his hands over his ears. He didn't want to hear them. He didn't want to hear his aunt ask her dumb questions. How did she get to come into their house and act like she knew them? She didn't know them.

And it was his mom who had been doing all the crying. Jenny had been there taking care of them, checking in on him, talking to him. She was with her friend because of the fight the two of them had. That Jen didn't want their crazy aunt and her two hellions to be staying with them.

Fresh wetness came. The pain in his chest returned, and he was wiping both snot and tears with his fist as he slammed his head into the window. It didn't break; he wasn't trying to. He could feel the pain push through the cloud that was trying to conquer his thoughts. He slammed his head into it again, and again, then holding his forehead against it, feeling the cool chill of the glass.

"David! Oh my god, are you okay?" He heard his mom say. He could hear the worry in her voice and even as her voice sounded miles away, he could feel her arms as they wrapped around his shoulders.

"Come here." She said as she pulled him back from the window and into her arms. He kept his eyes closed, closing them as hard as he could, trying to stop more tears from coming. He didn't want more tears. He didn't want more pain. He just wanted it all to go away. Let this all go away and bring his dad back to him.

* * * *

Jen had fought with Harley about going out, telling her she was in no mood for a movie, or to go anywhere. She did not have the energy, nor the desire, to get her mind off her pain. She wanted her pain. She needed her pain. She was hurting, and angry, frustrated that everyone couldn't just leave her alone.

That wasn't going to happen though. Jen found out that it was her mom that had been reaching out to Harley, trying to get Jen out of the house. Which explained where the shopping and movies plan had come from. That was always more of something her mother enjoyed. Probably came from her mom being a part of that whole "mall" generation, where everything could be solved by a trip to one of them fossils of commercialization.

What Harley had said to her to actually get her out, to get her motivated to leave the safety of her room, was, "Hey, screw all that other stuff. Why don't we just head over to the gym?"

Her friend got her. Her friend understood what she needed, and what got her there. Still, standing there in the large gymnasium of the local "Y", she felt crowded. There were too many boys dribbling balls up and down the courts. There were four courts in total, and one of them had a group of old guys in their forties who were playing aggressively. The court next to them had a few teenagers shooting hoops for fun. The other two courts had a group of younger kids just running rampant and screaming. It was pure chaos, and there was no room for her to just casually toss a ball through a hoop a few times.

"Yeah, maybe this wasn't the best of ideas. You know, with it being a workday, I wouldn't expect there to be so many people here." Harley said, as she watched one of the old guys push another one. He slammed into a third, who was dribbling the ball.

The ball went wild into the other court, and the guys were paying it no mind as they had devolved into just yelling at one another.

"It's okay. We can go." Jen said. They were sitting in the bleachers that were only partly pulled out, providing minimal seating.

"Okay, well, this is your pity party. Where do you want to go?" Harley said, already reaching to grab her cell phone that was sitting next to her.

"I don't know. I just want to hit something. I want to take a bat and slam it into something hard and just keep smashing."

"O-kay Miss destruction. Well, I don't know if we could do anything like that, not without getting arrested, but what about hitting a punching bag? One that's not me or anything?"

"Sure."

"Perfect. Let's check on studio B. If there's no class going on right now, we could use the punching bags in there. You can hit those."

"Yeah, but don't we need permission or gloves, or something like that?"

"I don't know, but what are they going to do? Kick us out? They'll probably never even know we're there. It's all the way on the other side of the building, away from the front desk."

"Yeah, but they got cameras."

"Do you ever see any of them watching them?"

"I don't know."

"Neither do I. Do you want to punch something or not?"

Jen had to admit, she liked the idea of just hitting something, anything. Finally, a plan that possibly had merit. Jen grabbed her own phone, quickly checking and seeing that there were two missed calls with voicemails from her mom. She dismissed the notifications and got up.

They quickly made their way from the gym and followed the maze of hallways back to the corner of the building and the seldom used studio B. The room was dark and unlocked.

"Time to tear it up." Harley said, as she let the door slam behind them. Jen wasn't waiting for her friend as she went to the closest bag and playfully threw the first few punches. Seconds later, she heard a beep. Her heart nearly stopped, thinking they had been caught. Then Imagine Dragons blared through the speakers from overhead.

"Death, the misery. Everyone wants fights with an enemy," rapped to them and Harley came sauntering up, grooving to the song. She stepped up to the other bag and started punching to the beat of the song.

"You hitting or dancing?" Jen asked, throwing another punch.

"Both. If you can't enjoy yourself while beating the crap out of someone, then what fun is it?"

Jen grimaced at her friend. She knew she was just trying to help and get her to cheer up, but why couldn't anyone get it? She didn't want to be cheered up. Her dad was dead. Her mom was a drunk. There wasn't anyone left to take care of her and her brother. It was all going to fall on her now. She was it.

She threw another punch harder, thinking about her mother. She had taken David out of the hospital away from the doctor that could help him. How could she be so dumb? What was it about doctors that had her so strung up?

Another punch, this one harder than the last. She thought about her dad, the last time she saw him. Had she told him that she loved him? She couldn't remember. It had just been another night then. She had no clue that it was going to be the last time she'd see him. She had come home from being on a date. He playfully ribbed her that next time he was going to sit out on the porch waiting for her, cleaning a shotgun. They both knew he wouldn't do it and that he liked Clara. They were both geeks and loved talking about all things horror, but her dad still liked to give her grief because they were dating. He was just being protective.

Her dad knew about her relationship with Clara. He knew that they were more than just friends.

Oh, hell, I wish Clara could be here.

Jen threw another punch, going back to a memory of him when she had come home after her date.

She had gone to her room, not thinking anything about it. She had gone to her room, watched a few online videos, listened to some music, and had fallen asleep. It had been late, and it had been just another night.

It would always be the last time she had talked to him.

She hit the bag two more times in quick succession. Throwing more of that anger into every punch.

She thought about David. He still wasn't talking. He hadn't shown any interest in people, anyone. He had given her mom that hug and hugged her when she forced herself on him, but he didn't come to any of them. Everyone seemed not to exist anymore. He was alone inside his mind, trapped there, not saying anything to anyone, and it hurt her as she wanted him to come to her. She wanted to help him. He was her little bro; she missed him. It seemed too much like she lost him as well, as he was now just a shell. Would he ever get better?

She hit the bag again and again, more thoughts flooding into her, pouring out through her fists. She wasn't sure or even trying to hit the bag like a boxer. She wasn't dancing around or working on any fancy hit and be hit moves. She was angry, and the bag was finally something that her anger could pour into.

It felt... not good, but it felt better.

The tears were starting to come with emotions she had tried to keep pushed down, rising to the surface. As they did, she kept hitting the bag harder and faster,

"Come on, come on, you bastard. Come on." Jen screamed at it, not sure who the 'you' was, but just wanting to pound something as hard as she could.

"You get 'em, Logan. Knock his block off."

Jen threw another punch, and then leaned against the bag, crying and breathing hard. She had to take a minute trying to catch her breath before she could look at her friend, mustering only one eye to open as sweat was drenched down into the other one.

"Logan? Are you really comparing me to that creep, Logan Paul?"

"I don't know. Isn't he, like, some big boxer?"

"I think so. Maybe."

"Yeah, so like him. You get 'em girl?"

Jen shook her head against the bag.

"Hey, are you two new to my class?" They turned as the lights flooded on in the studio. A tall, athletic red-haired man stood there smiling at them. He was wearing shorts that were too small and emphasized his package. Under his right arm, he was holding a box where a pair of boxing gloves could just be seen poking out.

"Because if you are, I need to check with the front desk, as they didn't say anything about new students."

"Oh, sorry, we were just..." Harley started to say but stopped and looked at Jen for some guidance. Jen wasn't in the mood to make up a story.

"My dad was killed, so we came in here to hit the punching bags."

Jen saw the color disappear from the man's face as well as the smile, and he was quick to get out of the doorway to set down the box.

"I'm sorry to hear that. Look, if you want to sit in on the class, it's okay. I teach boxing and self-defense. I take it you were hitting the bags?" He said, nodding to the bags behind them. Jen nodded.

"I think we're done. Thank you, though." Harley said, as she was already quickly making her way to the door. Jen didn't move at first, holding the man's gaze. A part of her wanted to say yes. She felt so helpless, defenseless right now. Maybe doing something other than sitting at home would do her some good.

Harley wasn't waiting for her, and Harley was her ride. Jen quickly shook off the thought and rushed to catch up with her friend.

"Maybe some other time." Jen said as she left.

"So, what was that about? And did you see those shorts? It was like a bad day in gym class." Harley said, nudging her friend as she normally would while walking down the hall.

Jen didn't play back, and Harley dropped her smile, choosing to walk with her friend in silence.

They made their way to the front, but as they were about to leave, she saw a familiar face walking in, a gym bag slung over his shoulder.

"Officer." She called out. He had his head down, not watching any of the people around him, but after hearing her voice, he looked up and saw her.

"Hey, how are you holding up?" Ellis said.

"Fine, I guess. I didn't know you had a membership here. I've never seen you, or is this more of that detective guy having you spy on us?"

"Me neither. Haven't been here in over a year, but just got a notification that my annual family membership was renewed." Jen watched as Officer Ellis momentarily lost his stoic composure, and a crack formed to show the hurt raging inside. Then it was gone, and he was looking back towards the door outside.

"Oh no, are you okay?"

"Yeah, I'm fine. Just figured since I had the membership, might as well use it."

"Yeah, well, there's a boxing class back in studio B if you want to hit something." Harley said, chiming in.

"I just might do that. Thank you."

"Hey, the funeral's tomorrow. Is that detective going to be there?" Jen asked, barely able to hide the disdain in her voice as she thought of the jerk who had tried to question her and her mom.

"Probably. He's still thinking it's drug related, so he'd be there to observe any known associates."

"Wait, really? Isn't that just like what they do in bad cop shows?" Harley said.

"Don't know, I never watch them, but it's a solid plan, especially when there are no other leads."

"Is there any way you could be there?" Jen asked.

"Me, why?

"In case he does show up and cause trouble. I don't know. Maybe I'm just being silly. It was just an idea."

"Um, well, I can be."

"Have you still been checking up on us?"

"I've worried about your brother, but no. Your mom made it clear. I didn't want to make her uncomfortable."

"I'll talk to her. Please come tomorrow."

"Okay, I will." Ellis nodded to them, then turned to head to the locker room. Harley watched him leave, then nudged Jen.

"He's cute if you like them as old as your dad."

"Not funny. Really, really not funny." Jen said and stormed out of the "Y". Harley followed her, apologizing as she did.

CHAPTER 13

Stephanie was ready to get home, kiss her husband, take off her shoes that no matter what brand she tried never seemed to hold up for comfort like they promised, open a bottle of wine, and crash into bed for the next sixteen hours. She had had enough; it had been hell for the last few days on the ward, and she was ready to unwind and enjoy a day off. It was long overdue.

"Dr. King, Dr. King, I need you to sign off on this." She heard a voice calling out behind her. She turned to see one of the nurses on her ward rushing down the hall to catch up with her.

"What's up?"

"Josh Stevens in 104, you were saying you wanted to change his meds. I need you to sign off."

"That's right. Good catch." Stephanie King looked over the change of meds order on the tablet Bailey handed her and confirmed it was correct, then signed her approval. "There ya go. Now I'm officially out of here. Not on call, not on duty, outta here. I don't want to see anyone's faces for at least thirty-six hours."

"Some worry. Next time Mrs. Deeters calls, I'll put her straight through to your cell phone."

"You do that. I'll have to tell Tony where you're stashing his chocolate."

"Hey now, I need those for the long winter nights."

"It isn't winter yet and you need to stop reading those trashy romance novels."

"Someone's got satisfy this lonely old woman."

"That's what's momma's special toys are for. Now you better check in with Tina, make sure she doesn't disappear back into her shell. Her and I made some good progress today."

"Will do. You go on, get some rest." Bailey said, quickly making a few notes on the tablet before heading back down the hall.

Stephanie felt the cool air against her face, the gentle wind blowing through the trees nearby, rustling in the early night. It was well lit as she made her way to her car. Her hand in her pocket wrapped around her mini pepper spray. Occasionally, she would look around as she walked.

Most nights, she wasn't overly afraid as she walked to her car. She always had the spray, and it was just force of habit that she held it while she walked. She considered herself brave, but only an idiot would walk alone and not have the slightest bit of fear. Women were attacked and raped far too often in this country. It was the invisible epidemic that society chose not to see. She was not about to become one of the hidden many.

Yet, as she walked, she knew that wasn't it. Something else prickled at her. Goosebumps ran along her arm, and she felt like she was being watched. She kept looking around but didn't see anything there. There were cars randomly parked throughout the well-lit lot, but nothing stirred. Still, the feeling remained. It was like a constant itch nagging at her, warning her something was wrong.

She didn't breathe easily until she made it to her car. She unlocked the door and, out of ridiculous paranoia, checked the back seat as well before climbing in, then immediately locked the doors.

Her phone chirped, and she felt her heart leap into her throat. She closed her eyes and took a breath to calm herself, laughing at being such a silly fool.

She checked and saw that it was a message from her husband. He knew it was her night off and he had tried to align his schedule to match hers. He was messaging to apologize that he couldn't, and that he wasn't sure how late it would be before he was home.

That feeling she had earlier stayed with her the entire drive home. It momentarily eased once she parked the car in the garage, but it returned as she walked to the house. Something was watching her. She knew it was silly, but she could feel a presence somewhere in the darkness and now that she was home, there were many more shadows to hide it.

Inside, she immediately turned on the kitchen and outside lights, scanning briefly to check that nothing followed her to the door. Visually satisfied, but the sensation persisted. She systematically went from room to room, turning on every light. She stopped near the stairs leading upstairs, feeling as if the shadows were going to slither towards her and grab her.

What the hell is with you tonight? Get your shit together.

She shook her head, hoping to break free from the certainty that she was being watched, knowing sometimes just doing the physical act reaped mental rewards. She didn't care that it failed her, that the nagging was still there. She tried to ignore it and went to the kitchen, pouring herself a glass of wine.

She knew it was cheap entertainment and if her husband was home, she never would have given in to her guilty pleasure. He wasn't there though, so she had the house and the tv all to herself. She made herself comfortable and tuned in to the latest episode of that doctor show. The tawdry one which was more about the doctors sleeping around than medical drama. It was terrible, but some of the male doctors were too cute not to gawk at, and she got to poke fun at all the inaccuracies.

She watched as five minutes into the episode, clothes were flying, and they were missing someone coding. It was so bad, and yet she was ready to see these two finally get together. The story had hinted they would for so long, but it was hard to know for sure. The actors had no chemistry, but the writing kept trying to force it.

The nagging sensation was forgotten, pushed down as she let her mind slip into the show as sex was on the horizon.

Then hot, searing pain shot through her from her shoulder. Her mind couldn't comprehend the sudden change. She was thrown forward. Her arm was ripped backwards, being torn from her body. She couldn't think through fast enough. She was dumbfounded when she looked, and it wasn't there. Her arm was gone. Blood was pulsating out of her. Her blouse was torn away. Where the hell was her hand?

She screamed then as pain clouded her thoughts. Then she fell through the coffee table. The wine flowed crimson red, mixing with the blood soaking into the carpet.

She wasn't sure how long she lay there, but could feel glass cutting into her exposed shin. Her face felt like there were a hundred small flames near her eyes. She reached up to wipe them away, and again the shock that her arm again wasn't there bewildered her muddled mind.

She felt something digging into her side and tried to turn and pull away from it. She heard more crashing, more glass breaking, but she also heard something behind her, a slurping sound coming from a source she couldn't see.

Something pulled her, and she fell back onto the carpet, looking up at what had once been her white couch. Half of it was red and wet with her blood, and there was a dark shape. She couldn't make out all of it. She saw sharp needle points protruding from its back and a long snout, with long fangs sticking out of it. Its skin was black with what looked like either scales or pieces of armor patch-worked together.

The creature was ripping something, using a long tendril like tongue that slithered out from its long snout to pull strips of sinew, then held it up and let the long strands drop into its open jaw.

It was eating slowly, enjoying the meal as it ripped into it piece by piece.

Stephanie tried to push herself away from the couch and work herself back from the thing, and it turned to look at her. It watched her for a moment, but didn't move to chase her. It let out a little snort and then turned back to its meal.

It ripped another long piece and then turned so she could see better what it was that it was eating.

In its claws, it held her arm. It had sliced it just below her shoulder, pulled it away from her and was ripping chunks of muscle from the bone. It was eating them slowly, savoring every bite, and it wanted her to watch it.

She kept pushing, fighting to push herself back, shaking herself viciously at the impossible monster in front of her. It was a thing twisted from nightmares. It wasn't there. There was just no way. It had no place in the real world. This thing belonged in the mind of her patients. It had no place at all in her house.

She refused to accept it.

She continued to push, though it was getting hard. Just breathing took a considerable amount of effort.

Her mouth was filled with the taste of iron and was filled with blood and bile. Somewhere, a sliver of rational thinking still hovered, and she knew she had bitten her tongue. It didn't matter, as that sliver was fading. She had stopped moving backward, her body hitting something hard she assumed was the wall.

The room was growing dark, and she struggled to make out the shape moving towards her. From a distance, she felt her body lifted into the air. The sensation, the pain, was getting farther away. She was drifting from it, towards a light that was coming closer to her.

Then the light was ripped away, and the world was alive around her. She could feel the pain vibrantly shooting through her as bright as all the colors were around her.

She was looking into the dark, soulless eye slits of the creature, the black orbs glaring back at her.

Its forked tongue burrowed into her other shoulder. She could feel it all. It felt like it was pumping acid into her, making her more aware, forcing her to feel all the pain over again, though now it was a thousand times more intense. She could feel herself screaming. Her legs grew warm as her bladder let go.

She just wanted all of this to end. She screamed for it to kill her. She begged for it to...

But instead, she felt the sharp pain in her other shoulder and felt herself drop as it tore away her other arm. She watched as it casually went back to her couch and started slowly ripping fresh meat from its new morsel of flesh.

* * * *

David sat up in his bed, screaming, grabbing whatever he could find around him, his stuffed animals that his dad and Jen had bought him, and clutched them to his chest. He was breathing in quick gasps, sweat dripping against the chill of the room. He was shivering. The cold penetrating through his bones and freezing to his core.

He couldn't stop screaming. The terror was not going away. He still was there, watching. He couldn't turn away; he couldn't get away from it. He was a part of the beast, and saw what it saw, felt what it felt, and savored what it savored. Now that made him retch with disgust, as he tasted the human flesh being chewed and slithering its way down its throat to be digested.

He had felt everything.

In his dream, he had seen the doctor. The scary one who had talked to him in the hospital. The one who had tricked him and distracted him while the big guy stabbed him in the arm to put him to sleep. She had got out of her car and gone into a large house.

He could smell her. She smelled like rotten meat, but he knew the smell was from her and that was how people smelled to it. It had been following David's smell, and his smell was still intertwined with the doctor's.

It had followed the doctor. It hungered. She was food, but she wasn't ready yet. She would only lightly satisfy it. It needed to prepare her, to season her.

It quickly made its way up her wall and found a window. Talons shot out and sliced through the glass, sending shards flying. Then it went into the darkness and followed the smell. She hadn't made it upstairs yet, though her odor was everywhere. It was all essences of her, none of it was what it craved.

It moved along the ceiling and found the stairs leading down. The smell was stronger down there. The monster went towards it. It saw her sitting watching the glowing screen. She never turned and realized it was there. She wasn't getting flavored correctly. He would need to pain her, then she would flavor.

She stretched out her arm, and he sliced through it with his talons. David wanted to scream in horror as he watched the large, sharp claw reach out at blinding speed and cut it away, just pulling the arm to its snout. Then he tasted the blood. It rained around him and he lapped it up.

The doctor was screaming, and he could sense her flavor improving as she howled in pain. He tore away her flesh, and she tried to get away from him. He didn't chase. He knew she wouldn't make it far. He was, however, disappointed as he felt her life flickering.

She can't go yet. He needed her. He needed the flavor to be complete. She needs to still beat. Her juices must still flow. Otherwise, the flavor fades. She can't go yet.

There. David couldn't see what it did, but he heard her scream as she sat up, fully aware and watching him in horror as he approached. He could feel her fear and salivated for more of it. Fear pulsating through her, flavoring her soul. The stronger it pounded through her, the better she tasted.

He took her other arm and savored that one as well. He ate it faster now that it was peppered with taste. Quickly, he could feel her fully seasoned and well prepared as he approached. He looked down at her, snorting out laughter at the frightened and pathetic way she was looking at him.

Then he tore away her head with his large snout. He felt her skull shatter as he chewed. She was delicious, but now he knew he needed to hurry. Once the head was popped, it only had a brief period to tear into her and devour the soul before it faded away. He tore viciously at her neck, burrowing deep, tearing through organs, swallowing pieces of her whole as he needed to get deep within her to find that spark of life before it faded.

Then, with delicate relish, he pulled it free from her. He felt it as it joined with him, and every part of it tingled with ecstasy.

David tried to scream harder, and that was when he had broken free from the creature. He felt his connection rip away. Its thoughts left his mind, but just before it was completely severed, he felt one last thought. It was filled with recognition and joy as the creature thought, "there you are."

Then David was back in his room, sweating. Jen burst in. His room flooded with light. She rushed to his bed and pulled him tight into her arms just like Dad had always done.

"It's okay. Okay bud, we're here." She said, just like he would have said. The tears were streaming, and he clutched at her.

"What the hell?" David looked up to see his mom had crashed into the door. Her hands were shaking, and her eyes were wet and red with tears. "I thought we were done with this shit. Can't you just sleep through the night like a normal kid? You're old enough. You know, this was the shit that killed him."

"Mom!" Jenny yelled, and David felt his own tears rising. He couldn't control it, and his own sobs hit him hard. He was nearly convulsing, as he knew she was right.

"You killed him. It was all because of you."

Jen hurried out of the bed and pushed her mother into the hall. David heard her fall to the floor, but Jen didn't go to help her. Instead, she slammed the door shut and went back to David's bed. She pulled him back into a hug.

"Ignore her. She's drunk. I'm here and I'll stay here until you're ready. Then if you want, I'll sleep in here if you need me. I can grab my sleeping bag and camp out on the floor. Okay?"

David nodded as he refused to release her. Outside in the hall, they could already hear their mom snoring, passed out where she had fallen on the floor.

CHAPTER 14

How do you say goodbye to your hero, to your mentor, to the person who, even though he wasn't home as much as you wanted him to be, was the person who was your solidarity in the changing world around you?

Jen wasn't sure. She didn't know how she was supposed to react. She was sure people around her expected her to cry more. It made sense that she would. She was the daughter; he was her father, and she should be an emotional mess.

But her tears were hidden deep inside as she watched her world get buried. Though it wasn't really her dad being lowered down in that casket, as they never found the body. Still, the finality was real. She knew he was gone. It wasn't like she'd read or heard about when people could feel their loved ones were still out there. She felt the loss. She knew that there was no hope he was ever coming back to them.

Jen didn't look at her mom. Unlike Jen, who was standing as the casket was being lowered, she sat there in the chair next to her. Jen refused to look at her as she held her brother close in front of her. She knew David was upset. Like herself, he was not one to show it, but he was. There was more going on with him, though. He still wasn't saying anything, so his silence was hard to read, but she could feel his pain.

"Come on, catch me. You're too slow, come catch me."

Jen looked up from her father's grave and watched as a boy the same age as David was running through the cemetery, chased by an older boy. Both of them dressed like they were going to church, which was to say they wore nice clothing, but weren't black in the way of traditional funeral attire. Jen recognized them and was instantly annoyed with her cousins as they chose to play games while she was trying to say goodbye. She wanted to yell at them to stop, but instead turned to look at her aunt, hoping to mentally burrow the message into her to take care of her kids.

The woman ignored her glare just as well as she ignored the bursts of laughter coming from the annoying pair. It shouldn't have surprised Jen as others at the funeral were making occasional glances at the children and then at the mother, the disapproval obvious.

All morning, her aunt and the little hellions had been at their house, having flown in from California. That made two of her mom's sisters in town, while the rest of her family had not bothered coming. Jen guessed none of them wanted to devote any time to comforting their sibling, most likely out of spite, as they had all been upset with her dad for moving them to the Midwest.

Her dad's family, however, nearly filled the grave site. She knew some of them, but her dad had a larger family, with most of them never leaving the area as he had when he moved to L.A. years ago. In fact, other than her father, all of them lived within fifty miles of where they were born, and from one another. They were a close family, and all of them were there to grieve with them.

Jen looked at the officer whom she'd talked to outside the hospital. She had called him before the funeral to see if he was coming. He had thought about it, and she had to talk him into it. She didn't feel comfortable being there without him. She slept on the floor of her brother's room last night and he hadn't slept well. She heard her him tossing and turning, occasionally whimpering in his sleep. Even with her there to comfort him, the nightmares never stopped.

Jen felt, well, she wasn't sure how she felt or thought. She was so confused, but when she woke up, she had the desire to keep her brother safe. She did not trust her mom, but the officer, he seemed like someone that could help. She had no clue as to how.

* * * *

Ellis tried to stay towards the back of the large funeral party, and out of Mrs. Carey's vision. Just because the daughter had invited him to be there, he doubted the mother would be happy to see him. He had already been planning to attend, not because the detective had wanted a police presence there, but because he was worried about the family. Whoever had killed all those people was still out there.

Price wanted people there to observe the guests, see who may be attending that could tie into the drug trade or some other clues as to where the money was coming from or who was involved. The detective wasn't accepting that Mr. Carey actually made movies and, while not a big name, did a decent enough job of making cheesy horror films to support him and his family.

As Ellis looked at those in attendance, there were a few shadier characters there, but the family resemblance was too strong from the photos Ellis had seen, for them not to be related.

So, what did happen? Were these people in danger?

Ellis wasn't sure. It was eating at him, which had prompted him to come. What else was he going to do on his day off? It wasn't like he had a family to be with or big plans to break. At least this way, he was there just in case anything happened.

Ellis watched as the priest was finishing his prayer and turned when he heard a car driving up the little pathway through the cemetery. He saw Price getting out of a car. Unlike Ellis, who had dressed for the occasion, Price was in his normal cheap suit that screamed police detective. He was walking toward the gravesite, and Ellis knew his chance of staying in the background had vanished.

* * * *

The screams were there now, every time he blinked or closed his eyes. It was like a thousand screaming voices all trying to be heard as they howled in pain. David couldn't seem to get away from it. After the dream last night, they lingered after all the other fear from the nightmare had faded away. Jen had stayed in his room, had eventually moved and slept on the floor. David had watched her as she tossed and turned, trapped in her own hellish nightmare. He had heard her call out for their dad multiple times as she tried to find comfort in sleep.

He never made it that far. Every time he tried to get himself comfortable and to work his way into sleep, the screams erupted, echoing off the surrounding walls. He wasn't even making it to sleep, just closing his eyes for the briefest of seconds caused the chaos of nightmares, new and old, to rampage on his senses.

David had been thankful when the sun rose and Jen woke up. He was tired but enjoyed that over the torment of trying to sleep.

With so little sleep, he felt almost zombie-like as he stood there with his sister's hands on his shoulder. He should be crying. So many of the people around him were, but his emotions felt like they were so far away. They were turned off, out of reach, no matter how hard he tried to access them.

Maybe that was a good thing. That was the thought that tried to wedge its way into his thinking as he turned away from the lowering coffin. He saw the officer that had saved him turn away from the ceremony, looking towards the cars, then start walking in that direction.

"Amen." The priest said and everyone started to move. Everyone was so much taller than he was, and it felt like none of them noticed him as they bumped into him, walking around him. Jen's hands had gotten separated from his shoulders, and he didn't turn to see where she had gone. He let the shapes move around him as he found his way, getting farther from the hole in the ground.

He found himself free from the masses and turned away. He didn't know where he was walking too, but instead felt the burning in his chest, the wetness at the corners of his eyes, for tears that threatened to fall but never came. No matter how much he wanted them to finally release and feel the pain, they stayed there, hesitant.

He didn't want to be around anyone. He didn't want to be a part of any of it. He didn't want to have to talk to any of them anymore, which didn't matter, as they never seemed to hear him when he spoke. He wanted to be alone, but he wanted people. He wanted to cry, but he never wanted to feel again. Everything raged inside of him and wanted to be let out, but the trap refused to release. How could he be in so much chaos all at once and still function?

The ground looked so comforting. What would it hurt to just lie down there in the grass and let the world just pass by, let all these feelings that bombarded him just go away? Everything should just go away.

"Do- do, we're talking to you."

"Hey, retard, why you gotta be so dumb?"

David barely registered the voices, and that they were talking to him before he felt the force come from behind him. He didn't have time to catch himself before falling to the ground and feeling the sting of slamming into the hard packed earth. He quickly turned around and looked up at his two larger cousins that were standing over him. They were laughing.

"Dingle berry doesn't even know how to walk; did you see that?"

"Bro, that was sus, he just fell."

"Right."

David used the closest tombstone to help him stand.

"Man, must suck losing your loser dad."

"Talking about living out here in Hicksville. How do you even survive, Ohio? Do you mess with your sister? Do you want to screw me? You guys all screw your cousin's out here, right?"

"Eww, That's gross."

"But that's what they do, right? Isn't your aunt like your grandma?"

David made it to his feet and started walking away from the noise behind him.

"Where you going, Ohio?"

Ohio? What did that even mean? David had no clue, as they were nowhere near Ohio. He shook his head, trying to get them out of his thoughts as he continued to walk away.

"Whoa, that's sus." One of them said. David ignored them, even as it felt like a breeze ran through the trees and chilled him to his bone. He shivered as the temperature around him suddenly felt much colder.

"Hey Ohio, is she one of your friends?" The other one said. David finally looked back at them and saw they were staring ahead of him. David turned around and saw what they were looking at. A girl roughly the same age as David stood in front of a tomb watching them. She was pale and wearing a gray and white school uniform.

Why would she be wearing a school uniform in the middle of a cemetery? She must not be with any of the other guests, but why the uniform? It wasn't a school day.

There was something familiar about her and the uniform that she wore. David wasn't sure where, but he knew he'd seen it before.

David stopped walking as he began to feel sick in his gut and the screams tore through his head. Their fever pitch grew louder and howled in the wind as it picked up around him. Fallen leaves scratching their way through grass covered graves before the wind fell silent.

And then it was too silent. David couldn't hear funeral goers anymore, or the distant road. It was like all the sound had been sucked away from what was around them.

David turned back to his cousins and could see that they noticed it, too. They looked nervous but were still walking toward the girl.

David felt his skin crawl and knew he was not taking another step towards her. She didn't move at all, she just stood there. She didn't appear to be paying them any notice, not turning her head as her cousins moved to flank her.

"It's like she's a statue."

"Telling you this is Sus, bro."

"Completely Sus."

"Yo, Ohio, who is she?"

"Who is she, bro?"

David kept watching her, goosebumps now running across his flesh as he did. She was roughly his height, maybe a little taller, though it was hard to tell unless he was to venture closer to her, something he was not willing to do. Her school uniform, a black miniskirt, white shirt and grey vest with a crest of what looked like a snake over her left chest was well fitted, though there was not a trace of anything playful about it. It looked very cold, businesslike, but that could be how the suit fitted her. She had on black dress shoes, and black socks that ran thigh-high, only showing a small amount of her pale flesh before it disappeared.

David looked back at her face. Her blood-red lips and white skin seemed to conflict with her shoulder-length blond hair and her eyes. He couldn't see them clearly from where he was at, but he felt he knew they were brown.

Where did you recognize her from?

He wished he knew. It was right there, on the edge of a memory just out of his grasp. He didn't think it was a good memory as he felt a nagging pressure on him to turn around and run. He wanted to get out of there. After all, what was she doing? She stood there so still, not even watching the two older boys as they approached.

"Ohio, say something, bruh, or get her to say something." The taller of the two boys said. David thought the boy's name was Damien, but hadn't met them before their aunt came today and hadn't paid attention when they'd been introduced.

The screaming was too much. Made it so hard to think or to pay attention. What was the other boy's name? David tried to recall what it was. Oliver? Was that it?

An intense screaming howl pierced through his thoughts, and he watched as something changed with the girl standing there. The boys hadn't seen it, but was she getting taller? No, that wasn't it. She was getting shorter.

David realized that wasn't it either and watched as the boys got nearer to the girl that was not a girl. They weren't looking at what they should have and were still getting closer to her. They didn't seem to notice as a line formed just above her stomach. They didn't watch as the line revealed darkness, but as it grew larger, it also showed a large set of teeth that ran along the rim of that void, teeth running as wide as she was.

By the time the eight purple tentacles emerged from the thing's midsection, shooting out to grab hold of the boys, it was too late, and they were too close to get away. David could only watch in horror as it grabbed them both.

CHAPTER 15

"What do you think you are doing here? You wanted me here, fine I'm here, but you knew you weren't going to be welcome." Ellis met the detective just as he got out of his car. Ellis was pissed, but it was clear the detective did not care.

"Things change."

"What do you mean, things change? You're never going to get anything out of the mother or the son if you keep pissing them off."

"Oh, we will sooner or later. Just might mean having her come in for formal questioning."

"Are you charging her?"

"I don't know. You think I should?" The detective had been walking towards the funeral party but stopped to look sternly at the off-duty officer.

"No, I think you should leave the family alone, or very least provide them protection. You're dead wrong on the drugs."

"I know."

That stopped Ellis, and the detective stopped with him.

"I got the studio's financials. Turns out you can make a lot of money even if I've never heard of them. I guess his stuff goes straight to cable, but he was in tight with a company out of California. It's all legit, or so they tell me."

"So, why are you here?"

"Because there are more people presumed dead, and that Mrs. Carey was seen arguing with one of them a few days before. One hell of a link, wouldn't you say?"

"Who?"

"You know what? I don't have to answer your questions to do my job. You're not needed here. Why don't you go home? I'll take it from here."

"You should be the one leaving." Jen said as she stormed up to the two men. "We just put my father's empty casket into that grave over there because you can't find a body or tell anyone what happened. You keep investigating my dad more than looking into who killed him. How dare you even show up here? I asked him to be here, just in case, and that's because you can't tell us a damned thing. You keep treating my family more like we are to blame and not the victims. Get the hell out of here."

"I'm sorry you feel that way, miss. We're only trying to do our jobs and right now we don't have much to go on. It wasn't just your dad that went missing. There were two security guards and two officers that disappeared that night as well. There are many more funerals than this one this weekend. Detective Hill's funeral will be held here later today. Their families want answers too, and it was your dad's studio. Your brother is our only witness at this point, and we need him to talk to us."

"He's still not talking to anyone." Jen said, a little quieter after thinking about all those other people, a sliver of guilt trying to cool her temper as she shifted her weight back. She didn't step back, not wanting to give this cop the satisfaction that he got to her, but eased off some of her aggression.

"I don't believe that. He's hiding something."

"Are you really that insensitive?" Ellis said. He glanced at the detective and then back to Jen. Motion from the funeral party caught his eye and he watched as the group turned to face them. The group parted, and Mrs. Carey was on her way as she pushed through.

"Mrs. Carey. I'm sorry for your loss," Detective Price said as she approached them.

"Why are you here?" She said as she glared at the detective, then looked at Ellis.

"I-" Jen started, but the detective cut her off as though he hadn't noticed she was speaking.

"We are just trying to get answers."

"And what answers are you going to find here? Trying to make more allegations about my husband? My sister told me you called the backers in L.A. Seems like you're investigating my husband more than trying to find his killer."

"We need to talk to your son. He's our only witness."

Jen looked around, noticing for the first time that David wasn't with them.

"Like hell you do. You vultures can stay the hell away from my son. I know how you are and there's no way I'm letting you subject my son to any of your police foolery."

"Mom." Jen said, though her mom's anger was intensely focused solely on the two cops. There was a fire there that she was not used to seeing in the shorter woman.

"Police shenanigans and hypocrisy. Just as bad as doctors. They have their fancy drugs you shoot people up with. It's all about the drugs.

"You think my husband sold drugs? Well then, you never knew my husband. Police making up stories about people. Police and doctors ganging up on people. Well, you can just get the hell out of here. We don't need any it."

"Mom, where's David?"

"Mrs. Carey-" Detective Price tried to say, but he was again cut off.

"You both need to leave."

Ellis turned to Jen. It was clear her mother was so caught up in her fire and brimstone damnation of the police department that she was paying no attention to her daughter. Jen was frantically looking around and Ellis picked up on why. With the growing group, there was one person clearly not amongst them.

"Mrs. Carey, Wh-" Ellis tried to say, but it was Jen who finally got her mother to stop and look at them when she yelled over all of them.

"Mom, where's David?"

"He was with you. I thought he was."

"He's probably playing with Joe and Damien."

"Those little demons?" one of Jen's uncles said to another uncle, quiet, but they could all still hear it.

"I doubt it." Jen said.

"Let's go look for them." Officer Ellis said, but then looked at Mrs. Carey. "If you'll let me."

Jen's mom was already succumbing to more tears and had leaned back into her sister, who had been standing behind her. She nodded at the officer.

"He's going to be okay. They're just playing. You'll see."

David watched as the first tentacle shot out, grabbed the closer, smaller of the two boys, and pulled him into that large split midsection that was now a drooling mouth lined with teeth. As the mouth opened wider, more rows of teeth appeared in what looked like a narrowing throat that was lined with them. Then, as the boy drew nearer, each row spun in different directions. It reminded David of saw blades rotating, preparing to slice through flesh and bone.

It was so quick, the boy, David finally remembered his name had been Joe, was pulled into the large mouth, and closed around him just as the boy started screaming. The scream was quickly cut short as blood oozed down the front of the monster girls' school uniform and the bottom half of the boy's body fell to the ground.

"Joe!" the other boy, Damien, yelled. David watched as Damien grabbed a large branch that must have fallen from one of the surrounding trees and ran towards what looked again like an innocent girl, though her front was dripping in blood.

The creature split open and again the tentacles reached out. Damien had not yet reached the creature, and was lifted off the ground, each tentacle grabbing a limb to support him. The branch fell uselessly to the ground, and the creature remained standing there, holding the boy.

David felt himself belch as his stomach twisted, watching the thing, and he knew he should run. He had to get out of there. So far it had all happened so fast, and he had been in shock, but he had regained himself. He should be running. His legs should be carrying him as fast as he could to get away, but he found that he was trapped there. Some unseen force held him, and he couldn't bring himself to turn away. He could feel the creature's hunger. It had been starving and was why it had quickly devoured the first boy, but now... now it wanted to enjoy the meal, to obtain that full flavor of the earthly morsel.

Even if he tried, it was so hard to think with all the screaming. Joe's screams had joined the chorus inside his head, and they grew louder as he watched it toy with Damien.

It brought Damien over to it so that he was dangling over the large teeth-filled hole of a mouth. It held him there, and David noticed that with all the screaming in his head, he wasn't hearing Damien scream.

Then David could see why. One of the tentacles had gone into Damien's mouth and forced its way down his throat. Damien's eyes were bulging as he struggled to scream around the appendage choking him.

Blood dripped from the side of Damien's mouth as the tentacle forced its way deeper. He was trying to thrash and fight against the slithering appendages, but more of them wrapped around him. They entwined around Damien's midsection, squeezing him.

Something red and sharp burst out of Damien's throat. David couldn't make out what it was, but it moved upward, slicing through the flesh of Damien's neck. It went through the jawbone without hesitation and Damien's tongue dangled free as the tentacle finished pulling itself free.

David could see the large fang that was at the end of the long tentacle and watched as it receded back into the flesh of the appendage, hiding in the purple tissue.

Damien was trying to scream, but with much of his neck and face mutilated, it was a gurgling wheeze. He was shaking violently, and David couldn't tell if he was being shaken or if it was him trying to escape. It seemed more like he was furiously fighting for his life as blood squirted from the gaping hole. One hand broke free from a tentacle, and Damien quickly reached to his other, struggling to pull free.

If he could see what David had seen, he would know it was futile. Damien was being lowered into the mouth of the creature; the spinning of the teeth already loud in David's mind as he watched them. Remnants that had gotten stuck were being thrown free, gore and blood flying everywhere.

Then the mouth swung closed, and blood erupted from the thing's mouth.

David could hear Damien's and Joe's screams mingling in his mind, adding them both to the chorus. They reached a crescendo then lifted to a tortuous peak that sent David to his knees, eyes closing in anguish at all the noise that pulsated through his skull.

His screams joined them, but these he could hear with his own ears.

Until they quieted.

He could still hear them, they were all still there, and now he could distinguish between each individual scream, but they had shifted to the back of his mind, just behind his thoughts. He could hear himself again, something he hadn't been able to do all morning.

David remembered the monster, realized he must be next, looked up to see that it was moving towards him. Its tentacles were now slithering on the ground in his direction.

His unseen restraints were gone. He was free. David didn't hesitate as he turned. He pushed himself up as one of the tentacles swished through the grass just inches from where his foot had been. He could feel them getting closer. He didn't turn back. He just ran and knew that no matter how hard he pushed himself, it was right there behind him. It was always behind him. He struggled, knowing it was always ready to pull him back into that large blood splattered mouth. It would pull him in and those teeth would tear him apart.

CHAPTER 16

"Joe! Damien" their mother yelled. Ellis winced as she was right next to him. He had learned her name was Lisa when he got details about the two boys before they started searching for them. Most of the funeral party opted not to join them. From what he observed during the ceremony, he understood why. It was hard to think that they were not off somewhere, goofing around.

Though, if David was with them, he doubted they would be playing or could have gone far. Ellis hadn't realized just how big this cemetery was. All the times he had driven by it on patrol it had seemed large, but now, as he was looking for the three young boys, its vastness felt like an impending doom weighing on him.

It seemed like the sun was mocking him, the blue sky too bright as he searched for missing kids. It felt like the weather was wrong for the day. The emotional tone was off. It was too sunny, too positive. It felt more like a day to be spent in a park with laughing children running around, teasing one another as they rushed up ladders and came down slides.

It was not a day to be spent in a cemetery for a funeral, and not one to be looking for missing children in a city that has had a sudden rash of the lost. The sun also played hell with the surrounding trees. The shadows danced and tree-shaped fingers ran between the graves. His head kept spinning as they walked, movement out of the corner of his eyes, ghosts or children, kept him alert. His own wife and child were buried there. Maybe it was their ghosts he kept seeing.

He had to struggle to pull himself from his memories. He wasn't there for them...

"David!" He yelled, as they passed another large monument commemorating some overindulgent rich asshole. There were so many in this damned place with row after row stretching for miles. Not only did it make the small headstones he had barely been able to afford for his wife and son seem so inadequate in comparison, but it made it difficult to search, as one of the kids could have fallen and incapacitated themselves behind one. Every one of them needed to be walked around and checked.

At least Mrs. Carey wasn't with them. When they'd broken up into groups, she had been quick to make sure she was alone with her daughter. She didn't want anything to do with either one of them, even though they were both out there searching for her son.

Knowing Price, he just wanted to find the boy so that he could question David without his mother around.

That couldn't be true. Deep down, there had to be some human traits in the asshole. Though if there were, Ellis hadn't ever observed them.

Ellis and Lisa passed another tomb and looked around the back. Again, there was nothing.

* * * *

"Why? Why did they have to be here? We're trying to say goodbye to your dad. They could have left us alone. They didn't need to come. They're just going to try to lock your brother away. They're trying to steal him from me. We've already lost so much; they want to take everything.

"I'm not going to let them. They don't have my parents making up stories this time. There's no one here that's going to send him away. I'm here, and I'm not going to let that happen. Not this time." Jen's mom said. She was in such a hurry that many of the words were on top of each other, making it hard to understand, not that Jen needed to. She'd been hearing various versions of this rant since her dad di-... went missing. Jen was getting frustrated with the whole mom-Karen-conspiracy vibe she'd been going through.

And all of this when they needed to be paying attention and looking for her brother. With how distracted her mom was, Jen was confident the woman could step over her brother's corpse and wouldn't notice. She had her head up, focused on spouting more vitriol for the police than calling out for her son.

"Davey!" Jen yelled, starting to get worried about not finding her brother. It wasn't that it was a large cemetery and would take them a long time to find the three boys if they were hiding, but that she couldn't see David venturing this far away from them, on his own or with his cousins. Even before dad, he wasn't adventurous. This wasn't like him. At least, this wasn't like him, to run off.

What if he was taken? But who in the hell scouts cemeteries looking for little boys? She couldn't imagine there were a lot of opportunities there, unless it was someone who had been watching them and followed them to the cemetery. They were in the news lately so could they be targets?

"He probably ran off because he saw them damn cops there. Probably reminded him of the hospital."

Jen had to bite her lip to keep from turning around and yelling.

Davey had better be alright, Jen thought as she fought against her anger.

She realized just how unlikely that would be when she saw the blood.

She turned the corner well ahead of her mother, partly walking ahead of the older woman to get away from the conspiracy garbage. She saw the large angel, its head buried in its hands, and she had walked around it to see a tomb a few feet ahead of her. Its cement entry way was covered in blood, some of it still dripping down the grey wall. There were stairs that lead into the tomb's depths with the bottom locked away by an iron gate.

As Jen got closer, her stomach already twisting into knots, she could see there was more blood on the stairs, and pieces of flesh, large clumps of it. Blood flowed around them as it ran down towards the entrance as though being pulled in by the dead.

She thought about her mom behind her and quickly turned, wanting to stop her before she saw the grisly scene. Jen was too late, her mother was already there, her mouth slightly hanging open, the little color she had drained from her face.

"No, no, it can't be David. This couldn't be. It just couldn't be. Just no way, not possible. It just couldn't happen. It wouldn't let it happen, no way."

"Mom, mom, you need to listen to me. We need to get the police. They need to get over here."

Jen tried to get her mom to listen to her. Something had happened, and Jen had no clue what she should be doing. Dammit, that needed an adult and lately she didn't feel like her mother counted.

Something shifted, and a twig snapped nearby. Jen couldn't be sure in what direction, but it had her look back at the flowing blood and the surrounding area. There was no body, so someone could be hurt and need help-

There's way too much blood there for that-

She should go and see if she could help them. She should, but she didn't move. Whoever did that could still be there, and they might not be done.

She sensed she was being watched. Someone was out there; she was sure of it. She didn't know how she knew, but she knew, and they were just waiting to take them next.

"David!" her mother yelled. Jen spun to face her, ready to scream at her to be quiet. The shout had felt like a firecracker going off in a library, as it was deafening in the stillness. Her scream died in her throat as Jen saw movement. Something dashed behind another tomb about fifty yards away. It had been hard for her to see, but Jen swore it looked like a girl wearing an odd outfit.

Jen looked at her mom and saw just how terrified she looked. The older woman was trembling, and looked like fresh tears were just moments away. Jen feared her mother was going to collapse again, just give up and crash to the ground in another unbearable emotional state.

"Come on, mom, we'll find him." Jen said, trying to release some of her anger. She wanted to shake the woman and tell her to snap out of it, but could already see her folding back into herself as it was. Jen needed to keep her mom in the present, and there with her. "We'll find him."

A scream echoed through the cemetery and while it sounded far away, Jen could feel it pushing like a force through her skull. Nails pounded behind her vision for a brief second and she thought she was going to be the one collapsing to the ground by the sheer force of it. She had to grit her teeth to stay standing, and reached out to her mom, using both of them together to stay standing.

When it faded, Jen opened her eyes to see that her mom had a small trace of blood, slowly moving down her cheek like a tear. Jen could feel the wetness from her own eyes. Now that she was steadier, she released her mom and checked and as she pulled her hand away, saw the red streak that matched.

"What was that?" Jen said, still feeling shaken by the ferocity of what had happened.

"David." Her mom said as she turned in the other direction than where Jen had seen the little girl. Then her mom started to rush in that direction. She was nearly at a run, moving faster than Jen had ever seen her move.

Jen was still faster and quickly caught up to her as they rushed through the cemetery. Her mom seemed to be following a path only she could see as she was working her way towards some kind of beacon that Jen had no way of sensing. Wherever they were going, Jen sensed that it was the right direction, as she could feel that they were on their way to finding her brother.

Though as she ran, she also felt something else. There had been something back there. Jen hadn't realized it at the time, but as they ran away from it, Jen could feel a tension release and she knew they were fleeing some trap that they had not realized they had stepped into.

* * * *

They found David back at their father's grave. He was there, surrounded by a few of their relatives from her dad's side of the family that had stuck around. Some of them had agreed to search, but the rest of them were just there, talking and telling stories about their childhood together.

David was sitting on one of the chairs near his father's grave. The crowd had initially tried to calm him down, but he had pushed them all away so he could sit alone, looking at the uncovered hole, crying, and wanting to climb down there so he could lie there as close as possible and be with him.

Jen was able to make it to him faster, breaking out into a run as soon as she recognized him amongst the group of family members and when she got to him, she initially just stood there looking down at him. He didn't say anything. He wouldn't even acknowledge that she was there, his eyes locked on the empty hole.

In return, she stood there quietly as well. She noticed that he was breathing in short gasps and goosebumps ran on the skin that she could see. She was sure there was more on his arms and legs, covered by the suit coat.

He was scared. She could smell the urine and knew he had pissed himself at some point, but there was no sign of a puddle beneath him. He had run from somewhere that frightened him.

He had seen the blood... She was sure of it. He may have even seen it happen.

David patted the seat next to him without even looking up at her, and she lowered herself down next to him. She had barely settled onto the cold, hard metal chair when he surprised her and leaned into her. He was trembling. She looked at him and saw he was sobbing uncontrollably, his lip quivering as he let it all out.

"I'm here." She said to him, at a loss for what else to say, so she just kept repeating it to him, softly, as she held him. "I'm here."

They had a few brief moments of peace, and she continued to try to soothe her brother. It would all erupt into chaos in a few minutes when the search parties returned, and her mom told the others about what they'd found. More police would be called, amber alerts would be issued, and they would continue to try and find the two missing boys who would never be found. Not the bodies. DNA would eventually show that the blood belonged to the boys and there was too much of it for the boys to have survived.

But for now, Jen had her brother, and she was there, as was he. And they held each other, sure they would get one another through whatever was going on around them.

CHAPTER 17

What had started as Ellis's day off had turned into OT, and he didn't see himself going home anytime soon. More body pieces, more blood, so much of it, like the scene he had arrived at just a week ago. So many similarities with the same family involved. Just now, the victims were most likely children, two boys aged ten and eleven who were not from the area but only in town for the funeral.

It was going to be a long night. The sun was just touching the horizon, and they'd already had the dogs out there as well as police search teams canvassing the surrounding area. Amber alerts with the boys' descriptions were being broadcast throughout the surrounding counties.

The family had long since gone home, though they had to be forced to leave so the police could do their work. Detective Price had made that call once the blood had been reported to him. Yes, they were searching for the boys, hoping not to find corpses, but they still needed to treat it for the worst-case scenario. They couldn't afford any mistakes. Not with the rash of murders in the area. Price had told him about the mess they'd found at the doctor's house and now she and her husband were both suspected victims.

How many was that now? Nine possible dead, maybe more. What the hell did they have, some sick serial killer on the loose? If that's the case, when were they going to call in the feds? Don't they have a division that handled cases like this, or was the BAU made for television bullshit?

"How are you holding up?" Ellis turned from where he had lost himself in a daze, staring at the open grave. With the investigation, the police hadn't let the large hole in the ground to be filled.

Scotty, someone Ellis had worked with many times over the years and was probably the closest thing he had to a friend on the force, came walking up to him. His blond hair and large mustache made him someone that looked like the butt of a bad joke, but he was a good-natured guy to anyone that he respected. Detective Price was one of the few not on that list.

"Doing the best I can. Find anything?"

Scotty looked at the scene around him, then back to Ellis. "Just came on. Heard you been here all day. Figured if there was news, you'd have it for me."

Ellis winced at his mistake. "Sorry, it's been a long day, week even. Thought you were coming up to give me some news."

"What, you make detective and not tell nobody? You know us patrols don't get updates. We give them." Ellis knew he was trying to be lighthearted and doing his best to make light of the situation, but he wasn't having it, and Scotty changed his stance and lost the smile. "Hey, I know this can't be easy for, not with all that's happened. I'd say I get it, but no one knows the hurt you must be going through and then to be a part of all this. It's unimaginable. Just know that we're all your family. We're here for you, whatever you need."

"You going to tell me to take leave?"

"Hell no, I'm not your watch commander. I can't tell you to do anything. Just someone who knows you is here for you and wants to make sure you know that."

"Sure, thanks."

"Besides, I know it'd be pointless. I mean, come on, aren't you off duty?" Scotty said as he pointed at the suit Ellis had worn to the funeral earlier. He did stand out from the uniform officers who were studying the scene.

"Yeah well, the daughter worried they weren't safe and asked me to be here."

"Oh, does she know something?"

"Don't think so. I think I spooked her by accident when we talked at the hospital. She just wanted to feel safer having someone here. And-" Ellis trailed off, not ready to explain the something else that had pulled him to being there. The protectiveness he felt for the boy he saved. He just wanted to be there to make sure he stayed safe. There was something going on, something strange pushing at his thoughts. Memories were eating at him, but couldn't break through the surface of recollection.

"Woah buddy, maybe you should go home and get some sleep." Scotty said, causing Ellis to shake free of the rabbit hole he was going down trying to place a missing thought. "Where'd you go there for a minute?"

"Sorry, I feel like there's something about this that I'm missing. Every time I think I'm close to figuring it out, it slips away again."

"Did you put your laundry in the dryer?"

"What?"

"Usually whenever there's something I think I'm forgetting, it's usually that I forgot to put the laundry in the dryer. Had to wear a damp uniform a couple times now."

"It's a wonder why you're single and still on patrol duty."

"And your excuse is?"

"It's where I prefer. Who wants to be a dick in a suit?"

"Speaking of, here comes detective prick now."

"Officer Scott, thought you were supposed to check in with me when you first got here? I had to call dispatch just to find out you were already on scene," Price said, frustration in his tone as he walked up to them.

"Hey Detective, just saw my man here and wanted to get an update."

"And the lead detective couldn't give you that update?"

"Well, not if I want the juicy stuff." Scotty said. Scott was smiling as he looked over at Ellis, but Ellis was not sharing the joke and looked over at Detective Price.

"I was just giving him some updates as to what happened earlier. He hasn't been here long."

"Fine, Officer Scott, they're shutting down the search for tonight, but they're going to need watch over the crime scene until morning. You pulled the short straw."

"Great, sitting in a cemetery all night keeping watch. Who hasn't seen that horror movie?" Scott said under his breath as the detective was already walking off, yelling out directions to the other officers.

"I actually don't think I've seen that in a horror movie."

"Fine, it wasn't cops, but wasn't there something in Return of the Living Dead? Or what about Cemetery Man?"

"You do watch too many horror films."

"Maybe. You go home and get some rest."

"We'll see."

* * * *

Ellis didn't make it to his car before he was stopped by Detective Price. He hadn't thought about it until then, but they had somehow avoided each other much of the afternoon. Ellis may have been actively avoiding the man, but Price seemed anxious while walking over to him. They both might have been avoiding one another.

"Officer Ellis, can I have a word with you?"

Ellis's keys were in his hand, and his car was right there. A part of him wanted to ignore Price and get in. He could take off and be done with the detective.

Curiosity got the better of him, and he waited for the older man to catch up.

"Hey, it's Tom, right? Tommy?"

"Tom works."

"Tom, hey, so," Detective Price was avoiding Ellis's eyes, looking at the cemetery around them and then the empty grave.

"This couldn't have been easy for you today. Thank you for being here and I think I get it. I guess, well, someone overheard us talking last week. I never knew you lost them. I'm sorry for bringing them up."

Ellis was taken aback and wasn't sure what to say. He didn't really have a chance as he watched Price's expression change. The few moments of empathy hardened as something behind Ellis caught his attention.

"We may have one of them." Price said as he rushed past Ellis. Ellis turned just in time to see what looked like a flash of white clothing catch the last bit of remaining sunlight before it disappeared behind a statue. Price was chasing after it, and though Ellis was exhausted from the long day, he found himself energized with a second wind as he took off to follow.

* * * *

It didn't take Ellis long to pass Price, not that Price was out of shape, but Ellis was a runner. He was out of practice, not jogging nearly as much as he used to over the last year, but the muscle memory and breathing techniques were still there. It only took a few strides for his training instincts to kick in and he was rushing towards where he had seen the shape disappear behind the statue.

"Be careful... It could... be the kids, it could be... someone else." Price tried to warn, but Ellis wasn't slowing down. The chance at finding even just one of the kids pushed him past the point of reason and he hadn't realized before now just how much he needed to find them.

Why did he need to find them? They weren't the ones who reminded him so much of Tyler. Why these two boys? The other one was the one who-

He reached the statue and tried to cut around as fast as he could. As he did, he was too close to the statue and didn't see that the angel had a tail. The tail was low and caught him in the knee.

He felt his leg pull out from under him and his balance shifted against his will. He was trying to compensate, but he had been running and it happened so fast. He put his hand out, but it was too late. His shoulder slammed into the cool, hard earth just a few feet from the base of a large tree. Its roots were a gnarled mess erupting from the earth to stretch around him. He had been lucky to miss their thick, hard irregular surface.

"Watch out!" He called to Price, but it was too late. The detective had managed to miss the statue's tail, but his foot snagged one of the roots and he came down not far from Ellis.

Ellis was already looking around them, trying to see any trace of movement, hoping the white shirt would catch some kind of light. It was hopeless, and he knew it. The full moon had been last week and with the sun fully set, the world around them was hopelessly dark.

"We're not going to find anything out here." Ellis said, reaching out to the tree to guide himself up.

"Fuck." Price said as he reached for the tree to do the same. He quickly recoiled his hand from the bark. "Shit."

Ellis looked over at him, and Price stood holding his hand. It was obvious the detective had cut it. His hand was bleeding, dark liquid dripping to the ground.

"What the hell did I cut myself on?"

"Can't tell. You better get to the hospital, get a tetanus shot in case there was any metal."

"Yeah. You get yourself home, get some rest. We'll find them."

"I'm not the family. You don't need to feed me the bullshit. We both know the chances this late."

"Yeah."

"Yeah."

"Well, still, try to stay positive. You're too young to become the grumpy ol' detective who's an asshole to everyone. Enjoy your time on patrol."

"Shit, you almost sound human, like you care."

"Caring's the problem. You care too much, you burn yourself out, family too. Take it from someone who knows, keep the job at the door." Price stopped and looked at Ellis, realizing what he just said. "Sorry, I shouldn't have said that. I know it's rough."

"I get it."

"Good. Go get some rest."

CHAPTER 18

"They're going to find them. The police are looking. They're going to be fine." Jen said to her aunt Lisa. They were both sitting at the dining room table. It was Jen's turn to watch her aunt as different members of the family had tagged in throughout the afternoon. It wasn't easy. Her aunt was not a pleasant woman and any attempt at comfort had been rebuked with snarls of anger. "Get the fuck out and look for him, you lazy fucks!" had been said multiple times to the lingering family members who stood and sat throughout the house.

"What the hell do you know, little girl? Just what the fuck do you know?" Lisa said without looking up at her, her head held in her hands as she continued to look down at the table.

"Well, I don't, but being a bitch doesn't do any good either." Jen snapped back and she could feel eyes on the back of her neck and realized she'd said it louder than she intended.

"Being a bitch is all I've got left, honey." Lisa looked up at her. "You don't get what it's like to have a part of you, something you gave life to, just ripped away. Like your smug ass father ripped my sister away from me. Now I'm in this shit hole of a backward town in butt fuck Iowa or Illinois, whatever this cornfield hell is, and have more ripped away from me.

"I hate you. I hate your brother; you're not my family. You stole my family from me. So why don't you go find that mistake of a brother and get the hell out of my face?"

Jen could feel her nails trying to dig into the polished wood of the table. It was too smooth and highly frustrating as she wanted destruction. Instead, she gritted her teeth and struggled to hold in the tears that threatened.

Hell no, she was not going to give this woman the satisfaction.

"You know, I can start to see why mom never talks about you. No wonder she moved here."

"Fuck you. Your dad let her get so drugged up, had her in and out of rehab all the damned time. I love my sister, but he destroyed her, slutting her around to get financing for his shitty films, telling her she was going to be a star. My sister used to be beautiful and loved acting. Now she has to play nursemaid to you two."

"You are a piece of work. We've been nothing but nice to you no matter how nasty you've been, and those demons you call children need a mother, not whatever the hell you are. You should have been watching them, but you let them run around and play in a cemetery while we were burying *MY* father. Who the hell does that? Parent your children."

Someone came up behind Jen, who was now standing, glaring down at her aunt. Jen's face was red with anger, but her aunt looked nonplussed, almost dead inside as she watched her niece yell at her. Whoever was behind Jen was trying to talk to her and pull her away, but Jen didn't step back.

"Talk about parenting. I'm the terrible parent. Your mother was in rehab when she got knocked up with mistake number two. She was in rehab. So, tell me, who's the father? Your mother went from rehab to counseling after that one. You remember all that time away?

"Oh, that's right, your dad was off making movies, so you were sent off to school. That's right. You never wondered why they were sending you to those private schools, but now they don't? Funny how that worked out, hun. Who sends their little six-year-old away for school?"

The hands of Jen's shoulders grew firmer as they finally pulled her back from the snarling older woman.

"Hey Jen, why don't you go upstairs and check on your brother? I'm sure he's probably forgotten to eat anything." Uncle Tim said. She felt his hot breath on her neck, and she tensed, not realizing how close he was. She shook it off before nodding in agreement.

"Yeah, I'll go see how he's doing. You can try to calm down the slug over here." Jen said, turning to nod at her uncle before walking away from the scene. She could feel everyone's eyes on her as she made her way to the front hall. She reached the stairway and grabbed the large wooden ball that topped the bottom post and held it tightly, taking deep breaths to calm her nerves.

Just who in the hell did she think she was, coming into my home and saying crazy shit about my family? Just who in the hell?

Jen released her tense jaw and rubbed at the soreness. She hadn't cried, though. That thought helped her to stand a little straighter, glad that she didn't give that snake the satisfaction of seeing her tears.

She chanced a glance down the hall and stopped as a stranger stood in the doorway that went into the kitchen. He stood there, blocking the path from the kitchen into the dining room, staring at her. Throughout the day, as more people arrived, a growing fragrance of home-cooked meals wafted through the house that had allowed there to be a sense of heart-warming compassion, one that her aunt had clearly not felt and Jen had grown accustomed to it. She was desensitized to it.

That was until the foul stench of sulfur mingled with the blessed vibes of pleasantness mixed into a gut-wrenching foulness that she could feel bile rising up to the back of her throat. As she stared at the man, she swore the stench was coming from him. He brought this wrongness into the house, and it was fusing with the warmth that was her home.

She stopped from going upstairs, her step on the first stair trapped there by his gaze.

He smiled. It wasn't a normal smile. It was full of teeth, and as she stood there watching him, it spread wider. The longer her eyes were on him, the larger it grew. As it did so, the teeth sharpened into points and his chin lowered so the smile reshaped into a "V" and the width was stretched until it was unnaturally wide and lifting to his ears.

When her Uncle Vince left the kitchen, he should have bumped into the man but somehow stepped through him. The man simply shifted into smoke, only to reform briefly. Then he was gone. Vince made no acknowledgment that he had even seen the man. He continued on, carrying a tray of deviled eggs as he disappeared out of her view into either the dining or living room.

Was that real? Jen had to shake her head, her brain mildly aching like after intensely focusing on an object and suddenly being pulled back to reality. She couldn't focus, as the world around her felt too bright and wanted to spin out from under her. Her grip tightened on the railing, and she had to put much of her weight onto it as she wavered.

"You okay?" She heard the hoarse, raspy voice of her Aunt Carol. Aunt Carol had spent most of her life as a heavy smoker and yet somehow was still around at nearly seventy. She was actually Jen's great aunt, but everyone had always just called her Aunt Carol, and it stuck.

Jen opened her eyes and looked down at the shorter woman. She had ashen skin that seemed close to the color of light smoke. Maybe it was because of all the cigarettes, as it felt like the woman was in a perpetual haze and wreaked of cigarettes so strong you could smell her from across the room. Her teeth were dark yellow, and Jen could see them as she smiled a comforting smile up at her.

Jen figured her aunt was trying to be nice. Her aunt was an overly nice person, but Jen also couldn't get the image of the man out of her thoughts. As she looked down at her aunt, she couldn't get the image of something old and decrepit looking up at her, ready to devour her down to her soul. Jen tried to shake away the image, but she swore she could see blood staining those yellow teeth and her aunt's eyes seemed darker, almost black, like the eyes of a shark looking at her.

"Jen, you okay?" Her aunt said again, shaking Jen out of her daze. She had been looking back and forth from her aunt to where the man had been and had lost track of how long she had stood there, not answering the woman.

"I'm fine. I'm fine. I was just on my way upstairs to check on my brother."

"You don't look fine. You should sit down. You look pale."

"No, I just need to check on him."

"You need to take care of yourself. No one's going to take care of you. Especially not that woman," Aunt Carol said, nodding to the upstairs. Jen guessed she was referring to her mom, as they had never liked each other. Jen had heard her refer to her mom more than once as "that crazy one" whenever it had been just her and her dad visiting. The more Jen looked around and started to realize it, none of her aunts and uncles from her dad's side of the family had been welcoming to her mom since they've moved there.

"We do what we can." That was all Jen could think of saying as she took a few steps up the stairs. She was only a few feet when she barely heard her aunt muttering under breath.

"Always odd. That boy never looked like his father. His black hair. Nothing at all. Not at all."

Jen raced up the stairs.

She made it to the upstairs hallway and past her room on her way to David's when she stopped. She could hear her mom talking to herself. She was in the bathroom and Jen could barely make out what she was saying. Jen tried the door, but it was locked.

"No. No, can't be. Not yet, not to him. He promised. None of this should be happening. Not the deal. No, no, this is all my fault. All me, all my fault. All me, all because of me. I can't do anything right. It's all my fault." She heard her mother crying on the other side.

"You. You aren't real. You're not his father, you're not real. You stay away from us. You stay away."

"Mom. Are you okay?" Jen said as she knocked on the door.

"Get away from me. You all get away from me. I don't need any of you. Get away!" Her mom was yelling, then crying again, frantic as to how she cycled through the emotions. Jen wasn't sure if she should go downstairs and get help, but who would she get? Lisa? Jodi? Carol, any of the rest of her dad's family? None of them seemed like they would be able to help her mother.

It was going to be all up to her, but what should she do?

She tried the door again. Nothing, still locked, so she knocked gently. Still no acknowledgement that she was even out there. There was just more of her mom's ranting.

Jen figured there was not too much she could do for her mom, not without making noise that would draw everyone from downstairs. She would need to get rid of everyone first, but she still needed to check on her brother and make sure he was okay.

"It's not time. It's not fair, it's not fair, it's not fair. You lied. You're a liar."

Jen moved away from the door, worried she was losing everyone in her life, and that her mom might not come back from all of this.

She found David in his room. He was sitting on the floor with his back against his closet door. As the last rays of sun filtered in, the room was getting dark, but David seemed oblivious to it. He kept his glare on his bed, or more specifically, the darkness underneath.

Jen felt her heart stab at her. How much of this did he realize? What was going on in that head of his? Jen sighed, frustrated with how little she could read him, those blank stares and the silence.

She wanted her little bro back; someone she could laugh and tease. She hoped that somewhere, that little boy was in there, though she feared that innocence was lost. No one knew just what he had seen.

She walked over and sat down next to him.

"Hey." She said, and at first it seemed like he wasn't even going to acknowledge that she was there. It took him a moment as he continued to sit there, looking off into an unseen distance before he slowly shifted. Her heart leapt, fearful he was going to pull away and leave her alone on his floor, but instead of pulling away, he rested his head on her chest. She felt his warmth and the quick breaths, but when she felt the wetness penetrating her shirt, she could tell he was crying.

She pulled him closer as she held him.

"Yeah, I know." She said, and she realized she did know. She let the fear of not being able to understand what he was feeling drift away. She knew, because she felt it too. All the pain of losing their father, the craziness of knowing someone killed him, someone that was still out there.

Jen understood her brother, and as she sat there on the cold hardwood floor with him, she finally allowed herself to grieve. The tears she had been holding back were finally released, and she pulled her brother tighter, closer, so they could finally cry the tears for their father, together.

CHAPTER 19

With her brother drifting off to sleep, Jen finally made it back downstairs and was surprised. It turned out she didn't need to push to get everyone to leave. Most of them were already gone, so that only her Aunt Lisa and her Uncle Tim remained. Lisa was in the living room, wine bottle in hand, as she staggered around looking at family photos. Uncle Tim quickly made his way to Jen as she descended the stairs.

"Everyone okay?" It was obvious he was uncomfortable being left alone with the demon woman from the west coast. Tim looked so much like her dad. They weren't brothers though, as her dad had been an only child. Tim was her second cousin, but her dad had never liked calling him that, so instead he was Uncle Tim. Much of her family was like that, as her dad had a lot of cousins that they often referred to as aunts or uncles.

"I think so. Everyone already leave?"

"Yeah, they're all sorry to have left without saying goodbye. I told them I'd wait around and make sure you guys didn't need anything." Her uncle looked at her aunt and then he moved in as though to whisper to her conspiratorially, "They needed to get away from her. I haven't met a person who could release such venom with her words. That woman is a nightmare."

Jen looked at her aunt, wishing she could will her to leave as well, though she knew that wasn't going to happen. They were stuck with her, as she was staying with them for the duration of her trip. Originally, she was supposed to be on a flight that night, but it was already too late as she would have already left to make her flight.

"I can't believe they all left."

135

"I'm sorry. You know your mom doesn't make it easy, and well, with you three not down here, many of them felt like they were being blown off."

"I'm sorry."

"Don't be. I know they left, but we are all here for you, anytime you need anything. We're just a phone call away. You and your brother.

"You know, it wasn't your responsibility to be down here. There's something wrong with your mom. Like I said, call us if you need us."

"You can't be talking about my sister like that." Neither of them had paid attention to her aunt and hadn't realized she had been moving closer to them. They both looked at her, wide-eyed, like being caught in a conspiracy, which, in a way, maybe they had.

"She's my mom."

"You're an ungrateful cunt. My angels are out there and none of you even care about them. We should be out there looking for them."

"I think I'm going to head out. Remember what I said. You've got all our numbers. Call if you need anything. Even if it's just to get away from here for a night." Uncle Tim said, looking at Lisa as he said that last part before he made his way to the door. She hadn't noticed before, but he'd already had his coat on the little table they kept in the entryway. He grabbed it and left before putting it on, choosing to face the early fall chill rather than the frost that was brewing inside.

"Asshole. This whole damn family can go to hell. Where's my sister? I'm getting her out of here." Lisa pushed past where Jen stood on the steps and headed upstairs.

"You can't just leave."

"You got your brother. I'm taking my sister and I'm finding my boys, and we're going home. You can all rot in hell like you deserve."

Lisa stormed up the stairs, and Jen rushed to follow her. As she did, she felt the vibration of her phone in her back pocket. She glanced at the notification, dismissing it when she saw that it was her girlfriend, Clara. Clara hadn't called all day, probably because she knew a little of what Jen was going through. She was probably checking in on her.

Jen would have to deal with that once she was done with Ms. Aunt psycho.

"Sis, where are you? Malibu Barbie girl, where are you? We need to get you out of here."

Jen could hear the slur in her aunt's voice as she spoke and noticed how she was swaying back and forth as she used the walls to navigate the hallway. She had passed the closed door of the bathroom and Jen momentarily held her breath as Lisa neared her brother's door.

When she passed it, Jen breathed a sigh of relief as she eased her way to the bathroom.

"Mom?" she said, speaking as softly as she could while trying to stay under the radar of the crazy woman. Her mom had stopped her rambling from earlier, but Jen could still hear her crying.

Something crashed at the end of the hall. Jen looked up to see the door to her parents' room open, and on the floor was one of her parents' photo frames, the glass smashed from being slammed to the floor.

"Fucking asshole!" Lisa screamed, and another framed photo flew into the hall and smashed against the wall. This one, Jen could easily make out as a wedding photo by the frames border which had been made up of metal skulls. Her dad had given it to their mom for one of their anniversaries and they had put what they had thought was their best photo together. They had both been dressed in all black, her mom's wedding dress included, and had made it a non-traditional wedding by being married in a cemetery. Her dad loved to play the spooky goth guy back then, though not much had changed over the years, other than her mom being less and less into it.

The glass rained down, exploding from the impact from the large frame, kind of like how chaos was showering on Jen more and more, life just shitting on her as she had to deal now with crazy mom and crazy aunt. There was even a dent in the wall from where the thick metal frame had slammed into it and one of the skulls was wedged into it.

Jen was getting pretty sick of putting up with her aunt's bullshit. Yeah, the woman was going through a lot, and Jen would be stressing about her kids too if she had any, but this was taking things way too far. The woman was going to tear the place up and wake her brother.

Something thumped and sounded like it fell over. Then more glass broke as something heavy was flung across the room.

Jen stormed down to the end of the hall and could see the chaos of the bedroom. Her mother's large dresser mirror was overturned and had smashed against the king's size bed, shattering where it had stuck the headboard. Makeup was scattered throughout the floor and mom's chair was overturned against the nearby wall. A tornado couldn't have done much more damage than her aunt had done in less than five minutes,

"I'm calling the police." Jen yelled at her, the fury building up inside of her as she looked at the chaos around her.

"Don't you dare!" Lisa yelled, trying to rush over to stop Jen as she turned to leave the room and get away from the unhinged woman. "They're looking for my boys. They need to keep looking."

Lisa tripped and fell towards the bed which was covered in glass and had the broken dresser strewn against it. Jen watched in horror as the woman fell into the mess of it. Glass sliced into her arm and Lisa slipped more, trying to keep from falling into the maelstrom, but instead found herself slamming her head into the corner of the mirror.

Lisa dropped to the floor, a bleeding unconscious mess. Jen looked at her, initially concerned her aunt had just killed herself, but saw the labored rise and fall in her chest as she tried to breathe.

"Holy shit." Jen muttered under her breath. She rushed down the hall to the bathroom and pounded on the door.

"Mom! Mom!" Jen yelled as she slammed her fists into the door.

Nothing.

Jen stopped knocking on the door and suddenly realized how much silence descended upon the upstairs. Her mom wasn't crying on the other side of the door anymore. There wasn't any sound upstairs except for the increasing buzz of the electricity as the quiet grew louder.

Jen pounded on the door harder, then started slamming her body against it. She could see the cracks in the wood as she slammed harder and harder. She tried the door handle, not sure why, but desperate to get into the bathroom, suddenly scared about what she might find behind the door.

To her surprise, the door opened with the twist of the knob just as she was coming in for another slam against the door. The sudden release of resistance nearly threw her off balance as it opened. She burst into the room, struggling to stay on her feet.

She didn't wait to regain her balance to take stock of the room, but immediately rushed to her mom, who was stretched out on the bathroom floor just past the entry of the door. Her face was pale, and as Jen touched her, the skin was cool and clammy.

Jen looked around and saw the empty bottle of pills in her mother's hand.

NO! She yelled to herself, not willing to accept anything at that point. There was nothing to accept. She needed to fix it. That's what she needed to do. Her mind was suddenly numb to everything else. She needed to fix this.

Her phone buzzed again from another notification, and she realized there was no one coming to save her and her family. If anyone was going to do the saving, it was going to have to be her.

She cleared away the notification, not paying attention to the line of text messages she had received, and quickly dialed the number for emergency services. Within seconds, her call was connected.

"I need help." She blurted before the operator had even finished asking what was her emergency. "My mom took some pills and is asleep on the floor and my aunt knocked herself out and is covered in blood. I need help."

The rest of it became a blur from there. The operator talking her through things to try while the ambulance was on the way. The voice on the other end of the phone line stayed calm as they tried to talk her through everything. The voice was reassuring and kept reaffirming that it was going to be okay.

Jen tried to stay focused on the calming voice while her aunt's voice tried to reach her from the hall. She had regained consciousness and was stumbling down the hall, looking for her sister.

All of it was a jumble of the outside, while internally she was lost in a fog, unsure if she could remember her own name.

Everything was happening on autopilot, and the world around her became distant as she struggled just to handle the moment.

"Watch him. Protect him. His father is coming for him. Protect him."

As the noise all blossomed around her, those words broke through, and Jen looked at her mom just before the paramedics took her away, loading her into the back of the ambulance.

When had the paramedics arrived? As she watched them leave, she struggled to remember.

CHAPTER 20

Detective Price heard the call over the police radio and recognized the address immediately. He heard the general details, heard that a police presence was not requested, though a unit was getting dispatched as a precaution, and he decided not to go. He knew how the family felt about him, and they were going through a lot. Right now, the last thing they needed was him to be there.

People often thought he didn't care. He knew he came off that way because, as much as he did care and worried about the people he tried to help, the job always came first. As he pulled up to his dark house and the empty driveway, it was a steady reminder of just how much the job always came first. His house was a tomb to that testament.

He cared for people. He took the job to help and did as much as he could. Even in times when he let cynicism take over his judgement, he still cared. It was just the longer you do the job, the longer you see how people betray your hopes and trust, the harder it is to believe people for what they say. How can you believe a mother who seems nice and protective when the next day you hear they tried to kill themselves, abandoning those she swore to protect?

He wished he didn't see it as often as he did.

He grabbed his phone from its holder on his dash and found the one number in his call history he hadn't added yet as a contact. A few seconds later, his phone rang a few times before he heard Officer Ellis's voice answer.

"Ellis."

"Hey, It's Price. Have you heard the radio?"

"No, was just getting home. Why?"

"Attempted suicide at the Carey's. Was wondering if you would be willing to go over and check in with them. I know you've had a long day and are off duty, but-"

"I'm on my way."

"Thanks. They've been through a lot. You know that better than me. Just want to make sure everyone's okay and I don't think they'd want me there."

There was silence at the other end of the call before Ellis responded.

"Roger that. I'll check in with them and keep you updated."

"Thanks."

The call disconnected, but before Price had a chance to put the phone in his pocket, he saw the screen light back up. Dispatch was calling him. Someone had probably put two and two together at HQ and was now calling him to see if he wanted to go over. He thought briefly about dismissing the call, but couldn't bring himself to do it.

Job first.

He accepted the call.

"Price here, thrill me."

"Detective Price?"

"Yeah, it's me."

"Sergeant Dekker. Sorry to call so late. I know you just signed off 10-42, but I'm hoping you can help me out."

"What's going on?"

"As you know, we're currently stretched thin, got county coming in to help, but I'm hoping you can do me a quick favor. I got a call for a wellness check, and it looks like it's two blocks from you. I'm hoping you can run over and make a quick pass of the place."

Price started the car.

"Name and address."

"Annette Marsh. She's at 986 Derry. Dr. hasn't been into work and not answering her phone. Co-worker says that it's not like her to miss her shift."

"Sure, I'll head over. Keep me updated if anything's found on the two boys. I heard there was a call to the house."

"Yeah, it's bad. Sister hurt herself falling down, and the mother attempted suicide. That family seems cursed."

"Yeah, well, just keep me updated.

142

Price disconnected that call and entered the address on his phone. The desk Sargent was off by a block, but still it was in his cul-de-sac. He backed out of his driveway and went to the address.

* * * *

Price came to a house nearly identical to his own, as just about all the houses in the area had that same generic design. It was only how people decorated the outside that distinguished the houses from one another. Unfortunately, this one was just as plain, with just as much a lack of individuality as his own. His was due to him working all the time, committed to his job, so what did that say about Ms. Marsh?

There was no car in the driveway, but one could easily be parked in the garage. All the lights were off, there was no sign of movement inside. Everything seemed clear that no one was currently home.

Price walked up to the front door, quickly scanning the neighborhood. It was his own neighborhood, so he was generally familiar with it on the day to day, but now, in his official capacity, he started to pay more attention. He looked at the houses around there, scanned how many were completely dark, how many had some lights on, and some had televisions going, easily visible through the large picture windows.

It was a regular, calm night with a cool breeze. Nothing appeared to be amiss. So why were the hairs on the back of his neck suddenly standing at attention and he had an unceasing sense that something was watching him?

He pushed the thought to the back of his mind, knowing not to dismiss it entirely. His years on the job had taught him long ago to never discount a feeling, no matter how out of place.

He rang the doorbell and listened as his only response was silence.

A car passed by on the street behind him and he turned to watch it go, still with that nagging sense that something was there studying him.

He knocked on the door and waited. Still only silence.

"Hello, this is Detective Price. I'm here on behalf of the Cronenberg police department. I'm here to do a welfare check.

Please open this door." He called loudly and saw lights in the neighboring house turn on. He'd gotten someone's attention, just not the one he was hoping for. He saw a shape at the window, but they weren't pulling down the shade for a better view. They were probably trying to be nosy without making it obvious.

He briefly debated on going over and talking to them, but there wasn't reason to canvas yet. If he troubled the neighbors and Ms. Marsh turned out to be fine, that could make it an awkward situation that could be avoided.

He dialed the number for the desk sergeant.

"Everything good there."

"Not sure. Nobody is answering. I'm going to start doing a walk around, see if I can see anything."

"Okay, keep me updated. Call me back if you need to breach. Time to start following protocol. I'm going to dispatch a unit to the location just in case. They're about ten to fifteen minutes out. They're just wrapping up at the Carey's."

"Roger that."

Price put the phone back into his suit coat pocket and started checking windows, looking into each one to see if he saw any signs that would indicate anything had happened there. He also checked them to see if there were any unlocked. It was doubtful, but if he had to enter, going through an unlocked door or unlatched window was better than having to break his way in.

He made it all the way around the house and was back on the front porch without seeing anything wrong or finding an unlocked entry. He wasn't surprised, just frustrated.

He checked his watch. It had already been fifteen minutes, with no sign of the patrol unit.

"What's the update on that patrol unit?" Price barked into the phone as soon as the desk sergeant answered.

"They got tied up. Had to follow the ambulance to the hospital as one of the women went into hysterics and started fighting the paramedics." Price felt like he knew which one was causing the trouble, not that both women weren't cable of it.

"Understood. Well, I'm going in. Log it, walked around, no unsecured entry points so will be forcing in the front door."

"I'll make a note in the log. I do have another unit dispatched; they will be there as soon as they can."

"10-4."

Price put away the phone and looked closer at the front door. There was paneled glass, so it looked like he could break one panel and reach in to unlock the door.

He looked around, trying to find something to protect his hand while trying to remember if there was anything in his car. He remembered he had his gym bag in the trunk and went for it. After he had grabbed it, he was walking back to the front door when that voice in the back of his head screaming that there was something wrong grew to a fever pitch.

He scanned the area again and noticed that there was a girl standing on the sidewalk across the street. She was wearing a school uniform, but he didn't recognize it from any of the local schools. Several thoughts ran through his head, such as, it was the weekend, why the uniform, why was she staring over here and not walking somewhere, what time was it, how young is she, why isn't she gone or with her parents? With the thought about the missing two kids earlier, it wasn't safe to just be wondering the streets like she was.

Price debated about going over to her and getting details, maybe call her parents, but she seemed okay for now and the patrol would be there soon. They could check in with the kid. He did live in a decent neighborhood, so she should be safe.

All of these he knew were rationalizations again rattling around because he had a job to do and was intent on doing it. There was more to it, though. That screaming voice that had been rattling around his brain since he had gotten there was a full-on siren now, telling him not to go over there.

Something was off about her; he just couldn't place what it was.

And she just kept staring at him, not saying or doing anything. She just stood there, unnaturally still.

He tried to shake off that feeling as he went to the front door of the house and, without any further hesitation, slammed his wrapped fist through the glass.

Thankfully, the glass wasn't reinforced and broke easily. He then used the remnants of the towel to clear away the shards so he could get his hand through and unlock the door.

CHAPTER 21

Jen had told the officers before they would leave that her uncle was on the way. They had demanded some kind of guardian for them. Her not being eighteen would have meant a night with civil services if they didn't have someone to go to.

She had been lying at the time. She had never called him. She acted like she had while the officers were distracted by their dispatcher. Jen had been worried they were going to wait until her uncle showed up, but an emergency call came in and they rushed to leave, claiming they'd be back to check in.

Jen nodded, and who knows, by then maybe she would have called him. She just wasn't ready yet. It was all too much. Too much noise and madness, of chaos swirling around her life. Her brother was asleep, and she just wanted some silence.

Her phone buzzed again, and she looked at it. Clara had been calling and texting, probably worried about her since she hadn't responded. It's probably been the longest they've not communicated since middle school and Clara knew everything Jen was dealing with today. Well, she knew everything that had been going on. There was a lot more, and Jen had no clue how she was going to talk about any of it.

Rather than reading through all the messages, she hit "call back" on the menu and heard the phone ringing. Before long, it connected, and she heard Clara's concerned voice.

"About time. How are you holding up?" Clara's voice sent a wave of comfort through her that reached deep down near into her soul as finally she had someone she could turn to. Though it was separated by cell towers, it felt miles closer to any recent conversation she'd had with her mother.

Just hearing Clara's voice made her realize just how badly she needed her there. Clara was the one she needed, not some uncle that she only somewhat knew. Clara, the one who was nearly always with her, and had to be away from for almost a week because she'd been out of town with her parents.

"Please tell me you're back."

"Just got home a few hours ago. Still tired from the flight, but I wanted to check in, see how you were holding up."

"Can you come over?"

"I just got home."

"Please. I need you. I really need you, not just phone voice you, I need to hold you. Please."

Clara must have heard the desperation in her voice.

"I'm on my way. Be there in ten."

"Be safe, don't be running red lights. I have too much other crazy going on and enough people I know are already in the hospital."

"I'll be safe. I'll get there when I get there. I'm on my way."

The phone disconnected and Jen looked at it for a minute, looking at the ragged reflection of herself on the screen. She looked like she was crazy, bags under her eyes and her hair was a mess.

Clara wouldn't care. She's seen her worse than this.

Jen heard a crash upstairs and rushed to get up there. She made it to the hallway, and the lights were flickering around her. The house felt like it was shaking, and sparks shot out from the outlets. A wind came from nowhere and blew around her, pushing her away from proceeding down the hall. She pushed against it to reach her brother's room to realize that the gale force was coming from there.

She had to fight to open his door, only for the wind to stop suddenly. She nearly lost her balance, but caught herself as the surrounding maelstrom calmed. David had been rolling in his bed, screaming as she had come into the room, but as everything died down, he turned over, sleeping as though the incident with their mother had never happened.

CHAPTER 22

Inside, the house was dark as very little of the light from the streetlamp outside lit the room. He scanned what he could see of the room before entering and did see a lamp nearby, but his instinct was to not touch anything. He worked too many crime scenes where the first cop on the scene messed up evidence by doing something dumb, such as disturbing the scene. So, as much as he wanted the extra illumination, he opted instead to use his mini flashlight as he pointed it throughout the room.

He made his way through the downstairs, finding no sign that anything was amiss. A brief scan of the garage showed that a car was parked there.

Price made his way back to the front of the house to where stairs led to the second floor. That was when he could hear the noise.

It may have always been there. It was so soft, almost imperceptible. Now, as the silence had set in, he could hear it coming from upstairs. There was what sounded like a wet, rhythmic thumping sound. It made him think of his dishwasher when it was running while he was on the other side of the house. There was that swooshing sound, the thudding as the blades turned inside, and then that long suck as the water drained.

Goosebumps ran along his arm, and he saw the hairs rise in warning. That growing sense of impending doom filled his chest, making each breath painful against his chest.

Maybe you should just go outside and wait for backup?

It seemed like a rational thought, but it was an unwelcome stranger. One that he cursed away. How would that look if he waited and there was nothing up there, or worse, what if that sound was her? What if she was lying up there gasping for breath and him not going up there was what allowed her to die?

At least have your pistol ready, the voice tried to reason. He shook it off. A person doesn't go into a welfare check with guns drawn. The kind of drama that could cause was incalculable.

He reached the second floor and took a deep breath, scanning the immediate area. The hall was short; the house being smaller than his and led to two doors. He guessed they were both bedrooms, and the sound he heard was coming from the room on the right.

He eased himself to the door and paused. He thought back to when he entered the house. It had been nearly fifteen minutes ago, but felt longer. He was trying to remember if he called out once he had entered the house. He called out while he was knocking, but had he announced himself upon entry?

The legal ramifications were one matter, but as he heard the sucking sound coming from the other side of the door, images of him storming through that door just to find Ms. Marsh sucking off her husband invaded his mind. He would never hear the end of it at the station. And word would spread. He wasn't sure how, but things like that always had a way.

His phone rang, the trilling default ringtone exploding in the quiet. He instinctively jumped back, his brain not registering at first that the sound came from him and there was not some danger lurching at him through the door. His heart was suddenly racing, and his hands shook. His hands never trembled, but yet here they were, and he had to struggle with getting the phone from his jacket pocket.

He pulled it free, and the light was bright against the surrounding dark. He looked at it and saw a number that he vaguely remembered, but had no name associated. Wasn't the desk sergeant, he was sure of that. He briefly debated on answering the call, but never got the chance as the ringing stopped.

He looked at the now quiet phone in his hand, at the screen that said, "1 missed call." His heart should be slowing, he should be catching his breath, but he wasn't. Something was wrong. As the silence grew around him, it took him a moment to realize that the sucking sound had stopped on the other side of the door.

Dammit, just pull the band-aid off. The thought resonated through his skull and internally he cheered it on. That was it. That was his old self, kicking it into gear. It was time to do this. No more hesitation. Kick those pussy thoughts to the curb, man-up, drop your balls and open that damn door.

He threw open the door, not caring if they were getting it on, as at this point, they would have heard him, anyway. At least then he could get a good show, and then explain to them what he was doing there. Having a cop barge in on them while doing some hanky-panky is what they deserve for him having to be there for this damn welfare check.

He stood in the door frame, trying to comprehend what he saw. The room was dark with only light coming in from the streetlamp outside. From that little light, he could see the shape of what at first seemed like two people, one holding the other as though they were in a deep kiss with one another, the man poised over the woman as she was bent back in his embrace. In the darkness that made sense, that's what he told himself he was seeing. It took a moment for reality to set in, for his perception to burst from what he expected to see to what he saw.

Reality crashed as Price watched the woman slowly slip away. She fell into pieces as first her head hit the floor, splashing in a pool of what he assumed was her blood that had soaked into the carpet. Then part of her arm fell away as half of her torso split off. Her remaining corpse slid down so that Price could finally see the true outline of the thing standing there in front of the window.

Its back was ridged with grooves and what looked like needle thin spikes protruded six inches from dark scales. Its mouth was elongated with sharp fangs that reminded Price of a wolf that was turning to face him, glowing red eyes on fire as they glared in his direction. What the torso had slid down now looked like it had been like a long tongue that was flickering wildly in the little light, and Price felt the wetness as drops of blood reached him.

It was hard for his rational mind to fathom just what the hell this thing was that had turned its attention on him, but its intentions were clear. While the one mutilated body that had just fallen to the floor had been its first course, he was next on the menu.

He didn't hesitate as he skillfully reached into his holster below his suit jacket and pulled out his pistol. He fired off three rounds into its expansive chest. It snarled at him in response, the red eyes flaring in anger.

Price stepped back, keeping his eyes on the target as he worked his way out of the direct line of sight, firing as he continued to move. His main goal was the stairs, and once he couldn't see the thing anymore, risked a glance over his shoulder to judge the distance. He guessed it was twenty feet. He should be able to make that. The thing hadn't even started chasing him yet.

Maybe he'd been wrong. Maybe it was full of Ms. Marsh.

He stopped firing once he broke the line of sight and within a few rushed steps, was halfway to the stairs. The thing still wasn't following him. Had he hurt it more than he realized?

He took a second to expel his magazine and check the count. Seven shots left. He'd shot over half a magazine into the damned thing. Maybe it was down. Maybe it wasn't as unstoppable as it had looked.

A rumbling growl shook the hallway and sent hanging photos to the ground, bringing his attention back to the door. The thing emerged into the hallway, hunching down to get through the door. It walked slowly on what looked like two hooved feet, its legs buckling in reverse as it walked. It moved slowly and maybe that was because of the confines of the hallway as the creature was so massive. Everything else was tiny around it.

It spread its arms, and they stretched the width without coming close to fully stretching and, as it did, so it expanded large claw-like hands. The talons of each were nearly a foot long. The expanding claw went from one talon scraping along the floor to another talon shredding into the ceiling.

Price swore he could hear a chuckle from deep within its throat as he felt his heart painfully trying to escape from his chest. He hadn't realized he'd stopped moving as he just stood there, his brain refusing to function as he was screaming at himself to run. He needed to flee, to turn around, to stop shooting and pissing the damn thing off and just get the hell out of there.

It took a step towards him; its hooves were loud and heavy as it moved. The wood of the old house creaked under the enormous weight, but the sound was soon lost to the eruption of more gunfire as Price started firing again at the beast. He screamed as he kept shooting, and as his clip emptied, the echoes of the shots died away so that his voice was all that could be heard.

That, too, died away as it took another step forward. From what Price could see, there was no sign that his bullets had done anything.

He reached the stairs, nearly tripping down the first one, his focus was locked on the creature as it took another step. Its pace seemed incredibly slow.

Maybe that was the answer. Price started to think it through. The thing was not moving fast, and it was heavy. It might not be that nimble. Price might even be able to turn around and beat the thing downstairs and outside.

He wanted to shoot it some more. Maybe he could aim for those red eyes or wait for it to open its snout. Maybe he could fire into the soft tissue of its throat.

That would require another magazine, which, as he was supposed to be off duty, was conveniently in his glove compartment.

He eased himself down a step, watching as the thing took another long step towards him. It wasn't moving fast, but it was making ground. Price had to run. He turned and rushed down the stairs, not fully thinking through a plan other than to race it to the front door.

He made it down the steps when he felt a crash in front of him, the sound of breaking wood exploding towards him. It was hard to make out in the darkness just what happened, but the hulking form that was blocking the front door was unmistakable. It must have leapt from the hallway upstairs, over him to now be in his escape path.

Price didn't hesitate. He saw the thing in front of him and shifted weight, jumping over the side of the stairs to land on his feet in the downstairs hallway. He raced down it until it opened into the kitchen. At least there was a little light from a nightlight plugged into an outlet over the counter. He barely had time to register the large island in the center of the kitchen, but was able to turn and avoid it.

He felt a stinging sensation at his side as he raced around. He brushed at it and felt the wetness. It burned, and he paused to look down, struggling to see what was wrong. He couldn't see much in the dim light, but the pain was spreading along his back and down his leg, letting him know that the creature had somehow got him.

He turned his side toward the light so that he could see it better and felt a tug of resistance as he did. His shirt was ripped open, and blood was oozing down the large gash. It felt like his skin was being pulled by something and he could see his shirt rise as he moved. It was like there was a string or something pulling at him.

He took a step closer to the light and nearly howled as more pain ripped through his abdomen. Now with more light, he could see what looked like a small red thread that stretched out from the gash and, as he strained his eyes and followed its path, he could see it led back to the hallway and the creature.

His stomach twisted and writhed in pain. He took another step away, working his way closer to the sink, and it felt like his insides were being lit on fire. He ripped open the front of his shirt and heard the sound of the buttons bouncing off the tile floor. He ignored the sound, focusing on his stomach.

He watched as he could see it just under his skin, his stomach covered in lines that looked like worms moving just beneath his flesh. They were slithering back and forth, what looked like a hundred of them, all branching out from the one strand that came in through his side.

"Fuck this." He grunted the clenched teeth. The pain as they tore through his midsection was unbearable.

He started pulling drawers open until he found what he was looking for. He pulled out a large butcher's knife and, in one clean motion, sliced at the thread connecting him to the beast.

As his pain numbed itself away, he heard the howl of pain from the hallway, closer than he would have liked. The walls shook as the creature thrashed in the confined space and he worked to ignore it. He needed to find something, anything else that could hurt it.

He briefly studied his stomach. He could see the lines as raised flesh from when it had been tearing him up, but they were now motionless. His bowels felt like they were going to let loose, but he could tell there was something wrong. There was a pain threatening on the horizon, and he didn't think it would be just shit when he finally did go.

Okay, what can you find in the kitchen that might hurt that thing? Shit, I don't know. Why couldn't this be the eighties? I could break for the bathroom, find some Aqua Net and a lighter to make a mini flamethrower, just like how it was done in the movies.

He needed to focus. What could he do? He tried to think of what people normally had in the kitchen.

Of course, there's the back door. He was only a few yards away. He could try to make a break for it.

The howling sound in the hallway reminded him why that was a bad idea. Once it saw him make for the door, it would rush to stop him, and it had the better path. He didn't think he could make it.

"Fuck this," He growled again but was caught off guard by a sudden burst of coughing that had him bending over, reaching out for the counter to keep his balance. His head spun, thoughts losing focus as he momentarily went grey, trying to get the coughing under control.

When he did, it took a moment for the sensation to release its grip on his skull. He was off balance now, and as he pulled back, he saw the drops on the counter from where he had coughed up blood. Spots hung at the corner of his vision, and little worms danced in his view that faded as he tried harder to breathe.

He wanted to scream. The pain growing from his side was stabbing deeper into him. Even though the things were cut off, they still stung at him inside. He could see where they were growing darker under his skin, his flesh turning black from their presence.

"Fuck. Fuck, fuck, fuck, fuck, fuck." He said and felt another coughing spasm on the verge of taking him. He tried to fight to keep this one under control, but his lungs were burning, pushing for the release of the liquid he could feel starting to fill them.

Just how the fuck are you going to get out of this? How are you going to kill that fucking thing? He tried to work it out, and the best he could do was think of looking under the sink, trying to find any kind of chemical that might be there, anything that might work on it.

He found two cylinder-shaped cans; one he could clearly read the label as "Comet" and set them on the counter, and then there was also a large gallon jug of some liquid. He pulled it out, wincing as the stabbing pain throbbed from the motion, only to be disappointed that it was only vinegar. He wasn't sure if bleach or ammonia would do anything against that creature, but felt a hell of a lot more confident than going up against the thing with vinegar. What was he doing, going to make a salad out of the damn thing, have some vinegar and oil dressing to go with that?

Stay focused. Drop the bad jokes. Focus. He tried to. It was hard to keep himself present as he could feel his side drenched in blood, and he was drowning in his own lungs.

He grabbed the jug from where he set it on the counter and turned to put it on the island. He stopped when he saw the thing was standing there on the other side, watching him.

He had the distinct feeling that it was amused in his attempts to fight it, and it was giving him time to prepare.

Fuck, he had no chance to kill this thing. What was he even thinking? He should have just tried running for the door. At least that idea had a chance before the creature was there.

"Suck on this," He hissed as he tossed the gallon jug of vinegar. He didn't have much strength left, and it barely made it to the creature just to be swatted away. Price wasn't done. He grabbed the canister of Comet and threw it. Again, the creature just swatted it away and Price heard the deep growl of a chuckle he had heard upstairs. It started to move to get around the island and it cut off his escape out the back door.

"Fuck." Price hissed as he flung the third canister at the beast. He didn't wait to watch it get flung away as he struggled to make it around the island in the opposite direction of the creature, which put him moving back into the house.

He barely crashed into the hallway, his cough making him unsteady, the pain racking through him, making it a struggle not to just collapse to his knees.

Behind him, he heard another howl, but Price immediately picked up on how this one was different. He chanced a moment to look back and see that the thing was covered in whatever had been in that last container. The container was split in two, having been busted open from when it attempted to swat it away.

Price was suddenly struck with the stench of eggs that had gone bad, and he could see smoke rising from its scaly flesh from where the container contents had touched.

This is your only chance. Get him. He didn't wait. He rushed in, knife high overhead as the thing was backing away from him, and brought the knife down into one of the glowing red eyes.

It screamed a high-pitched noise that shattered the window above the kitchen sink as it sliced through the air with those large claws. Price thought he was lucky when the sharp part of those talons missed him, but he was still struck by blunt bone and tossed away like a rag doll, thrown back into the hallway.

Wind and lung blood was forced out of him, and he quickly turned onto the side. At first, it was only coughing up more blood, but it quickly turned into retching up bile. It didn't take long for him to throw up more blood as well as pieces of what he hoped was not his own stomach.

Fuck this shit. I need to get out of here. He pushed himself up, leaning heavily on the wall. He was nearly blind with pain and could barely stumble as he tried to get his own feet to lift from the ground and shuffle forward. He wasn't sure why he was fighting so hard, as all he could think about was the different ways he hurt through his body. It was hard to even focus on what wasn't working.

His right leg refused to lift, and his discordant body failed to catch it. He stumbled forward and slammed into the stairway railing; the ball shaped decoration catching him in his stomach.

More blood erupted from his mouth, and he had a quick passing thought, wondering just how much more of it was left as he sure felt like he was losing a lot.

He slid forward, using his momentum to take the next step. His arm reached out in a painful stretch of his body as he found the next railing and used that to keep him upright. He kept going. He had momentum. He just needed to make it a little further. Once he made it outside, he would be safe.

How do you know that? What's keeping that thing from just following you out there and killing you on the front lawn?

He fought to push away the thoughts, which was easy enough as another slice of agony cut through his insides, and he felt his bowels finally release. He could smell the defecation and feel clumps of shit sliding down his leg. Intestines were probably mixed in there for all he knew, with how much his insides hurt.

The door felt cool to the touch, and he quickly pulled it open. It swung inward. He could feel the cold night air. He was free. He was going to make it. The monster, he could hear it still howling in pain in the kitchen. He just needed to make it to his car, radio in for help, get more bullets to shoot the damn thing. All of this was now possible. He was almost there. He was alive. He just might make it after all and halle-fucking-lujah to that.

He hit the outside wall hard, his triumph of making it outside quickly thwarted by the exhaustion it had taken him to get there. His breath came in short gasps, his lungs continuing to fill with blood no matter how much he coughed it up. His vision was becoming blurry. He could barely make out the schoolgirl from earlier.

She had crossed the street from the last time he had seen her and was now right there between him and his car, blocking his way.

"Please..." he gasped, "help me."

She watched him, devoid of any emotion, her face a blank slate as he struggled to move closer.

Then her midsection opened wide, exposing the rows of teeth. Large purple tendrils emerged from that hungry, waiting mouth and shot towards him. He barely had a moment to comprehend what he was seeing before they wrapped around him, and he was lifted into the air, being pulled towards it.

"Fuck me."

CHAPTER 23

David tasted the sweet, sweet taste of fresh flesh as the monster took its time devouring each morsel. It had been days since the last time it had feasted, and this one was a welcome blessing.

Though the creature had noticed that this one had been different. It wasn't as well seasoned as the last meal. She had not given in to as much fear as he would have thought. She actually seemed to be prepared for its arrival.

Still, he had done what he could, and now was enjoying the delicacy.

Though as he ate, he could feel things, changes happening to his... no, its own flesh. Her fears had come through and he could feel that he was changing to it. That it fueled him to modify his appearance... No, its appearance.

Those thoughts are not yours. You are not him. David fought to keep himself, his sense of self, as he was merged into the creature's mind.

It took another long strip of flesh and David felt it as it slowly ran down its throat. This time, the creature hadn't bothered with slicing it and let it slither into him whole.

David sensed that it could feel him as a part of it, but didn't think it knew who or where he was. Not yet.

But it sensed someone else. It ignored it, though as it came close, he could smell that it had already been claimed by another who was nearby.

It went back to its waiting meal...

* * * *

When Clara arrived, Jen immediately pulled her into a tight hug that lasted for an eternity of emotions. It had started with Jen desperately needing her girlfriend and ended with Clara's shoulder drenched in tears.

Clara had tried to break it a few times, but Jen had just held tighter and let it out. Eventually Clara had stopped struggling and returned the embrace.

"What happened today?" Clara asked. Jen shook her head as a response as she sniffed back more tears and pulled away.

"Not down here. I want to check on Davey and we can talk in my room.

"Sure thing. My brother gave me a ride over. I just need to say good night. I didn't want him leaving in case you needed me to send him to the store."

"That's nice of him."

"He's worried about you, too. We all have."

"I know, I'm sorry." Jen wiped away more of the tears. All week she had to be the one who was keeping it all together. She was the one under the surface pressure, not able to let herself feel the deep torrent of emotions raging through her. Her inner turmoil had been tearing her apart, but with Clara there, she didn't have to be the strong one. Finally, she had someone she could talk to, could release some of this pain, too.

"Hey, do you think he would mind staying and hanging out for a bit?"

"Really? You want Andy to stay?"

"Yeah, just for a little while. If he's okay with it."

"I'll go ask him. Are you okay?"

Jen could only shake her head, suddenly unable to find her own voice.

"Okay. I'll be right back. Or should you come out with me? I could call him. Maybe I should just call him." Clara was already swiping at her phone and a second later there was the trilling sound of it calling out.

"What, you couldn't come out to say goodbye? Love you too Sis."

"Don't be like that. Hey, you mind coming in? She's really upset and wants you to stay. That okay?"

"Be right in."

Andy was at their door a few minutes later. It was always strange to see the two next to each other. Andy, being the older of the two, did not make him the bigger of the two. He was shorter, scrawnier, and had an unhealthy pale complexion. He would never be mistaken for an athlete, and he was not one anyone would ever expect to be called upon as a knight in shining armor. He looked more like he would be the worst knight imaginable's third string squire. Jen had once seen a bully put his hand completely around Andy's biceps just to prove how little muscle he had. She had to pull more than one bully off as they had tormented him in the past, but to her he was near family.

Clara and her had been dating for over a year and before that, they had always been good friends. She knew Andy well, and had remembered the year she had grown, and he had not. Since then, her "older" brother was almost like another younger brother who needed to be watched out for and protected. Knowing what she knew about him, she also knew he had the heart of a lion and knew she could rely on him.

He was surprised and nervous as he bounced from foot to foot in the entryway to the large house.

"Hey Jay, how are you doing?"

Jen wasn't sure what to say. She kept trying to tell them much of what had been happening. It felt like she hadn't seen either one of them in forever, but every time she tried to tell them, she kept losing herself to more tears.

They tried to get her to go into the living room, but she nodded to the stairs instead.

"We can talk in my room." She had said. David was sleeping upstairs, and she didn't want to be away from him for too long, not with his night terrors. She knew he could wake up at any time.

Clara and Andy started up the stairs, but Jen paused as she again smelled bad eggs, the odor twisting her stomach in disgust. She briefly looked around, sure she'd see that creepy old guy from early, but that was her just being silly. Someone had probably left eggs out earlier and they'd gone bad. She would have to check the kitchen later and take them out to the garbage.

CHAPTER 24

Ellis arrived at the house and parked out front. There was already a car he didn't recognize in the driveway next to the rental he had seen earlier. He assumed the rental was the sister from out west.

He had called the hospital on the way and had found out the sister had already been discharged under protest and was now waiting for a ride back to the house. He'd overheard her shouting at the hospital staff, demanding the ambulance take her back there and issuing her own verbal assault on them. If Ellis had heard correctly, her cell phone had been left at the house, and she was worried about missing a call about her boys.

Ellis felt for her. It couldn't be easy, what she was going through. He had known that his wife and son were gone, and it was the worst feeling on earth, to know that a part of you was forever stolen. How much harder was it to have those pieces of your heart ripped away, and not knowing if you would get them back or if they were permanently gone? Not knowing had to be so much worse.

He debated about whether or not he should knock on the door and check on them. It looked like all the lights in the house were on, and he didn't blame them. The family had been through enough. Deciding he should at least make sure they were okay, he got out of the car. The cool night blew gently against him, and he heard the rustle of leaves sing the song of fall. Halloween was still weeks away, but the early signs were there. Some houses were already showing signs of decorations that would soon be lit, illuminating the season with cheap dollar store skeletons and ghosts.

Tyler had loved this time of year. He loved dressing up in costumes. Every year, his wife would thrift shop and buy every character she could find that he liked. He would wear a different costume around the neighborhood playing every day he could. And when they ran out of store bought, they would craft with his wife to make their own special creations.

His phone was full of photos that hurt too much to look at. He tried to avoid bringing back those memories, but sometimes life had other plans like walking down a street by the light of the streetlight and remembering the years he would take Tyler trick-or-treating.

Ellis walked up to the door and stood there, frozen by the memories of his own dead wife and son.

Why am I even here? Detective asshole should have called over some on duty officers. This was bordering harassment, and you know it.

How did he explain to them that he just had this feeling in his gut saying this wasn't over? He stood there, not sure what he should tell them. Maybe he should just go, maybe he was just being irrational and misplacing feelings of his own to keep him close to this family.

He should go; they don't need him there.

He looked back to the streetlight and watched the quiet neighborhood. In his mind's eye, he was watching as he walked with his son down the sidewalk. Tyler was carrying his little purple octopus, swinging it around and occasionally bumping into daddy and daddy would grab him, pull him in tight with the occasional bending over just so he could kiss the top of his son's head.

* * * *

Jen wished that when she was done, that she stood in her bedroom, getting the tightest hug she had ever received. Instead, she was barely into her story before Clara started getting upset.

"What a bitch?"

"Which one?" Andy asked. Andy was sitting in her beanbag chair that had been thrown into the corner. It was more like a large plush chair than a true bean bag, and to be fair, it was probably the most comfortable thing Jen owned. Of course, it had been something her father had bought her. "You said she attacked you?"

Jen lost her place in what she had been saying. Talking about it all had brought the maelstrom of madness she had gone through

164

earlier back into focus. Her chest hurt to breathe, and she felt like it was a struggle to pull in every gasp of air. That sensation from earlier where she felt like she just wanted to collapse onto the floor and let a river of tears flow through her while simultaneously screaming and taking a bat to anything relating to her mom or her aunt.

So much chaos tried again to tear through her that she felt herself closing in, her mind shutting off from thinking and a fog just pressing in from her temples. How could someone feel everything and nothing all at once, but yet there was no other way to describe just how she felt? How could she ever put that into words?

"I'm fine." She barely said as she sat on the bed. Clara was sitting next to her and tried to pull her into a hug, but Jen had gone stiff, lowering her gaze to her hands.

"Okay, but that's not what I said. Your aunt really attacked you?"

"Andy, let it go. Maybe... maybe don't tell us everything right now. We'll just hang out for a bit."

"Yeah, we don't have anything better to do." Andy said. He was already flicking a baseball Jen had left sitting on her dresser. He was tossing it into the air and trying to catch it. Most of the time, he failed, and the ball would sink into the chair around him.

Clara gave him a look as she sat there.

"I should go check on David. He was having trouble sleeping before you got here. I don't want to leave him alone for too long."

Jen didn't move. She'd told them about her aunt, and about her cousins. She hadn't told them about her mom. They knew she wasn't there, but- wait... had she told them about her mom? She tried to remember just what she had told them. It was so hard to think. Her jaw was starting to hurt as her mind was working against her. Her jaw, her temples, her crown. Pain was coursing through them as she struggled.

"Jen, when was the last time you ate or had a glass of water?"

Jen looked at Clara. Jen had started to stand, to go check on her brother, but somehow found herself back on the bed.

"I don't know. Why?"

"Because your lips are chapped. You look thirsty."

"I don't know. I might have had a glass of OJ this morning. I think."

"Andy, could you go down and get a glass of water?"

"Sure."

"It's going to be okay." Clara said. Jen wasn't sure. She thought Clara had already said that. Maybe she'd said it a few times. Maybe it was the first time. Everyone kept telling her it was going to be okay. When they had first gotten there, it felt like it might be.

Then reality returned.

Jen sat in the bed; she had no idea for long. She just kept sitting there as time passed her by. The smell of bad eggs getting worse, somehow rising from the kitchen.

Somewhere in the distance, she heard a loud gong sound that reverberated through her skull, pulling at her sense of familiarity. Not that she heard it too often, but as the loud bell rang again, she recognized it for what it was. Her father and his obsession with creepy things had long ago replaced their doorbell with a bell that he felt sounded like an ominous sound of doom. It had delighted him anytime it rang. Her mother had hated it to the point she would often put a sign over the buzzer advising people to knock rather than ring the bell.

The sign must have blown away.

"I'm sure Andy will get the door." Clara said.

"What now?" Andy said, walking into the room with a glass of water. "Damn, what's that smell?"

"I think some eggs were left out downstairs in the kitchen and they went bad?"

"I don't think so. The smell is coming from up here. I didn't smell anything downstairs."

"No, it can't be coming from up here. I smelled it downstairs earlier." Jen said almost dreamily.

"I'm sure of it. Here." He handed her the water, and she looked at it like she had no idea what it was. The gong sound echoed again.

"No way you can sleep through that. That's going to wake up your brother," Clara said.

"Fine, I'll go down and get the door." Andy said, frustrated about having to go down the stairs for the second time.

"We should check on your brother."

Jen nodded and allowed Clara to lead her out of her room.

Jen was trying to pull herself back. She wanted to push all these unwanted thoughts and emotions away, but somehow couldn't find the strength or motivation to do it. She could feel that there was a part of her that felt like she deserved all this and that she should hurt.

Clara led her to the hallway and to her brother's bedroom door. They could hear moaning from the other side and the rustling of him tossing and turning.

"He's having one helluva bad dream." Clara said as she put her hand on the door.

Jen was pulling herself out of it. She could hear the sounds her brother was making and knew he needed her. He needed her in there to be with him. She didn't have time to be there wallowing, worried about their mom.

She suddenly felt awake again as Clara pushed the door and it gently swung open.

Neither of them moved or said anything at first. They were stuck, standing there and watching as what looked like a giant eyeball roughly three feet in diameter appeared to be hovering just above her brother's bare feet. Which, if the floating eyeball hadn't been creepy enough, a large tongue emerged by the eyeball splitting in half, revealing large teeth as pointed as the spikes that ran the eye's width. The tongue ran its gooey self along the surface of the eye and then disappeared back into the mouth so that it appeared again to be just a free-floating eyeball.

It was hovering just above his little toes, perched above them like it was ready to start eating.

"They can see me. The monsters are coming. They can see me," David said. His eyes were shut, and he thrashed as though something was chasing them, while he was oblivious to the horror just above him.

CHAPTER 25

Andy opened the door and saw a stranger standing on the front porch of the house. The man looked nervous, like he was unsure if he should be there or not.

"Can I help you?" Andy asked.

"Hey, is Jennifer Carey home? I heard about earlier and wanted to check on her and her brother."

"What, did someone put out a notice that creepy old guys are just to stop by?"

"Sorry, no, Officer Ellis. I was the one who found David." Ellis said, suddenly realizing how that sounded to a stranger when he tried to put it into words. It did sound like he was being creepy.

"Oh, you're a cop. Let me just let you in so you can do whatever you want." Andy acted like he was going to open the door. He stopped part way through and brought the door back to being barely open. "On second thought creepy guy, you're not wearing a uniform. No, I think you just need to get out of here. You're probably some reporter trying to get in, or some pervert. Are you? Are you a pervert?"

"No, I'm not a pervert," Ellis said. He was already reaching into his coat pocket for his badge and wallet. He saw the moment where Andy must have seen his service revolver in his shoulder holster as he saw the boy tense up.

Ellis showed him his badge.

"Oof, sorry Chad. My sis told me there's been a lot of Ohio's around."

"Chad?"

"Never mind bruh. It's jelly. So, what's up?"

"May I please speak to Ms. Carey? Or is there an adult here that I may speak to?"

"Bruh, no adults here. Why don't you check back laterz."

"What's your name?"

"Why?"

"Because I like to make sure I know the names of annoying little shits who piss me off."

"Ooh, that's good. Think maybe I should post that to my insta? See if it'll go viral."

"Yeah? You're not too bright, are you?"

"I don't think you are. You go viral, you get cancelled po-po."

"Yeah, little hard to do with your phone in your pocket," Ellis said as he patted the rectangle shape in Andy's pocket. "Bruh."

"Hey, that's assault. I'm going to report you."

"Stop watching all those cop shows, kid. Now, can you please let Ms. Carey know I'm here?"

"Na bruh, go be martial law somewhere else," Andy said as he started to close the door in Ellis's face.

"You can close that door, but I'm not going anywhere."

"Yeah, bruh, well, we'll see about that." Andy said, reaching into his pocket to pull out his phone. "And this time, I will be recording, nazi-popo."

Andy nearly had the door closed when the screams cascaded down from upstairs and he paused to look back. Ellis didn't hesitate. He was trained to react.

Ellis burst through the door, slamming Andy back so hard he fell to the floor. He didn't slow down but did call over his shoulder as he rushed to the stairs.

"Call 911. Tell them 10-103, Officer Ellis is on scene."

Ellis took the stairs two at a time until he reached the upstairs hallway, where he paused. The screaming had stopped, and Ellis surveyed the scene. Two doors on the left, one door to the right, and then a door at the end of the hall. All of them were open and dark.

"Get away from him!" He heard a familiar voice yell. Ellis worked his way down to the door on the right, scanning the open doors on the left as he passed. A bathroom and a bedroom, both without anyone there. He slowed as he neared the third door, his hand hovering over his service pistol.

Something crashed against the wall, and he could see the photos on the wall shake. Glass was shattered and then something heavy crashed to the floor.

"This is Officer Ellis. I heard a scream and have entered the-" he called out, but was quickly interrupted by a new voice.

"Hurry up and get in here!" The voice yelled.

He rushed into the doorframe and quickly took in the scene. Photos frames were scattered on the floor, a dresser was toppled over, two girls were crouched down to his left and they were working their way to a twin sized bed that was against the back left corner of the room.

He stopped looking around when he saw a large free floating eyeball half the size of himself hovering towards the end of the bed.

The eye turned from looking at the little boy, focusing its attention on him. The center split and Ellis suddenly found himself looking at spikes stretched in what had to be teeth, each one longer than his trigger finger. The mouth was large enough to bite him whole

As the mouth opened wider, Ellis found himself drawn to looking into the darkness that was swirling around inside. It was like a black smoke that spun. He found himself mesmerized by it, suddenly not thinking about those large teeth that were waiting to bite him in half.

"Officer!"

The black smoke just kept twirling around. It was getting larger; he was getting closer to it.

"Officer!" He heard a pair of voices calling out to him and he found himself blinking away the darkness, pulling at his thoughts. He was midway into the room with no recollection of moving from the hall. The eyeball was now only a few feet away, and he saw as a large tongue licked the surface of the eye in preparation of its feast.

He looked over briefly at the voices, never completely taking his eyes off the thing. Two girls were toward the head of the bed. The boy was asleep but tossing wildly, as though caught up in his own nightmares.

Ellis had his gun pulled as he took a step back. He fired into the mouth of the creature, one shot, then two. Both seemed to be lost in that void. That darkness started to swirl, and he started to feel its slithering tendrils pull at his thoughts again. He quickly looked away, focusing instead on just above the mouth. He took another step back.

The thing slowly moved toward him, and he noticed for the first time that it wasn't free floating like he had initially observed. There was a long, thin strand of light color that was hard to see in the dim room at first. He only noticed when a strand pulled away from the supporting fiber and somehow floated to a foot closer to him before it landed on a new spot on the ceiling.

"Holy shit!" Ellis recognized the boy's voice from downstairs and knew he must be behind him.

"Get out of here!" He meant it for all of them, but could tell the girls were not going to leave David. As the thing shifted itself, so it was gently moving towards him, Ellis fired another two shots. These aimed at the white of the eye just above the mouth.

The mouth immediately closed and the large eye floated back from the shots, the holes black where they had hit it. It was rotating away from him and turning to look back at the sleeping boy.

How is David able to sleep through this, the yelling, the gunfire? Whatever nightmare he was trapped in couldn't be worse than the one happening around him?

Ellis took a step forward and readied himself to fire another shot, while taking a brief second to count his shots and subtract from what was loaded. He figured he had eight shots left.

The eye turned back to look at Ellis and Ellis realized he'd made a mistake as he saw how it was swinging back on the thread that held it to the ceiling, another thread splintering off to bring it closer to him. Ellis quickly took two steps until he was back to just inside the doorframe.

"Shit!" the boy behind him called out. "I got this."

Ellis feared the boy was going to do something stupid, but then caught out of the corner of his eye, the kid running for the stairs. He disappeared down them.

Ellis took a breath and focused back on the large eyeball moving towards him. He started to fire but paused. The bullet holes were gone. It couldn't be, but they were, and the thing was still moving closer to him, the eye again splitting, revealing those large teeth.

It was only a few feet away, moving faster towards him as it had continued to use the momentum his bullets had caused to swing link a pendulum toward him with those tethers attaching closer and closer as it did.

Ellis stepped back into the hallway, not sure what to do, and pissed at himself for letting the thing get between him and the kids.

Though maybe you could use that? Keep leading the thing away from them. If you do that, then you can keep them safe.

It was a plan. Not a good plan, but a plan.

He started backing down the hallway. Not too much. He wanted to keep it so the thing was close, but not too close. It hadn't made it to the hallway yet, and if he got out of view, who's to say it wouldn't turn around and go back to the kids?

The eye made it to the door and paused.

Ellis waited for it to come for him, holding his breath, debating on what he would do if it turned back around.

He watched as the thread worked its way over the frame of the door until it found the hallway ceiling. It was about to pull itself across the threshold when the kid reemerged at the top of the stairs with a canister in his hand.

"Get the hell out of here!" Ellis yelled.

The eye stopped moving towards him. It rotated back and forth like it was trying to decide which one it wanted first.

Andy didn't pause. He ran down the hall and launched the contents of the container toward the eyeball, a cloud of white flying towards the creature.

As soon as it made contact, the thing visibly shook in pain and thrashed in agony. Smoke emanated from where the white powder touched, and the white of the eye was turning black, sizzling as though it were burning.

Ellis lowered his gun as he watched the thing twist on its thread. A howl emerged from deep within it, and as the smoke darkened the hallway around him, he could smell the sulfate as it grew stronger.

"What are you doing? Shoot it. Shoot it!" The boy yelled.

Ellis raised his gun and started firing at the thing. His first two shorts hit where the eye was unfazed and, like his earlier shots, nothing happened. He readjusted and fired into the dark areas and the eye turned its glare upon him. Its mouth was twisted into a snarl and the eye was turning red, blistering from the powder.

Ellis aimed his final shot at the largest of the black areas that were expanding. He fired. In response, the thing's tongue shot out, reaching for him. It was stretching, trying to get him, and Ellis watched as the tendrils were slithering on the ceiling, pulling itself in his direction.

Ellis also watched as the darkness was moving along the threads, spreading from where it had been shot. The darkness only made it partway up when the threads snapped, and the large eye fell to the floor. It did so with a soft, wet plop as it collapsed in on itself. As it sunk into the carpeted floor, it continued to hiss and bubble as the dissolving tissue disintegrated.

Ellis walked towards the bubbling mass on the floor. It was no longer recognizable as anything. As the smoke faded, the bubbling stopped. Ellis stood over it, watching, waiting for any sign of movement.

The boy was excited, laughing and jumping around, cursing challenges to it. "Come at me bruh," and "that all you got, eyeball bitch!"

Ellis turned away from him to look into the room. The girls were on the bed. Jennifer sat near her brother's head, running her hand through his hair. He had stopped thrashing in the bed, his eyes were open, and he was looking at Ellis.

They were safe. They were all safe, but just what in the hell was that thing?

CHAPTER 26

What was that stuff?" Ellis said, looking over at the kid who was still doing some kind of gyrating hip thrust dance. The kid noticed that the cop was talking to him and stopped.

"What else bruh? Salt. How else are you supposed to stop a demon without a demon blade? You never watch Tv?"

"It's like you're from another planet. Speak English." Ellis said as he went into David's room. The boy was breathing heavily, watching him as he walked closer. Ellis could have sworn he saw anger, then fear in those eyes, but as he neared, all of that seemed to fade away as the boy's breathing steadied.

"Is everyone okay?"

"They don't prepare you for how loud those things are when you see them in movies." The unknown girl said, her hands covering her ears.

"What about you two? Davey, you okay?" Ellis said. The boy nodded, then looked over his shoulder at his sister, who had her arms draped around him.

"Yeah, I think so. What was that thing?" Jen asked.

"Hey squirrely, you seem to know. What the hell was that thing and speak English for us non-illiterates?" Ellis said, looking back at Andy coming into the room. He jumped over the hissing spot on the floor.

"Whatev po-po." Andy said.

"What is that?"

Andy held up the cylinder container. The top had been cut off, but the girl with an umbrella logo was unmistakable.

"Salt? You poured salt on it? What was it, an eyeball shaped slug?"

"Na bruh. You still not getting it?"

Ellis took a deep, calming breath.

"Then what was it? I'm missing a few steps here. Who are you?" Ellis turned to Clara, "who are you, and what the hell was that?" He ended with pointing at the spot on the floor.

"Not telling you my name po-po, but I'll tell you, you're right. From hell, Vee. The thing was from hell. I think at least. Unless it was an alien and then we just got lucky, but I don't think it was."

"Was what?"

"An alien, bruh." Andy said, exasperated.

"Andy, stop. Give it a rest." Clara said. "Hey, so yeah, I'm Clara and that idiot over there is my older brother who was supposed to just give me a ride. When he's not being an asshole, he's a complete geek."

"Stuff it." Andy said.

"Okay, so you're Clara, you're Andy. What was that?"

"If I had to guess, I'd say it was a demon." Andy said.

"And why do you say that?"

"Well, earlier, smelled like rotten eggs up here, right before we saw it. Had to be it, bruh. So, when I saw the thing and remembered that smell, made me realize we were smelling sulfur, which is like, demonic. So must be a demon."

"And salt kills demons? How did you know that?"

"Tv. Ain't you ever watch tv? And it didn't kill it. Nah bruh, it just hurt it. Salt cleanses, right, like crystals and vibrations and all that, or maybe it's like the Bible, salt of the earth, you know, right? It didn't kill it, but it hurt enough that you got it, bruh. And you know, like, I don't know if you killed it or not, maybe you just sent it back to hell and now it's down there pissed off at you and such, but it's gone from here, right? We're safe now?"

Ellis looked at Andy for a long second before shaking his head.

"Talking to you makes my head hurt."

Ellis turned back to the girls and David.

"I don't know what's going on here. I heard about your mother and I'm sorry. I wanted to check in on everyone and make sure you were safe. I'm not sure what to make of this?"

"I get it. I heard Davey having a bad nightmare and came in here to check on him. Then there was that eye thing. It was just floating there, watching him sleep, hovering over his feet like it wanted to eat them."

Ellis saw David tense up at the mention of the monster eating his feet, and he didn't blame him. The thought of something like that hovering over his bare feet was enough to make him shutter, something he was working desperately not to show these already frightened kids.

"And you smelled sulfur?"

"Well, I smelled bad eggs. I smelled it earlier when there was this weird guy downstairs and then again up here shortly before that thing."

Ellis felt like he was putting together pieces of a puzzle he wasn't sure he truly believed. Hell and demons meant that god and heaven existed. While a part of him wished his family was tucked away safe in heaven, he struggled with his own beliefs.

As a cop, it was hard to believe in the existence of an entity that allowed a methed-out mother let her baby burn to death because she was too high to notice the fire. It was harder to pray to a god that did exist and allowed it to happen. What, was letting evil shit happen to good or bad people indiscriminately just heavenly crowd control?

It was easier to believe in nothing, as then there was nothing to disappoint him.

He walked over to the spot on the floor and studied it. He did smell the sulfur stench emanating from it, and he couldn't discount how it had reacted to the salt. Slugs had a similar reaction, sure, but that didn't explain that he had just gunned down a free-floating eyeball that had been the size of a small child.

Ellis looked back at David. The boy looked frightened, and why wouldn't he? Who knew how much the boy had seen over the last few days?

It had to have been this thing.

Ellis let his foot hover over it, fighting the temptation to stomp the thing deeper into the carpet. The hissing was fading, but he was fighting with his own fear. It had to have killed that boy's father and the others that had gone missing. The two boys, the cops. All of them.

Ellis thought of that large mouth and how his bullets seemed to have just disappeared into it. What would have happened had one of them been swallowed?

Ellis holstered his gun, having forgotten that he still had it drawn, and then walked back to the kids, all of them now sitting on David's bed.

"David, was that what killed your dad?"

David shook his head and lowered his chin to his chest.

Ellis looked back at the black spot.

Just what the hell does that mean? Are there two of them?

"Yo, quit being a baby, bruh." Andy said, gently smacking David on his chest.

"You can go now if you'd like." Jen said, anger obvious in her voice as she stared daggers at Andy.

"I thought you wanted me here?" Andy said, hurt.

"The officer is here. You can leave."

"You upset because I made a joke."

"I said you can leave. My brother's not a baby, you can just leave."

Andy stood up slowly and looked at the spot on the floor. He looked at Ellis, who watched the exchange with interest before turning back to Jen.

"Hey, I helped."

"And now you can leave."

Ellis knew he would regret his next words.

"Maybe he should stay. Maybe you should all stay together. David, am I right in thinking there is one more of these things?"

Without looking up at him, David nodded his head.

So, there was another one. Where was it?

"Has anyone seen another one of those things?"

He looked around at the scared faces. They all shook their heads no.

Maybe it wasn't there? Maybe this wasn't the one that took the children at the cemetery. If that was the case, then how would he stop it? It wasn't like he could call this in. He couldn't think of anyone on the force that would believe him. He couldn't think of anyone at all that would believe him.

You try calling this in, they'll think you've finally cracked. How many of them have looked at you differently since last year? How many of them are just waiting for it to happen?

He wished it wasn't true, but he'd seen them look away as he walked down the hall, the conversations that ended when he walked into a room.

Even Scotty wouldn't back him up. He was a nice enough guy, but he was a flake himself. Even he wouldn't believe him.

Maybe a priest would...

That was the best thought he had, and even then, he didn't like it.

His thoughts were interrupted when he heard a baby crying from the other room. He looked up at the people around him and saw their confused faces.

"Is there a baby sleeping in your bedroom or your parents' room?" Ellis asked.

Jen shook her head. "No, only us."

"You had a bunch of people over earlier. You sure one of your aunts didn't leave a baby with your mom to watch?" Clara asked, but she was desperate. It was clear with her paper-thin smile and how she kept looking towards the door.

"We should get out of here." Andy said.

"I don't suppose you have any more salt in the house, do you?" Ellis said, looking at the empty canister on the floor.

"If we do, I have no clue where it is. Not sure where Andy got that one, to be honest with you." Jen said. Ellis turned to look at him. Andy shrugged in return.

"It was in the cabinet in the kitchen, but I only saw the one."

The crying grew angrier, louder, pulling Ellis's attention to the door. He wanted to unholster his gun, but while it would comfort him to have it in his hand, it would unsettle the kids. Besides, he was out of bullets and his spare magazine was at home in his gun safe.

"Are there any weapons in the house?" He was hoping Jen would say there was a gun cabinet somewhere, though even if that was the case, the chances it would be unlocked were low. He wasn't surprised when she shook her head.

"Bruh, you're trippin'. You got all kinds of stuff." Andy said.

Ellis looked back and forth between the two of them. It was clear Jen didn't understand him or knew what he was talking about.

"No, I don't."

"Yeah, you do. Your baseball bats, your hockey sticks. You got all kinds of stuff."

"Yeah, you think going up against that thing with a thin piece of wood is going to do anything?" Clara said.

"More than you think. You ever been hit with one? They hurt." Andy scoffed at his sister.

"Okay, stick close to me. We'll check her room. If clear, we'll see what we can use and go from there."

Ellis went to the door and from there, he could tell that the crying was coming from the end of the hall, in what appeared to be a master bedroom.

"Which room is yours?"

Jen reached around him and, thankfully, pointed in the other direction.

"Okay, you guys go to her room. I'm going to watch the hall and make sure nothing attacks."

"You sure that's a good idea, po-po? Thought you were going to check her room."

Ellis gave him an annoyed look.

"Sure, but that would leave you guys wide open if some big bad came out of the other bedroom, right?"

"But it's just a baby crying?" Andy said.

"Anthony Kishner Davis, have you never seen the meme about the baby crying? Serious." Ellis looked at Clara and smiled, glad to see he was not the only one getting annoyed with her brother.

"No."

"Baby crying is so sweet and cute, until it's waking up, four in the morning and you live alone. It's one of those two sentence horror memes. Seriously, you've never seen it."

"I'm not into all that spooky stuff like you two."

"Seriously, you can binge Supernatural all weekend."

"Yeah, because Dean's legit."

"Can you quiet it down, please?" Jen said, and Ellis nodded his agreement with cooling down the two siblings.

"Okay, you three ready to go?" Ellis said. Jen pulled her brother in tight to her, and he realized his mistake. "Four. You guys get to the room. I'm going to take a walk down to your parents' room, see what I can see. Any sign of trouble, I'll rush to your room."

"Why aren't we just running for the stairs, bruh? Let's just get out of here."

"Because right now you seem to be caught up in something, rather it has your scent or whatever it does. But something seems to be after this family, and I don't think whatever it is willing to let you go just because you're not a part of the family. Got it?"

"Sure thing bruh. Got it."

"Stay together, keep safe, and we'll get through this."

They nodded, and he watched them as they moved swiftly down the hall. Once they were in the other bedroom, he turned and focused his attention on the room at the end of the call. The room was dark, but the anguished baby crying removed all doubt that there wasn't something down there waiting for him.

CHAPTER 27

Ellis made his way closer to the room at the end of the hall, the crying growing louder, angrier as he did, but as he neared it, it also sounded familiar. He thought of Tyler and waking up in the middle of the night. They had been lucky with him; he slept through most nights, but on the rare occasion he cried out, and Ellis was home, he had gotten up with him.

His wife had been suffering from terrible postpartum depression and was always tired. He tried to help her the best that he could, though being a rookie there were many nights he wasn't home. When he was, he tried to be the one to take his turn.

Tatiana had sometimes woken up in the middle of the night on her own trip to the bathroom to find the two of them in the easy chair, Tyler on Tommy's chest, both snoozing.

A baby crying. A baby who needed some attention, or love. There was something in the darkness of the room and it was calling out to him.

"Join us daddy." A voice echoed in his mind. Then another,

"Hey hun, don't you want to be here? I'm here and so is Tyler. You can come and meet your new son. I named him Max, after your father. I know we had talked about it. Join us. We're here waiting for you."

Tommy felt the tears streaming down his cheek as he reached the threshold. He grabbed the sides of the door, trying to crush the wood beneath his grip as he gritted his teeth. He closed his eyes, hard, trying to make them hurt. He wanted it all to hurt. His nails, his head, his jaw, all of it to force away the voice of his wife as it rattled around his head.

And he could see her there in his mind's eye. In the darkness of thought, he could see her standing there holding a baby boy. She was smiling at him, and oh God, he wanted so much for it to be real so he could run up to her and hug her, kiss her and feel her touch.

"It can't be real." He said it through gritted teeth, but in his mind, she stood there plain as day, just how he remembered her. Her long auburn hair, her brown eyes, those dimples as she smiled at him that always made his breath catch at how beautiful she was.

And in her arms, what looked like a baby not more than a couple days old. Its eyes were closed, but it kept opening its mouth, craving its next meal of breast milk.

She was talking to him, and he could hear her, but he also heard something else shifting around in the room. It sounded large and heavy. He tried to focus on the sound, but the baby was crying again, both in his mind and from the room. It was loud enough that it felt like it was tearing through his mind, ripping away his thoughts and memories.

"Officer!" He heard a voice from far away yelling. It sounded like it was from miles away as he could just barely hear it over the cacophony of shrieking.

"Would you like to hold him? He wants his daddy. Come here and hold your baby boy. Come hold him, soothe him. He needs you to put him back to sleep." His wife's voice said, echoing through his thoughts.

He squeezed his hands tighter, feeling his fingernails rake along the wood trim of the door. Around him, he could feel something grabbed him, tightening in its grip. It was pulling at him. He briefly remembered seeing the long tongue of the eyeball earlier and could imagine briefly its long form wrapping himself, pulling him into the dark depths of the room.

While the pressure tightened, the memories of earlier faded, making it hard to concentrate on what was real and what was going on in his own head.

"Max loves to be held. He wants to meet his daddy. Help me put him to sleep. You were always great with Tyler. Remember how he was just a baby and would sleep on your chest while you watched football? I'd come out of the kitchen and find the two of you both asleep in the easy chair before half time. He always loved to fall asleep on you. You made him feel safe."

Ellis tried to take a step forward. His wife and children were waiting for him, and he wanted nothing more than to hold his son. He wanted to meet his new baby boy.

Every day for the last year, he has struggled with not eating that final bullet, finally believing his end of shift so that he could be with them. Some days, he was closer than others. Most days he could push it to the back of his mind, telling himself there wasn't anything after this life. If he ate that bullet, he wouldn't be joining them, he would only be ending his own pain, and his father never raised him to be selfish. Taking his own life to end his own agony, that was a weak act, the act of the most selfish.

He tried hard to take that step forward and could feel as the pressure around his stomach grew tighter. He worked to put as much of his weight into it. He needed to get there, to be with them. He could finally join them. They were right there, just outside his grasp. He just had to move a little further forward, and he could touch them.

"Officer! Come on!" He heard from a mile away.

"What is that!"

"I can't see it."

"No, but whatever it is, it sounds enormous."

"Officer! Little help here!"

All the voices were there. He could hear them, but the words dissipated before he could grasp what they were saying. They were so far away. Why should he let it bother him? He just needed to make it a little further so he could reach his wife and child.

Then it was all suddenly ripped away from him, and his mind screamed in agony as though part of it was just forcefully pulled away. His brain was on fire, his skull physically hurting as though it had been scalped.

He had felt a loosening around his midsection, and then was slammed by a force that knocked him to the side, pinning him to the ground.

As he turned around, he saw that they were all in the hallway, looking at him, the boy, the girl, and that annoying kid. They were all ashen, looking at him with eyes full of sadness and fear.

Behind them was the door to the room. Something inside there still wailed, though there was now a deep angry howl as well. A loud crash shook the walls, and the few remaining hung photos crashed to the floor. The kids turned to look back at the door, already inching away. On the ground was an assortment of hockey sticks and baseball bats, and they grabbed them as they moved to get away from the door.

Ellis was slowly standing from where he had landed after being tackled. Jen was already up, having been the one to tackle him. She grabbed the aluminum baseball bat from the floor and reached out to help him up.

Something slammed into the wall from the other side of the door and cracks formed, stretching the width of the hallway.

"We need to go," Jen said. Ellis nodded his agreement, and they all rushed to the stairs. A cackling laughter echoing from what felt like the house itself as they ran. Ellis tried to push himself harder, and the kids were already there by the time he made it. David was crying. The rest of them, he could see, were on the verge of it.

They were halfway down the stairs when the house shook again, and Ellis could hear more cracks in the wood. He didn't need to look back or see that whatever was in the room was trying to break free and chase them. Damn, the thing had to be nearly the size of the room itself, trying to get free after them.

"When we get outside, get to my car," Ellis called down. Clara was already at the door and pulled it open. Andy was only a few feet behind her.

The door opened, and they both stopped, looking at the girl in the school uniform standing there. The girl smiled at them, the thin lipped smiled slowly expanding wider than what should be possible. The skin around her mouth tore, blood streaking down her jaw as it just kept growing.

Ellis saw her and saw her wrongness immediately. After everything that happened so far, he didn't pause to question, quickly calling out to the kids at the door.

"Get away from her. Head to the back!"

Jen grabbed David as soon as they reached the bottom of the stairs, quickly pulling him back from the door and already moving him towards the back of the house. "Go, go, go." She tried to yell, but David stopped and looked at the schoolgirl. Jen lost her balance and tried to pull him with her, but he slipped from her grasp.

186

"...see me" croaked quietly from his mouth.

"Come on!" Jen yelled as she reached again to pull him. This time he didn't fight her, and they were rushing down the hall.

The schoolgirl's grin grew wider, and her mouth opened to reveal that swirling darkness Ellis quickly recognized from before. He immediately turned his gaze from looking directly at it, focusing on the other two. Clara was still standing there dumbfounded by the girl, but Andy had turned away. He had started to run back with Jen and David when he realized that his kid sister wasn't behind him.

He rushed back, noticing how she was staring into the abyss of the girl's mouth, and worried she was about to do something. He kept from looking at the widening mouth of darkness and wrapped his arms around her.

"Clare-bear! Come on!" He yelled at her as he started to pull her back away from the door.

Neither of them had noticed the opening midsection. The purple tentacles reached out and grabbed them both. Andy screamed as he felt the slime covered appendage wrap around his waist. Then he felt another tentacle wrap around his leg. The tentacles pulled him away from his sister, separating them but keeping them firmly in its grasp.

Ellis looked around for anything he could use as a weapon. He saw Jen and David. They had stopped in the hallway before reaching the kitchen. She had David pulled around her so that she stood there holding the bat in one hand and the boy protected by her body with the other.

"Toss me the bat," Ellis said as he leapt over the railing of the stairs, putting himself between the thing and them. He held his hand out, expecting her to toss it over to him. Instead, she shook her head no.

Ellis wanted to run to her and take it from her, but the grunting behind him turned him back to the siblings.

Andy was trying to use his hockey stick the best he could. He was stabbing the blade of it down between himself and the tentacle, fighting to get it in any kind of gap. Ellis figured he was trying to use it like a wedge to work himself free.

Clara was closer and still mesmerized. She seemed oblivious to what was going on around her. The wooden bat she had been carrying had fallen free from her grip and had rolled to the far corner. Between him and the bat, there were multiple tentacles holding the pair, and a couple that just flailed casually in the hallway.

It was waiting for him to make his run for the bat. He could feel it as it watched him. He knew he had to do something. There had to be some other option.

He turned away from the creature and ran down the hall, quickly passing the stunned girl and her brother.

"Stay back." He heard her yell, but he ignored her as he burst into the kitchen and started rummaging through the different cabinets.

"Clara!" Jen was yelling. He tried to look back down the hall but could only see the boy. He didn't have time; he needed to keep searching. He found a cabinet of seasonings and pulled the contents out. Chili powder, various forms of pepper seasonings and garlic salt crashed to the floor.

None of the cabinets had any more salt. Sure, there was onion salt, garlic salt, flavor bomb salt, but no other large blue cylinders of table salt.

He heard more screaming from the other room that was tangled in painful, tearful sobs and knew he had to hurry back to try something. He should never have just left them alone with whatever that thing was.

He left the kitchen frustrated, and as he stood in the hallway, he noticed the dining room to his right, with the long dining room table. There were four ornate glass shakers, two of which seemed to glow with the crystallized substance filling them. He quickly pulled them from the table and rushed to get back to the kids.

He found David alone in the hallway. Jen had abandoned him, rushing to fight the thing. She was swinging her aluminum bat hard against the tentacle that held her girlfriend and screaming, sobbing as she swung.

"Drop her! Just drop her!" She yelled as she kept swinging. She never saw the tentacle that was at her feet, slowly rising, wrapping around her without making its presence yet known. Once it was completely around her, it tightened and lifted her off the ground.

"Come on!" Andy yelled as he tried to wedge his hockey stick. He saw how the thing had ahold of Jen and shifted, pulling his hockey stick up to bring it down. He swung it like a bat to hit the tentacle that now had her. It didn't have any more effect on it than Jen's bat had.

Ellis ran past David, working to open the caps on the two shaker bottles. There wasn't a lot and knew he was only going to get one chance as he ran forward. He kept an eye on the three remaining tentacles that were flailing on the floor as though looking for a target, waiting their turn to grab someone. They seemed to pull back as he approached. He was sure it was to lure him into a trap, but could he also be sensing fear from the thing? Did it know what he had in his hand?

He doubted the thing feared him. What had once been innocent-looking brown eyes had fully gone black since the tentacles had emerged, and he could feel them as they watched him approach. No, it didn't fear him. It was hungry for him. It was lusting for all of them.

He ran towards it, ready to go kamikaze and straight in for the kill. As he lumbered forward, he saw as one of the tentacles tensed, then slipped to his side. It was giving him an opening, but he could see out of the corner of his eye how that tentacle was racing to get around so it could wrap around him, pull him in like it had done with Jen.

He kept running. It took less than a few seconds, but as he experienced it, the world seemed to crawl to a snail's pace. He saw the tentacle to his side snap towards him, but he ignored it. He wasn't focused on himself. Instead, he only needed to get close enough to the body. Even as he felt the purple tentacle swirl around him and get tight, he was still pushing forward. He made it to only being a few feet from the thing, and he threw the contents of the jar at the face of the girl.

As soon as it struck, her face erupted in smoke and fire, a scream erupting from deep within the gut that bellowed forth, reverberating the surrounding walls. The creature upstairs heard it, and the walls trembled with more ferocity, as there was a loud crash from up there.

Ellis felt the tentacle around his waist squeeze, then release before he found himself falling to the floor. He landed hard and rolled off balance on top of someone else.

"Bruh!" he heard exclaimed beneath him and rolled off with hands under him, trying to push himself off faster. Ellis struggled to get free and was hit hard with a flailing tentacle that had him fall back, his second saltshaker clattering to the floor. He heard it hit the hardwood floor but couldn't see it through the mesh of tentacles and limbs, as Jen and Clara had both also been released and were floundering for their balance. Jen was quick and the first one to her feet. She was trying to help Clara, but Clara was still not fully there, her eyes glazed over, and she kept looking around as though she couldn't quite understand where she was or who they were.

A tentacle slammed into Jen, and she was pushed back onto the stairs, landing on their uneven edges. Ellis could hear the air get knocked out of her from where he was across the hallway.

He was still trying to stand, using the wall behind him to get his own balance. The thing had hit him like a freight train, and he was pushing away the stars that danced at the edge of his vision. Another tentacle swung past him. He felt the breeze of it just missing him. It wasn't trying to hit him, and they seemed completely out of control, the thing flailing as it fought the fire rampaging its fake face.

He tried to survey the madness, but more tentacles were swinging around. Andy took a hit and was slammed into the corner. Ellis knew they needed to get away from it. Whatever their next plan was, they needed to get out of reach first. Then they could try escaping through the back. Where they would go from there, he had no clue.

Andy was the closest. Ellis got low and started to work his way towards him. He was feeling along the wall, keeping his back pressed against it. That way, nothing came from behind and gave him additional support, as he loved. The fact that he was getting older, and his knees hurt to squat like that too much, had nothing to do with it. He tried to convince himself of that as he moved closer.

Ellis reached him as Andy was still shaking it off and pulled to get him to go with him. Andy fought him at first, but stopped when he saw it was Ellis.

"Come on!"

Ellis got him to his feet and was pushing him down the hall when he noticed that the air wasn't as chaotic as it had been. He pushed Andy hard toward the hall and turned to face it. The left side of the thing's face had melted away, or so the part of it that had looked human. Underneath, there were black scales with red glowing light spilling out from between them. The light seemed to fade in and out, growing dim and then bright, pulsating.

For the first time, that face showed signs of emotion, as he could see the anger that glared from those black eyes, the ones that were locked on him.

"Run! Go, go, go!" Ellis yelled at Andy, who had turned and was standing dumbfounded in the hall. He looked at the creature and then looked at Ellis before he turned to run. Ellis was trying to take measure of how he was going to react when those tentacles launched towards him. He even hunched down as though he was a linebacker going to take out the running back, coming straight toward him.

Out of the corner of his eye, he watched as Jen was helping Clara get away, moving to the base of the stairs. *Damn*, that wasn't far enough, and it cut them off from any good option. No, there was no good option for them. Jen was right, she had nowhere else to take her as there was a tangle of tentacles between her and the hallway.

The tentacles twitched in unison. He flinched, then tensed again, trying to anticipate its next move.

CHAPTER 28

For all the scenarios he played in his head, he was wrong. The tentacles all moved at once and at the first sign of their movement, he leapt to his right, reaching for the living room and the aluminum bat that had rolled there. He landed, hard, on the floor, half expecting at least one of the tentacles to catch him. He never expected to reach the bat, but figured there was always a chance, and the distraction may have opened a path for the two girls. At least with him pulling it away, they should all be able to escape.

It's not like you have anyone waiting for you at home. Save the kids. Save them at all costs.

Not only was it the job and his duty, but it was also his mission currently to get them all out of there, so they'd be safe.

When the tentacles didn't grab him, he quickly stood and ran to grab the bat, turning once he had it, ready to swing at the first tentacle that came for him. He could hear shouting and the shuffling as tentacles were moving and being fought, but none of them were around him.

"No! Don't you take her!" Jen called and Ellis was quickly running back to the hallway. Just as he was close enough to see what was going on, he watched as a tentacle slammed into Jen, launching her into the far hallway wall. She slid slowly to the ground, her legs giving out, supporting her.

The rest of the tentacles had grabbed Clara. It held her, and time slowed as no one moved. Ellis held his breath, waiting for it to turn its attention to him. The thing did turn to him, those dark eyes trying to pull him into one of those mesmerizing stares. He avoided it by looking just above the eyes, avoiding a direct look into those two black holes. It was looking directly at him, but the tentacles held Clara.

Jen was slowly waking up, her head shaking as she pulled herself back to where she was. She must have realized it quickly as her eyes shot open and she was immediately pushing herself back against the wall to give herself distance from the thing. The thing turned from looking at him, to looking at her. That wide unnatural smile somehow managed to grow larger as one of the tentacles wrapped around Clara's head and twisted.

The sound of Clara's spine snap could be heard across the room, but then it didn't stop. The tentacle continued to tighten on Clara's head, wrapping itself around it as though it was a boa constrictor, tightening on its prey. The sound of the skull as it was being crushed, and then the bones grinding together into powder, was sickening.

Brain matter was oozing out from between the tentacle and dripping onto the floor. Clara was gone, but as the tentacle continued to squeeze past the point of the life being taken out of her, her arms and legs were twitching.

Jen briefly burst into tears, but they weren't there long. Ellis watched as the moment of mourning passed quickly and the rage stormed through her, quickly pushing it away. She wiped away the tears with a swipe of her arm as she stood, her eyes locked on the thing.

He figured she must be doing as he had done, as there was no getting sucked into the abyss. She kept that fire burning and kept her focus on the creature.

Tentacles reached out for her, and she let it, only making a move to raise her arms as it wrapped around her, keeping her arms free. It grabbed her, pulled her off her feet and brought it towards her.

Jen showed no fear, only that burning anger.

The thing seemed to pause. It brought her closer, but stopped before pulling her into that large mouth in its midsection. It dropped Clara's corpse to the floor and brought the brain splattered tentacle closer to Jen's face.

When Jen didn't react, it ran the tentacle along her face.

Still, only the anger burned. Her fists tightly clenched as though she was going to try to box the thing. Her breathing quick, almost like snorts. She reminded Ellis of a bull staring down a matador.

The monster and the kid were locked in their own test of will, and Ellis was surprised to find that he wasn't sure who was going to flinch first. The creature seemed to have no idea what to do next. It was almost like eating Jen, or whatever it did, just wasn't enough for it. It needed something else from her, some other kind of nourishment, and Jen just wasn't providing it.

It needed her fear. She wasn't afraid of it. She was pissed off. She was too angry for her to be scared. She wasn't giving it the fear it needed. That must be why it wasn't coming after him, either. He had charged it. He had been fighting it, but he hadn't thought about being afraid of it.

They didn't give it what it needed, either one of them.

Yeah, but if it can't feed from her, it's just going to kill her, like it had for the other one.

He knew what he had to do. He raised the bat, and he charged forward.

It turned to face him and raised its tentacles, ready to smack him away.

And that was the opening that Jen needed. He hadn't seen her pick it up. He hadn't realized that she had been holding it. With her clenched fists, it seemed natural with her angry posture. Ellis hadn't thought about what had happened to the other saltshaker until he realized it was tightly clenched in her hand.

Jen twisted the cap and threw it into the large open midsection mouth of the creature.

As soon as its contents made contact with the darkness within, the mouth closed. It was quick and sudden; the tentacles releasing her and pulling back from how they were attacking. Then the creature was backing away finally, giving them the opening they needed, and Ellis didn't hesitate to take it.

He quickly ran over to Jen and grabbed her arm. She still wanted to fight, but was also so caught up in the retreating monster that she initially tried to push him away. He had to dodge her attack on him and then pulled again. This time, he pulled harder, nearly pulling her off balance as he was turning to rush down the hallway to Andy and her brother.

"Let go of me!"

"Come on! We are getting out of here," he called. As they approached, he scooped up David into his other arm and rushed to the kitchen. He didn't pause for Andy, but made eye contact with him as he rushed by, making sure the kid knew to follow them. Andy got the message.

Ellis was familiar with houses like it. It was a common design for the area, and while they were not all the same, most were. He knew if he went into the kitchen and through it, there would be a back door.

They quickly made their escape, the creature behind them howling its pained scream in their wake.

CHAPTER 29

The moment the cop let loose of Jen's arm once they had made it outside, she stopped for a moment to catch her breath. For all the sports she played, nothing had been as intense as back there had been fighting for her life.

As she did so, as she was bent over gasping for air, the realization that she had just seen her girlfriend murdered was sinking in. The anger that had previously fueled her ebbed, giving way to the sadness that was trying to invade. Thoughts of when they had first met, their first kiss, late nights hanging out in her room, they all flooded her in the few seconds as she tried to suck in air.

She could feel the goo that was drying on her face. That had been a part of Clara just moments ago. She was covered in her dead girlfriend's brain matter. She couldn't stop herself. Vomit erupted from her.

"We have to go before that thing comes after us," the cop said, coming back over to her. He'd checked on the rest of them, her brother, Andy. They had all survived. Why couldn't Clara be there?

"Yo! Bruh, where my sis?" Andy said as he rushed up behind the cop, pulling him around to face him, turning him away so that none of them could see her second eruption spewing from her.

"She didn't-"

"No bruh, where is she?" Andy pushed at the cop and in other circumstances, it would have seemed comical, the short wisp of a teenager pushing the large, broad-shouldered man as though he had any chance of moving him. However, with the tears that were starting to dampen the corner of his eyes, and the desperation etched on his face, no one would find this funny.

"Andy," Jen started, and he immediately turned to her. She could feel a chunk of something at the edge of her lip and could only imagine how she looked to him as she wiped it away. She felt beaten and tired, her face wrecked, and tears streaking through the grime.

"We don't have time for this. We need to keep going." The cop said. He glanced back at the house and then back at them.

"My sis, I'm going back for her." Andy said, and he stepped away from the cop to go to the back door. The cop reached out and grabbed him and wrapped his arms around Andy's head.

"There's nothing you can do. We need to get out of here or you're next."

"It's not the only one. There are more. There's another one watching us right now. It's the one that killed Dad," David said, his voice rough and weak from not being used for nearly a week.

"Davey?" Jen said, rushing over to her little brother and crouching down to look him in the eye. "What do you mean?"

"Who cares? I need to get in there." Andy said while trying to fight his way free from the cop, who squeezed harder before letting the kid go. Andy fell to the ground and Ellis left him there to walk over to the boy.

"How do you know that?" Ellis said

"Davey, are you alright?" Jen asked him, but he wasn't looking at her. He was looking at Ellis as he approached and lowered himself down to David's level.

"How do you know? Where is it?"

"I don't know. I see them. When they... feed, I see them, and I feel weird after."

"Weird? How weird?" Jen asked.

"I don't know, just different."

"Where is it?" The cop demanded, suddenly alert to the surrounding darkness. When they escaped into the backyard, it had triggered the motion sensor lights. That was good for the immediate area they were in, the lit area, but it made the dark around them much harder to see.

He turned his attention back to David.

"I'm not sure. I can feel it. It's close, but the other one is in so much pain. It hurts so much. It makes it hard to think."

"Wait, you feel its pain?" The cop said. Jen pushed him out of the way, and sniffled back the tears, struggling to push down her emotions. She had to be strong. She had to be there for David.

198

"Davey? Are you okay?" Jen said.

Before David could answer, the cop called out, "Hey!" Jen turned to watch him chasing after Andy as he was trying to run to the house. Andy was unsteady on his feet. His run looked more like a drunken jog, but it wasn't the cop that kept him from going back into the house. As he neared the back door, the back of the house collapsed, stopping them both.

They both stood there and could hear the sound of a baby crying coming from under the broken boards and in the smoke of the rubble.

"Bruh, we need to get out of here." Andy said, wiping away the tears. He was stumbling back from the house, afraid of what would happen, what would emerge if he took his eyes off of it.

"Gas. We need to run. There's bound to be gas leaking." The cop yelled and was pulling at Andy to get him moving. By the time they caught up to the rest of them, they were all running across the alley into the neighbors' backyard.

None of them saw the creature that had watched them from the shadows. It had watched them all, drool dripping from its long snout. It knew it could devour them all quickly, make quick work of the group, but what kind of flavor was that? No, it could wait. It wanted to make sure they were properly prepared. He wanted to make sure he seasoned them just right.

So, it followed them, sticking to the shadows, preparing for his meal. It would get them ready for its feast.

CHAPTER 30

David could feel it watching them. He knew it was close, and at times, could even see through its eyes. How it watched them as they moved through the neighborhood, walking down the sidewalk on one of the side streets.

They looked pitiful. All of them looking tired, roughed up, the tall one carrying the bat while the short one had a hockey stick. If it wanted to, it could devour them outright, might even get some flavor by the second or third morsel, but it wasn't a proper meal. The flavor was all in the seasoning and it just took patience to get them just right.

David could feel the other one, too. It still burned with anger, just as the false flesh had burned from its face. It felt cheated. It wanted its meal. It had been left with scraps of seasoning, no substance, on the body it had devoured, and it wanted them.

For a while, David had felt the other one from the house, but it had felt wrong. All of them were unnatural, evil incarnations upon this existence, but something about that felt not fully formed as body, but powerful of mind. That one had tried to take over David's thoughts rather than share this unholy connection. David was relieved he didn't feel that one anymore. It was just... gone.

There are others out there. Most David could just barely feel, some far away while others were closer. Most of them were not so closely shared with him, though there were a few close by that he could feel and had that same familiarity.

It scared him how much he felt around him. He knew they were all coming, and somehow, he knew they were all out for him. They were all coming to get him.

"Where are we going?" Jen asked as she was rushing to keep up with the officer. David watched as she did. She had been staying close to him, and he worried about her. She thought about what the monsters thought and knew they hated her. He had to fight that hatred as it kept clouding his own feelings.

He remembered when the officer had killed Lumy, how it had woken David, cleared his mind, but had also filled him with such anger. He had wanted revenge on the officer for killing it, but then the feeling had faded.

Though David still felt something different now when he looked at the officer.

"Anyone else feel like it's too Ohio?" Andy said.

"Ohio? Can't you speak English?" The officer said.

"Strange, bruh. Strange. It's so quiet. Doesn't that seem wrong?"

The officer looked up and down the street. It did seem quiet, but as David also looked around, he saw families inside, large screen televisions visible through large picture windows. It was quiet, but also unnaturally normal. As they were moving, trying to escape from monsters, the rest of the world seemed like nothing was going on, that everything was as it should be.

"It's just a quiet neighborhood," his sister chimed in. "This is how it normally is this late."

"It's not even late." Andy said.

"It is for this street. Once the streetlights are on, everyone's home and having dinner."

"Just don't seem right."

David looked at the house closest to them. They were watching some boring cop show. The family seemed happy talking to each other as they were watching it.

He wondered why they weren't going up to the door, trying to get their help. They were being chased by monsters. They needed help. Why wasn't the officer taking them to the door and knocking?

"She has a point. If anyone had heard the screaming, that was a block over. I'm sure someone heard the back of the house collapse. Until emergency services show up, there's probably not going to be a lot of ruckus yet," the officer said.

"Hey officer, I just-" his sister started.

"Call me Tommy. Better than just calling me officer, okay?"

"Sure. Tommy, what if people had heard the house collapse and called over to check on us?"

The officer stopped and looked back in the direction they came. It was obvious he had been so caught up in their survival, he hadn't thought about other possibilities, such as what would happen if someone came across the girl monster and it decided to eat them.

"She's not there anymore." He said, which got everyone to turn and stare at him.

"Davey, how do you know that?"

David didn't like the way his sister looked at him.

"Because I can sense her. I can't tell for sure where she is, but I know she's also coming for us. She's coming for me. They're all coming for me. I'm sorry."

"Why do you think that, buddy?" Tommy said, as he walked over to David. He put a hand on David's shoulder as he lowered down to meet his eyes.

"I feel it. They're looking for me."

"Why?"

"I don't know." David said, and he knew it was true, that the things were coming for him. He didn't know why. He was just a kid who woke up with a monster in his closet. Maybe that was it. Maybe it was because he discovered them. There were so many of them out there that he could feel, all hiding. Somehow, he had found them and now they wanted to get him because of it.

And odd enough, it no longer scared him or made him cry. He wanted to... He wanted to feel sad that they were coming for him, that they had killed his dad and were going after people. He felt like he should feel sad about it.

He just didn't.

The officer, David had a hard time thinking of the older man by his name, kept Davids's stare. Finally, he released it and stood, looking around.

"Bruh, you're a cop. Why don't you just call for backup?"

"Okay, let's do this." The officer started walking towards the closest house. David saw the elderly couple still inside turned away from them, not noticing as they neared. They were caught up in watching that cop show.

"Emergency services will be on the way soon enough. Until then, we need a phone. I'll call in and get us some help."

"What are you going to tell them?" His sister asked.

"I have no frickin' idea, but I can call for Detective Price. Maybe by the time I get him on the phone, I'll think of something that doesn't sound like I've lost my mind and kidnapped a group of kids."

"Why not use your cell, bruh?"

Ellis pulled something from his back pocket. David guessed that the mangled piece of metal could have been a phone at one time.

"I felt it break when I was tossed back there. You?"

"Yeah, out of minutes, didn't bring it with me."

David and the officer both turned to look at his sister expectantly.

"In my room, charging. Wasn't expecting to be out here running from demons." She nodded towards Andy, and David wondered if that was in acknowledgement of him calling them demons earlier or something else.

"So, we're going to call in the army?" Andy asked.

The officer looked back at Andy as he rang the doorbell.

"You talk too much." He said in response as he backed up and watched the door, occasionally looking around, scanning for any signs of movement for the monsters stalking them. David stayed where he was. He knew the ones that were stalking them were not the ones to be afraid of. He recognized the feeling for what it was now and turned to look at the large picture window.

Already he could see the cloud of darkness that was filling the room. It was flowing out of some dark shape David couldn't see in the center that had just appeared out of nowhere. The old couple had already been up, on their way to respond to the doorbell, but now they stood there, watching the evil unfold in their own living room.

Then the screaming started. Blood was splattering everywhere in streaks of crimson. Something that looked like it could have been a severed hand slammed into the large window.

The officer, once he heard the first scream, briefly stepped further back to see through the window and once he did, ran to the front door.

"Get back to the street. Stay there." He yelled as he reached the front door. He checked it first and confirmed it was locked. Then he leaned back just enough to bring his foot down on the door.

"Nah, bruh, what you doing?"

"Stay out here!" The officer ran into the house. Inside the window, David could only see darkness filling the room. It was nearly completely black, and the officer was leaving them to go in there.

* * * *

This is really dumb. Just what the hell do you think you're doing? Ellis was chiding himself as he entered into the front hallway of the house. He didn't want to leave the kids alone, but he couldn't just stay out there when people were getting hurt.

There's nothing you can do for them. Get the hell out of the house and keep trying to save the ones you can.

But he knew there were other reasons why he chose to go in there. Through the darkness and the screams, there was something he was looking for. Something they needed if they were going to survive.

* * * *

Jen had to come up and pull her brother back from the window. She wasn't sure what the hell was going on with him. He was suddenly acting so strange. To go from not talking for a week and now he was convinced he was connected to these things. What were they? Aliens, demons, none of this made sense with everyday reality.

She didn't know what was going on inside there, and she didn't care. She just needed to keep David safe. He needed her.

He didn't resist her, but he didn't turn to walk with her either as they made it back to the sidewalk, and then joined Andy on the side of the street.

She looked around at the surrounding darkness. It felt darker without a full moon lighting the sky. Between that and they were in the middle of the block, so no streetlamps to stand under kept them as a part of the shadows.

She felt like she could see things moving in the darkness. Did the shadow from that car parked in the driveway move? Was the pool of light around the street lamps smaller? Everything looked normal, but yet it felt so wrong.

You're letting what Davey said get into your head. Stop that.

She tried at least, as she turned back to look at the house, holding her brother close to her. He never took his eyes off that window, but then she felt him shift. He turned to her suddenly and grabbed hold of her in a tight hug. Her heart skipped a beat as she suddenly feared he knew something had just happened.

Oh my god, the cop just got killed, flashed through her thoughts just as the large picture window exploded and with it, a large round object crashed out onto the front lawn just twenty feet from them.

At first, it just looked like a black soccer ball had landed in front of them, but then it started to unspool itself and long strands of thin wire started to swirl around, cutting through the night air. They spun faster and faster until they were invisible, but Jen could still hear them. There was the high buzzing sound, almost a whistle as they sliced just above the ground. As it did, the grass was getting mowed by the wire, cleanly, as sharp as a blade.

The circle of cut grass was growing, the diameter ever increasing from the center ball. As it grew, Jen realized it was getting closer to them. The ball wasn't moving; it kept swirling around with more of that wire stuff unspooling from the center.

A squirrel started to run across the yard. It started towards them and then stopped. It was trapped between the thing and them.

As the growing circle neared it, a dark fog of black smoke emerged from the ball. The smoke somehow moved against the wind and went after the squirrel. The squirrel, sensing the wrongness of that smoke, ran, but not away from it. It ran from them, into the growing circle. It was like it was sucked into the engine of a jet. The moment the wire struck the squirrel, it was gone in an explosion of blood that somehow made it as far as them, raining on them droplets of squirrel fur, flesh, bone bits and blood.

"He's dead. We need to get out of here." Andy said.

Jen adjusted her brother so that her body was between him and it.

"Go where?" she said, trying to exhume more calm than she had, as she didn't want David to freak out over what they saw. Watching as the dark cloud of smoke was staying where the squirrel had died, as though it was trying to suck out whatever essence it had left behind. Who knew what for sure? It just stayed there for a few seconds, before it started moving again, this time towards them.

"Not here. That's a start. We could go to that old church, the one on Cunningham. Maybe they won't be able to get in there."

Jen looked over at Andy, surprised. That was actually not a terrible idea. If Andy was right, they couldn't get into a church, could they?

Then what, wait for priests to save them?

That idea twisted in her stomach. The idea of relying on old men and their God did not fill her with confidence. They needed to find something else that could stop these things.

There was a sudden screech, a wail as something was in pain. The smoke stopped moving in their direction and Jen could hear the buzzing sound quiet as the wire slowed. Then there was a crack that reverberated through the neighborhood and the wailing ended.

The cop stepped through the dissipating smoke with a canister of salt in one hand and a handgun in the other. The gun was shiny, well-polished gold and looked large in his hand.

"God, I love the second amendment." The cop said with a smile.

"Hate to burst your bubble douche, but this isn't some cheesy action movie. We have things chasing us. And it's not the gun killing these things, so you can blow the second amendment out your ass like all those other cult maganites."

"Bruh, bet you don't like the second amendment when you're pulling someone over. Not when you're on the other end of the barrel."

"We don't have time for this. Sorry I said anything. We need to get out of here."

"Where to?" Jen asked.

"Emergency services should be almost to your house. I say we go back there and get help. Safety in numbers."

"Andy has a good idea."

"Oh, bruh?" The officer drawled out the 'bruh' full of sarcasm and Jen realized that this officer was starting to get tired of them or of all of this, she wasn't sure.

"There's an old church on Cunningham. It's not too far from here. We should be safe there, right?"

"Why the hell you asking me? You're the one who learned everything by watching tv. I don't know what the f-" the cop caught himself mid-sentence and looked at Dave before he continued. "Heck, any of this stuff is."

Andy looked hurt and looked down at his feet. The cop noticed and softened his tone.

"But we are all out of our league. I doubt anyone in emergency services will know anything or any other officers. Maybe a priest will have some answers."

Jen looked around. She noticed a dark shape walking up the center of the street. The shape was over a block away and hadn't reached the streetlight yet, but even at this distance, she noticed there was something wrong with it. She wasn't sure what it was, but how the shape moved, it seemed off.

"I still think we should make it back to your house first. I think getting around more people will keep these things back, and we can get my car. We'll get there a lot faster."

"I don't think people will scare them off." Andy said.

"Um, guys." Jen said, not taking her eyes off the approaching figure. They all turned just in time as the creature was just stepping into the pool of light from the streetlamp and she got to see it for the first time.

David spoke up, and she pushed to keep him behind her.

"They're here."

CHAPTER 31

Jen briefly thought about David and how he just said 'they' in that singsong voice when referencing the beast stepping into the pool of light, before her thoughts were lost to taking in the massive creature. She realized as it came to stand under the steel lamp that it was tall enough for its large, wolf-like head to brush against it.

It seemed to want them to take in its massive sight as it stood there for a moment, taking deep breaths, allowing its massive chest to expand and release. Black smoke erupted from its nostrils with every breath.

It opened that large snout and a tongue that looked to be nearly six feet long looped down and then rose back up to run along the fangs bared at them.

The thing wanted them to watch it. Jen realized, seeing how it was trying to stoke their fear. What was it David had said before, that they were only good to eat when they were terrified? Something about how fear made them taste better. Fear provided this thing with its nourishment.

It wanted them to be afraid. She watched as it took a step forward, its hoofed legs bent backwards, ready to leap at them whenever it chose, and though large, she imagined it was fast to.

It spread its arms wide, and they expanded to the width of the street. Its claws fanned out, spread like that they were as wide as she was tall, with the sharp glistening talons each looking to be a foot long.

This thing was large enough to eat all of them and still be hungry. The sheer size of it was something she struggled to comprehend.

"How much salt do you have left?" Andy asked as he was already backing away down the street.

"Not enough." The cop said. He wasn't backing up yet, but he wasn't taking his eyes off the thing either. "We need to get out of here. Where's the church?"

Jen realized that the creature was between her house and them. There was no chance they could go back for his car.

Car, she hadn't even heard it come up behind them until she heard the roar of its horn. The sound of it cutting through the stillness of the neighborhood and causing her heart to leap into her throat. She was too on edge; the damn thing nearly made her scream. Andy did, and she saw the cop had tightened his finger on the trigger ever so slightly.

They quickly got off to the side of the road instinctively before Jen realized they were getting out of the way just so that the car could drive up to the beast.

She quickly ran to catch the car, but it had already sped past them, watching them as it did. At first the guy behind the wheel was flipping them off, then he saw the gun in the cop's hand, and she saw the fear register on his face. The car went faster, and she could imagine how he was suddenly reaching for his phone to call the police on them. She doubted he ever looked up, that he never saw the death he was driving into.

Clouds of darkness erupted out of the monster like two large wings that unfolded out from its back. They took shape and then wrapped around the car. She heard the screeching of tires. Then she couldn't distinguish between what was louder, the sound of screeching metal as it was being clawed, bent, and torn apart, or that of the screaming man as he was being devoured from the car.

It continued. The man kept screaming, and all they could do was stand there and watch. They had no way to save him. Not from that thing. Not when it could just tear apart cars like they were Barbie dolls, ripping off limbs and discarding pieces. At one point, a foot came flying in their direction and landed just a few meters from where Jen stood.

"What is going on out here?" An angry voice yelled, and Jen turned to see a silver-haired woman standing just outside her front door. She had her front porch light on, and Jen could tell the moment she realized that something wasn't right. The woman's hand rose to cover her mouth. She stopped looking at them, looking instead at the writhing black cloud that hung below the streetlight. The pool of blood that had fallen from the cloud was forming streams in the street. Various pieces of what had once been a man landed in her own front yard.

That was when Jen noticed the purple tentacles emerging from the shadows of the bushes that lined the front of the woman's house. They were coming up behind her, separating her from getting back inside.

"Get away from there!" Jen yelled to her, and the woman shook with a start, with her body visibly quivering. Jen remembered the mesmerizing qualities of that dark fog, as she was certain they had all fallen victim at some point. The woman looked like she had completely forgotten where she was and had no clue of the danger wrapping around her.

The false girl emerged as the tentacles tightened around the old woman. The woman was suddenly aware of where she was and cried out as the creature approached. Those screams grew exceedingly frantic as she fought against the tentacles that had her firmly in its grasp.

Around them, more front porch lights went on. Moments later, screams erupted from inside. The houses around them were going dark.

Just how many of those things were out there?

It was an alien attack. It had to be. ET was finally there, and it was determined to make them dinner.

"We need to go." The officer said.

Jen didn't say anything, she just nodded her head, unable to stop watching as the woman was being torn apart, being eaten piece by piece as the thing was content in taking its time.

With the screams erupting around them, it was clear they were all taking their time and enjoying dinner. So many they have not seen, so many monsters surrounding them.

The once quiet neighborhood was now a cacophony of noise that they needed to escape.

＊ ＊ ＊ ＊

As they ran down the street, David kept looking back at the darkness surrounding the monstrous creature that was ripping apart the car and the man inside it.

He recognized the beast, though it looked so much different from when he'd first seen it a week ago. He knew that was the thing that had killed his dad, but it had grown, changed, evolved.

Each new fear it experienced kept pulling itself in. Its food was nourishing, but it was also changing it, shaping it to more terrors.

David wasn't sure what that meant for them, but knew it wasn't going to stop until it had them. None of them were, and there were so many more of them now.

And all of them were coming after him.

CHAPTER 32

Ellis was out of breath, and from the ragged breathing he heard behind him, he knew the kids were just as tired. They needed to rest, but where? How? Who knew how close those things were, and what would happen if anyone else got near them?

He needed an idea, some sort of game plan. Problem was, he'd never been a planning kind of guy. It's why he was a beat cop. Sure, there were times when he felt like he should have been a detective and he could be a decent investigator. He thought he could be that guy, if given the opportunity.

Well, here was the opportunity, and he had nothing.

They had made it to the busy street that turned into the neighborhood, and none of the things had caught up to him. They were back there, though. The screams behind them, faint in the chorus of the distant highway and other night sounds, were still there and were a constant reminder of what waited for them if they stopped running.

"The church is this way." Andy said, pointing to their right. Ellis looked in that direction. Neither direction looked appealing. Ellis had patrolled this area enough to know that the church did not take them to a good part of town. He was surprised the church was still there with how the area had gone to hell. More and more reports of people getting beaten, mugged, robbed and even the occasional shooting.

There were not going to be a lot of people to come across on their way there, and the people that would see them would not be much better than where they were running from. Either way, their chances of survival were not good.

Other directions had them going into nicer neighborhoods, but that meant more people. More lambs to be led to the slaughter.

Every fiber in his body had him wanting to turn left and head there, where there was a sense of safety, no matter how false that feeling was. He had just come from one neighborhood, similar to the one he would find there. There was nothing keeping what happened back there from taking more of those people.

They had to go right.

Starting that way along the sidewalk, it already felt like everything was getting darker. Could be because there were fewer working streetlights. He looked up and noticed about every third or fourth one; the bulbs were shattered.

They truly were heading into the dark side of town.

Ellis hadn't consciously done it, but he had stopped running. As they had turned to walk down the sidewalk, he had slowed to a brisk walk, and strangely enough, the kids did as well. Though they were all tired. Exhaustion could have had something to do with it.

But there was also traffic. Cars were speeding down the four-lane street, many of them going twenty over the posted speed limits. The whoosh of them as they passed had never been as reassuring as they were now. Signs of everyday life, proof that there was still normalcy in the world, that it wasn't all some nightmare they had drifted into.

The sidewalk was getting darker, which had Ellis scanning around them. They had come upon a stretch with a fence that ran along it, so there was no way of seeing what was on the other side. Across the road was a field that acted as a short barrier before the airport that sat in the distance.

"Hey look."

Ellis looked at Jen and then ahead to where she was pointing.

Ahead, there was a light shining brightly in the darkness. It was hard to see the building as it was away from the road and the fence line hid it from view, but the two rows of gas pumps were hard to miss. The light came from the overhang and the large parking lot.

"Hanks!" Andy called. Ellis smiled. He'd forgotten about the gas station and convenience store. He never filled up there, and while he'd heard calls for it everyone once in a while, it wasn't regular enough that he'd ever been called in to the scene, and they may not have been at this location. The company had locations on what seemed like nearly every street corner, though not as many in the rougher neighborhoods.

"Yeah." Ellis's pace picked up.

"What are we going to do when we get there?" Jen had slowed, pulling David closer to her. Ellis looked at her and could tell the idea of being around people was not appealing. After clearing the hope he allowed himself to feel for that brief second, he remembered why they hadn't gone the other way.

There's just no way. There was no way they could get through this and avoid people completely. Eventually, they were going to need help. He knew this, so why was it turning his stomach thinking about going to that gas station?

Acceptable losses. Wasn't that the military term for it, but who gets to choose who is an acceptable loss? Just because this was a rougher side of town, did that make the people living there any more of an acceptable loss?

Ellis knew there were those in the department that would feel that way. Having been one of the kids who grew up in one of those rougher neighborhoods, he didn't feel that way. No loss was acceptable.

"We have to go in there."

"Why?" Jen said, now stopping from going any closer to the gas station.

"Well, salt seems to be a good defense against these things. They should have some. They have camping supplies and general grocery; I can't imagine them not having salt."

"Yeah bruh, they have it. I know they do."

"So yeah, we're going there and getting salt. We'll get in, get out, and then get to the church. We should be safe there, right?"

Jen looked uncomfortable, but he could see her weighing what he said. He didn't wait for her to come to any conclusion. They didn't have time to debate; they needed to get prepared. They weren't there yet, but he could sense they were coming. He didn't have that sixth sense for them like the kid, but he had cop sense, and that spidey sense was tingling that they were on their way.

It was that gut feeling that kept him on edge until he felt the glow of those fluorescent lights washing over him. He stepped into that parking area, and in the cool night, he swore he could feel warmth filling him. Whether it was imagined or not, he couldn't help heaving a big sigh of relief at having made it there.

"Let's get in and get out. We don't want those things catching up with us here." Ellis said as he rushed to cross to the store.

"Why not bruh? Let's bunker down and call in the backup."

"Because she's right. We don't want anyone else getting killed because of us. They're after us."

"No bruh, kid said it-"

"His name's David." Jen interrupted him, but he ignored her and kept on.

"it's after him, bruh."

"Yeah, and you what? Want us to leave the boy alone? That's not going to happen. You come with us, fine. You're following us, fine. But we're getting in, getting out and moving on. You suggested the church. Right? Now it's the best idea we've got. Don't confuse this place as somewhere that we're safe. This is just a buffet on the larger menu if these things get here and find us."

Ellis looked over at Jen and was glaring at Andy, who, for his part, looked like he was ready to get away from all of them. He looked back and forth between her and him. Then he let his gaze land back on the boy.

The wheels were turning, and Ellis knew the kid was weighing his options. To be honest, Ellis was surprised it had taken this long for the kid to do the math. If Ellis was in his shoes and was a young kid who hadn't sworn to protect, hell, if Ellis had more to live for, he might have second guessed himself. The kid didn't have any of that. He only had to worry about his own survival.

But would these demon things stop chasing Andy just because he stopped running with them? Ellis knew that was the question Andy was wrestling with, because even Ellis wasn't sure of the answer. Though he suspected David knew something about it.

Ellis thought about the octopus in the hospital. David had been holding it. None of them knew where it had come from, but Ellis recognized it. It had been his best friend, the one they'd won for him at a carnival. It was just a cheap little toy, but Tyler had wanted it. Ellis had spent nearly thirty dollars to win it, but the joy that lit his son's eyes when he handed it to him... Ellis would have spent a thousand dollars to see that smile again, that happiness.

But those purple tentacles, the ones from the fake girl. He knew he had thought there was something similar to them. Purple tentacles like that of a once given purple octopus.

Jen and David had rushed past him when he had stopped to see what Andy would have decided. Ellis could see Andy finally run the numbers and decided he was safer to stay with them rather than go his own way and followed them. Ellis, however, paused for a minute. He turned to watch them go into the gas station, watching as David clung to his sister as she held the door for him. Ellis watched as he turned back to look at him.

Those were the eyes of a child, so lost, full of fear and confusion, sadness for all that had happened in the last few days. Those eyes looked at him, and Ellis pushed away all his questions about him. There was something off about him, but he still needed Ellis. They all did.

CHAPTER 33

Ellis grabbed all the cylinders of salt they had on the shelf, which were a lot of them. He was able to grab six himself, and Andy, who had been sticking close to him, grabbed the remaining three. Jen and David had separated, Jen taking him to the back of the store where, if he remembered correctly, there was a small section that had a few toys.

It was not unlike when we shopped to go camping for a weekend. There was always the last minute stop off for gas and supplies they'd forgotten when they had packed. I'd go grab the supplies, and she would take Tyler back there.

This wasn't the same Hanks, and he wasn't there with his family. He needed to get his mind back on what they were doing, though memories of them kept floating back into his thoughts.

They made their way to the cashier, Andy not saying much since their talk outside, but as they neared the register, he leaned in to speak quietly.

"We should go. We should go now. If we get out of here, the demons are only going after him. We need to get away from him."

Ellis stopped abruptly and turned to glare at the kid. He didn't say anything. He couldn't say anything. Anything he wanted to say would have turned into a thunderous, raging retort. He could hear it in his head.

"WHO THE FUCK DO YOU THINK YOU ARE? GET THE FUCK AWAY FROM ME. I'VE FUCKING TOLD YOU I AM NOT FUCKING GIVING UP ON THEM. GET THE FUCK OUT OF MY FACE AND GET THE FUCK AWAY FROM ME, BRUH."

No, Ellis didn't say a thing. He just glared. He clenched his jaw and slowly turned away from him and focused on the tired-looking older woman who was standing behind the counter. She was watching them with the "please don't get in a fight, I really don't want to have to call the cops," gaze that conveyed just how much she didn't want to be there, and she didn't want to have to deal with anyone.

He nodded at her as she neared and put the salt down on the counter so he could hold one of them up to the barrier glass between him and her. She scanned through the glass, and he heard the familiar beep of it registering the barcode. Outside, he could hear a couple of cars pulling up, their engines revving. He could hear the yelling back and forth as the youths taunted one another. He couldn't make out the words but registered the cadence. It hadn't escalated yet to where there would be trouble, but it was hard to tell sometimes.

Had he been on duty and not on the run from demons, he would have paid more attention.

"Here, get these."

Ellis looked down to see the brightly covered package on the counter as he was reaching for his wallet. "Balloons" was written in childish letters at the top, with each letter being a different color.

"Do you need a bag?" Ellis quickly looked at Jen before turning back to the cashier.

"Yes, please." He said, pulling out the card from his wallet.

"Hey, what's that?" One of the girls in the group outside yelled.

Ellis looked over to see that the teenagers getting gas were all looking back in the direction his group had come from.

"You just insert the card, sir."

"Can you add these please? Did you scan them?"

Ellis ignored them both, Jen and the cashier as he kept watching the kids outside.

Then everything went dark.

Andy screamed, "Oh shit!" The store became hard to see. Barely more than outlines of their surroundings remained lit from the outside.

Outside, the lights over the pumps had gone out as well. In the distance, Ellis could hear a sound that was getting louder. It was a deep roar, but beneath it, what sounded like thousands of pieces of paper being slowly torn, or like old television static that overlapped upon itself, could be heard.

"Not now." The cashier said. "Dammit Tony, you were supposed to make sure the backup generator was fixed."

"We need to get out of here." Andy whined as he looked around, jumping at the slightest twitch of a shadow.

"You can't leave yet. You still need to pay, and with the power out, it's cash only."

"That's not going to be an option." Ellis said, still watching the group. The loud gnawing sound grew louder.

"Don't make me call the cops." The cashier was already holding up her phone, showing she had 9-1-1 already entered and her finger hovering over the call button.

"Yeah, that's not going to help." Ellis said as he flipped open his wallet to reveal his badge opened for her inspection. "Calling them is just going to get them killed."

"Bruh, they're almost here."

There was a loud crash from the back room of the store that caused the glass barrier to shake and some of the more over-stock shelves spilled their contents.

"What was that? Who's back there." The woman said, lowering her phone. She started to pay more attention to them and their harried state. "Are they with you? Are they chasing you?"

Ellis turned to look at the woman. The loud chattering was getting closer and the kids outside were getting visibly worried. Everyone except those actually pumping the gas had gotten back into the cars. The woman behind the counter was looking back and forth, from them, to the cars outside and to the back room. Finally, she looked down at what he presumed was security cameras and froze.

"Miss. Miss, what's your name?"

She didn't look up as she stammered, "An- Anne."

"Anne, your name is Anne? Is that short for Angela?"

She nodded.

"Good. Can you tell me what you see? Is that a security camera feed? How does it still have power? Is it on a battery backup?"

Anne nodded again, still not looking at him.

"Is that a feed for the back room? Can you see what's back there?"

Anne shook her head.

"No."

"No? Is it a feed for outside?

Anne nodded and looked up at the cars outside. He followed her gaze just in time to see the first of them come into view. It wasn't just one of those monsters that came. It was a whole swarm of them.

CHAPTER 34

Jen had been watching the cop talking to the cashier, Annie, or something like that, and grew frustrated. They needed to get ready to protect themselves. This cashier wasn't going to do anything for them.

So, she grabbed one of the packages of the balloons and a thing of salt and turned to head to the bathroom in the back of the store.

That was when the first wave of those things ran towards the hot-rodders out at the pumps.

They weren't like any of the things they had encountered so far. No flailing tentacles, no rows of teeth, at least none that she could see. These were almost like spiders. Lots and lots of spiders, but with only four legs. As far as she could tell, they were about three feet in size, four multi-jointed legs that came to sharp ends, almost making each leg look like one long black talon. They skittered quickly across the parking lot.

There had to be at least twenty or thirty of them that ran across the parking lot and as soon as they got within a few feet of the teens outside who were pumping gas, they leapt into the air and landed on them, knocking them down.

Then those talons tore into flesh, and blood spurted. Pieces of tissue flew, body parts were ripped away, and that clicking sound of insects grew as the next wave reached them and went after the cars.

She turned away from the carnage and grabbed her brother's hand, pulling him with her to the back.

"We need to do something about these windows. Do you have anything to cover them?" Ellis was asking the cashier. Jen didn't turn around, but as she passed one of the stacks of shopping baskets in her path, she grabbed two. They rushed as fast as they could to the bathroom, and once in there, were thankful when the overhead lights came flickering to life. She closed the door and took a good look at her brother.

She expected him to look terrified at all the monsters and demons, but those large, brown innocent eyes of his looked up at her expectantly, watching her.

"You okay?"

He nodded, and she nodded back, taking a deep breath, issuing a long sigh as she did. Then she turned and got to work.

She grabbed the first balloon, poured a decent amount of salt into it, then put the lip of it over the bathroom sink. The balloon quickly filled with water. She tied it, then tested it by gently tossing it up in the air and allowing it to slosh into her expectant hand.

She looked at it again briefly, inspecting her handiwork before carefully putting it into the shopping cart and moving on to the next one.

* * * *

The lights flickered to life and Anne exclaimed, "Thank you, Jesus," while crossing her chest and lowering her head in prayer.

Ellis briefly looked at her before turning his attention back to the carnage outside.

He saw the creatures tearing through the metal to get to the kids. Already the area was red with blood as it not only flooded across the cement lot but covered the gasoline pumps and the cars. There was so much of it. The lot was growing dark as it quickly spread.

"Oh, Heavenly Father!"

Ellis tried to ignore her, though she was not making it easy, her volume getting louder as though she was trying to pray over the increasing noise of the things outside. She must be trying to make sure God could hear her, he thought as he turned away from the monitor.

They had to do something about all the windows. He called out to the cashier, but she was lost in prayer. Maybe reality too. He had to find something himself, but there wasn't much.

As far as he could see, the only thing they had was the large metal shelves the store used to make the aisles. They looked bulky, but there just weren't any other options.

"Hey kid," he pointed to Andy and then the closest shelf. "Help me with this thing." Ellis started to pull on the shelf to separate it from the next section, hoping the sections were not attached.

The cashier pulled herself out of her prayers to call out to them. "You can't do that. What do you think you're doing? That's Hank's property. You need to stop that."

They did, but it had nothing to do with Anne's request. As far as he could figure, the sections were attached. It was either that or they were just too heavy with all the foodstuffs still lining the shelf. It would take too long to clear them, and they didn't have time to separate and break them down.

He inspected the backing even closer and could see that it was just a pegboard. Even if they did get the shelves against the windows, it wouldn't take long before those things would get through.

"Damn it!" Ellis kicked the shelf and immediately regretted it. He wasn't wearing his normal steel toe boots as he'd been off duty. The not as rigid shoe sliced into the metal, and he felt the pain shoot through him. He gritted his teeth, ready to launch another curse into the air, when glass shattered, covering him with a spray of tiny shards.

He turned and saw one of the large, deformed spiders standing only a few feet away from him. He could finally see its hardened shell-like long snout, that was lined with glowing red eyes along the top and pinchers along the side, ending in large mandibles.

It turned towards the cashier, and she screamed as she dropped behind the counter. The thing jumped toward her and slammed into the reinforced glass, bouncing back from it. Ellis was surprised the glass held as it had, and the spider was visibly stunned.

As it recovered, another one emerged from the shattered door, pausing momentarily, studying its fallen brethren. Then it raised up those front two talon like legs and brought them down on the other creature's back and started ripping into its hard shell. An unearthly shriek rattled the shelves as the top creature viciously brought its mandibles into the exposed flesh and started ripping away shreds of the viscus underneath.

Ellis was backing away from it, keeping himself facing towards the front of the store. He couldn't help but watch the carnage, disgusted and terrified about what would happen once it was done, just who would be next.

He realized he wasn't going to need to wait for that one to finish. Another one came through the shattered door and seemed to take in the scene.

Ellis realized that Andy had backed away from that carnage just as he had done, but he had gone in the wrong direction. When Andy tripped backwards over a chip display, the creature turned in his direction, but it wasn't the only one. Andy had been backing up the row closest to the front of the store, the row that ran along the front windows.

"Kid!" was all Ellis got to yell before the window behind him erupted inward, and two talons reached through, piercing the racks above the shelves. They were only inches away from tearing into Andy as well. Ellis turned his back to the front door carnage and ran to the back of the shelves and the opening that allowed him to make his way to the front row. The kid met him there, having turned to run from the thing still fighting to free itself from the rack. Andy didn't have to wait for that one though, as the one who had come through the front door was rushing towards him.

Ellis raised the bat in his hands high above his head, preparing to strike, and Andy, stricken, jumped to get past him, out of the way. Ellis wasn't waiting. He was already bringing down the bat in a lethal blow that, if human, its skull would be shattered.

There was a satisfying crunch when the bat struck that outer shell, but it didn't sink home, deflecting away and throwing Ellis off balance. The thing itself wasn't fazed and fell onto its back talons to bring the front two forward. One stabbed into his leg and the other caught him on his right side. Both of them went through his flesh. The one through his leg came crashing to the ground, pinning him in place. The second was through his side, probably his kidney, and it held him upright.

Ellis screamed in pain until it became too much. The creature had him held there like a pincushion, completely at its mercy, though looking at the nearing mandibles, he knew there was no such thing.

"Back!" He heard someone yell, but it was hard to focus on the voice past his own pain. He could feel his thoughts slipping away, the tearing flesh of his own body being the only things keeping him present. Every movement the thing made sent more ripples of agony.

He could feel his foot jiggling. Such an odd sensation as he also could feel that it was his own muscles twitching, and he had no control. It moved, dancing to its own beat and as it tapped, it sent ribbons of pain from the tip of his toes to the center of his back, which felt like it was a bursting volcano of pain.

He felt a splash of something wet wash over him, and he knew it had to be blood. He was blinded by pain, but he could feel the thrashing around and, as it did, it was pushing, then pulling frantically on the talons embedded in him. It was shaking more violently, and he felt waves upon waves of pain as it did.

He heard it squealing over his own howls of agony. His insides felt like they were being torn apart. He tried to grab the one talon lodged inside his leg, but it felt like steel, sharpened to a razor's edge as evidenced by his burning hands that were covered in his own blood.

The world was beginning to spin around him. The grey that ebbed into the edge of his vision was turning black and growing. It was getting harder to breathe, and the world outside his own mind was slipping further and further away.

He was trying to fight it. The kids, he had to save the kids. He had to get this mother fucking thing off him so he could keep the kids safe. He had to keep fighting. He had to find a way.

His back twisted again; was he being spun around? He wasn't sure, but as the last of his vision blurred out of existence, he could hear laughter. It was a giggling sound of a child's laugh, and it got louder. It grew until it was so loud it was all he could hear and feel as it echoed to a point of pain throughout his head, a needle being ripped through his brain.

And then it was over.

CHAPTER 35

Jen watched the creature she had thrown her second water balloon at writhe in pain. She hoped when she had thrown it, that it would pull its legs back from the cop and she could get in there to save him. Instead, it twisted and turned, squealing in visible agony as it frantically fought against the salt water that had exploded upon its shell.

Then Jen watched in horror as the legs sliced through him, tearing him apart.

"Hand some over! Hand some over!" Andy was yelling at her, and Jen had to look away from the cop. She saw the moment when the fight had left him, and his body had gone limp. He was gone. They no longer had anyone to protect them.

She looked down at David. She had tried to keep him back. She didn't want him witnessing this brutality, but he had watched, and she could see those innocent eyes now looking up at her.

No, there was no one there to protect them anymore. It was going to be just her, and she was going to protect her brother, no matter what.

There was a loud scream, and Jen looked up from David to see that there were half a dozen of them things swarming around the cashier's counter. They were all pecking at the thick glass, and she could see where there were holes in it. Once the first hole appeared, they grew into a frenzy, tearing at it.

Jen wanted to rush over there and launch her water balloons at them, but there was no way she had enough and there were more of those things coming. Two more crashed through the door, fighting with each other to get through the opening, but once inside, they split, with one going for the cashier, the other racing to the sizzling carcass of the one that killed the cop.

"Jen, give me some balloons!" Andy yelled as he reached down to grab from her shopping basket. She wrenched it from him and stepped back, feeling the wetness on her leg the moment she did. She looked down to see water dripping from the basket. Another balloon must have popped. She had to be more careful.

With her other hand, she pushed David back behind her and took another step back. She could feel David keeping close to her.

Andy was terrified. She could see it in his face, and he kept looking back at the creatures. Two of them ignored their fallen brethren and had been slowly coming up the aisle towards them.

Jen and Andy could both see the mandibles twitching as the creatures got closer.

"Jen, please!"

"Slowly get behind me." Jen whispered forcefully, trying to not give these things a reason to jump toward them. So far, they seemed content with slowly approaching. At least behind them narrowed into the hallway that led to the restrooms and the emergency exit.

Andy kept his eyes on the approaching things and followed Jen's direction. She tried to watch it all. She watched the things; she watched Andy, and she kept an eye on his hands as they twitched. She saw his eyes.

He kept looking at the basket that wasn't overflowing but still contained enough balloons to come to the rim. He was looking back and forth at it to her, as though he was waiting to catch an opportunity to grab the basket and run.

"Andy, don't you dare. Get back to the door and get ready to run."

She turned away from him. She had to, as the skittering bastards were getting closer. She slowly reached into her basket and pulled out a red balloon that fit perfectly in her hand. The water inside swooshed around as she raised it, getting ready to throw. She knew once she threw the first one, she'd better be damned sure to grab the next and throw.

She felt the basket lighten and looked down.

"You can't get them both." Andy said as he grabbed one of the balloons, staying at her side. She wished she felt relief at having him there, but he wasn't the cop. He had let the cop die; was the reason the cop was killed, but he was also right. As much as she was willing to try it, she'd never be able to get the second one. Especially with how the last one had taken two balloons to go down.

"Okay. Fine. On two," Jen said, looking at Andy to catch his nod of agreement.

"One...two," she threw her balloon the moment she yelled "two" and it connected squarely into the mandibles to the closest one. She wasn't sure which one Andy had thrown toward. His went nowhere close to either one of them.

"Shit!" Andy screamed, as the one that was unscathed quickly jumped in his direction. He fell back to get away from it, and Jen quickly threw another one of the balloons. This one caught the monster on its side, and it crashed into a shelf nearby. The shelves gave way, and the bags of potato chips behind them exploded, raining chips of every assortment down on the thing. It screeched in pain, as it shook, trying to get away from the salt filled snack that covered it.

There was movement and Jen turned in time to see a third one was making its way towards them, this one moving much faster.

"Go" she yelled. David was already rushing towards the door. Andy was struggling to get up, but was not far behind him.

Jen grabbed another balloon and launched it at the creature. It saw her and moved out of the way, the balloon landing harmlessly to the tile floor. Quickly she grabbed another, then another, throwing them in fast succession as more of them were continuing towards them.

The closest one kept trying to escape from the balloons, but she caught it in the leg, and it backpedaled away from her, only to have the one behind leap on top of it and start attacking its shell. The next one kept coming for her and dodged the next balloon she sent sailing its way.

Behind her, an alarm sounded but was cut short by an explosion outside. The lights again went out, but now there was an orange illumination coming from behind her. In the flickering light, she could see the creature leap towards her. She quickly raised the basket, not thinking about what she was doing, and held it to block. It crashed into the basket and the remaining balloons exploded, dousing the thing with the saltwater contents.

The creature shrieked and fell onto its back, its legs twitching as smoke rose into the air.

She didn't linger to see if there were any more coming. She knew they were, and they had to get out of there. She turned and ran to the open door, rushing as fast as she could.

CHAPTER 36

The cool breeze struck her the moment she emerged from what was becoming the hot and suffocating air of the convenience store, though there was no relief in being outside. The second thing that struck after her escape was Andy's scream, that was quickly cut short. The door slammed behind her, and she knew those things would be coming, but it was hard to focus on them and take in the horror she saw emblazoned in front of her.

There was a large fire blossoming from some small machine house close to the back of the store and the fire had already jumped to burning up the back wall. It allowed her to see the purple, tentacled bitch that had killed her girlfriend. The thing had Andy wrapped in one tentacle and held him in the air. Jen didn't see her brother anywhere and turned around, trying to find him.

"David!" she screamed as something crashed into the door behind her. She quickly fell back against it just in time to feel it as the thing on the other side crashed into it again and again, starting to break through to get her.

"David!" she screamed again. Crying now and she fought against the door. She couldn't see David. He'd gone through the door first, Andy had followed him out, the bitch would have grabbed David first, but she had only seen Andy.

The bitch had to have already eaten him.

Jen struggled to push down the wave of grief that tried to cloud her thoughts, though as she did, the anger tried to replace it.

Something slammed so hard on the other side of the door that she felt herself being pushed forward. She struggled to keep her weight against it and the door slammed shut.

She felt something wet as something slammed against her side of the door. She could feel whatever the wetness was covering her face and wiped it quickly away just for her hand to come back covered in red. She looked down to see what had slammed against the door and saw Andy's head and part of his upper body where it had landed on the cement. His broken, locked in horror face was looking up at her, though one eye had been ripped viciously away so that only one lifeless eye was staring back at her.

Jen looked up at the bitch who still held the rest of Andy in its tentacles and was using different ones to pull at different appendages, ripping them off and drop into its large mouth, occasionally choosing to lob one in her direction, making sure that it had her attention.

Damn, she wished she had more of those balloons. Or had grabbed more of the cans of salt from the cop. They had all those canisters. Why hadn't she grabbed more? They were gone now, or impossible to get to, probably still sitting there on the counter.

The only thing she figured she could do was run. She just wasn't sure if she should run away or run towards it and try to tackle it. She wanted to go after it, though as much as fear and anger wanted to take control, rationally she knew she didn't have a chance no matter how well she played rugby.

But where would she run? Why? If everyone was gone, why keep fighting?

Her jaw hurt as she ground her teeth as she glared. She was daring it to come after her. Her fists were clenched. She was ready to fight.

One of the sharp talon-like legs pierced through the metal door she was pressed against. It was to her side, just above the waist. It had missed her, but not by much.

Andy's foot plopped to the cement by her own shoe, and she grimaced. The thing was taunting her. Jen could feel it was messing with her. Maybe it was trying to make her afraid, make her taste better as Davey had said. Whatever it wanted, it was only pissing her off even more.

"Come on, you she-bitch, let's go!" Jen screaming having had enough. She didn't have her dad, and she didn't have Davey. Then hell with it. She was going to go down fighting.

She grabbed the hockey stick Andy must have dropped when he was taken and ran straight to the tentacled beast. She went in, flailing the stick in the air, swatting at the purple appendages as they tried to take her. She was able to keep them at bay and thought that she was going to make it.

She stopped swinging the long stick and brought it up for a powerful blow on the creature when the remaining tentacles cleared out of her path, and she realized she was running straight into the large open mouth; the teeth shaking with excitement at its impending meal.

She tried to stop, shifting her weight and leaping to the right. The stick was knocked away, out of her hands, and she felt the tentacles wrap around her, keeping her from falling to the ground and rolling away. They lifted her into the air and her breath was forcibly squeezed out of her. She struggled to pull in air, gasping for it, but the more she struggled, the more she saw stars forming in her vision dancing around her.

"No! Not... like... this." She was barely able to get the words to escape from her lips and then she couldn't do it anymore. There was no more air to pull into her lungs.

And then there was plenty of air. It struck her with gale force, and she could feel air pushing its way into her lungs. She took in deep gulps of it, as much as she could as the darkness pulled back from around her. The fire she could see was being pushed by the wind. It flickered at first, but then danced along the side of the building, devouring more of the wall like a ravenous beast starving for its next meal. It made it to the edge of the wall, where Jen could just make out the edge of some wire cage, though what it contained she had no way of seeing. The fire seemed like it was running towards it, pushed by the sudden wind.

Then the air was being torn out of her again, the thing howling in frustration that Jen had been given that last bit of hope. She could feel her ribs rubbing and her bones on the verge of breaking under the crushing force around her.

"1...2... No mo... re bre.. ath for... you." It was a raspy voice, almost a whisper, coming from the thing, and the words were broken up, like it was feeling them out as it tried to speak.

She could feel herself slipping away, her eyes finding it harder to stay open.

Then there was laughter. A child's laugh echoed through her skull. It sounded vaguely familiar, but was from another time, something she couldn't quite place. Even that was fading, though, as she could feel her life being crushed out of her.

CHAPTER 37

The explosion changed everything. She felt life fill her again as she was suddenly able to suck in air. She was tossed free, or so it felt as her mind was still trying to catch up to everything around her after having been without oxygen for so long. The world around her was bright as the sun on the other side of the building was ablaze with warmth and light. It was a fireball of immense intensity that was quickly expanding, but then sucking itself back in.

Reality hit home, hard, when she crashed into the ground. She didn't know how far she had been thrown or at what velocity, as she'd been near unconscious when it had happened. She did know that the ground had hurt, and that the force of it had caused her to roll for a few feet until something stopped her from continuing on.

She was gasping for air. Her lungs were the first to burn with the need for it as her body and mind found themselves waking back up. As more thoughts came to her, she realized that the rest of her body felt like it was on fire. Needles of white-hot pain spread. The worst of it was on her knees and elbows.

Where's the she-bitch? Jen thought as she started to move and test herself and her surroundings? She rolled partially back so she could push herself up and felt all the scrapes on her palms, her forearms and her side. Everything hurt, and she had to fight against it.

She heard the she-bitch howl and looked over to see the fire burning bright behind her, her tentacles flailing angrily as she was thrashing, fighting against something. Jen wasn't sure what, but she guessed it was those spider-like things, as a few were on fire and jumping from the roof of the building.

"Jay jay."

Jen swirled around hearing her brother call out, instantly recognizing the little nickname he had for her when she was younger.

"Davey?"

She couldn't see him. She did see that she'd been thrown to the other end of the back of the building, to where the parking lot was stretched back to the large dumpsters. What had stopped her from rolling any further was a large yellow barrier that kept cars from driving back there. Thank gods, had she rolled any further, she would have been rolling across that unforgiving cement rather than the grass she had landed on.

"Jenny, over here."

She heard his voice again and swore it was coming from the dumpster. She started crawling in that direction, trying to work her way to standing, but her legs were unsteady. She would try to stand but would have to ease herself back to her knees as the world still glittered at the edge of her vision. She felt a ringing in her ears, and she felt nauseous craving a soda. Her mouth had gone dry, and she fantasized about the fountain drinks inside the convenience store. Through all of that, she kept fighting. She kept making her way to where she heard her brother calling out for her.

"Davey!" she called out again, attempting to stand as she did so. He hadn't responded the last time she had called out, and she still didn't see him. The flickering light behind her was casting a lot of shadows, making it hard to keep track of the dancing shapes in front of her. "Davey?"

A sensation of hopelessness washed over her, and for a moment, she wanted to give up. To lie down there and just cry the rest of it away. To have this be where the she-bitch got her, killing her where she lay.

The moment didn't last long because she was not in the habit. She was not in the habit of letting people win or going down without a fight. She took first place, or if she lost, she did so fighting. That she-bitch was not going to take her down waiting for her.

She made it to the dumpster and used it to finally stand. She was unsteady, as evidenced by how she kept falling back down without the support, but once she was up, she stayed. She turned to face the bitch. Her balance wobbled when she pulled her hand away from the support, but she quickly reached out and kept from falling.

"Jen." She heard his soft, innocent voice next to her, and Jen turned to see David standing there, hidden in the shadows behind the dumpster. He was alive, hiding right there.

All sense of balance was suddenly restored as she reached out and pulled him into the tightest hug she had ever given. This time, she let the tears fall, and she didn't care if it made her look weak or girlish. Her brother was alive. She had been so sure she'd lost him, but he was right here.

"Davey." She said, just as another explosion happened on the far side of the building, and then another. Jen didn't turn, she just held her brother.

"They're coming. They're coming for me. I can't hide." Jen could hear the fear in his voice, and she looked down to meet those tear-filled eyes. She wiped away her own tears, reminding herself why she had to keep it together and be strong. She needed him to know she was strong. She had to be it for him.

"Okay. We have to get you somewhere safe. We going to make it, okay?"

"But the offic-"

"Don't worry about him or anyone else. We're going to be fine. You and me. Just as it has always been. You and me, we are going to be fine."

The she-bitch howled in pain, but Jen didn't look in her direction. She could hear it though, the sound they had heard when those skitterers had first arrived. She sensed that more of them were coming, and whatever they were, they seemed to be going after the she-bitch just as much as they were going after anything.

"No, we won't."

"We will. We have each other. We just have to make it to the church."

David was crying even more, and she sensed he was hiding something from her. He looked at the monster, and Jen followed his gaze to see that the she-bitch was fighting with the spider-like things just as they had each other.

Skitterers. Jen didn't know where the name came from, but it seemed right. She watched as the she-bitch was trying to toss the skitterers into the fire so that she could continue after them. More and more of the damned things kept emerging from the burning building after her, and it was more to Jen's point that they needed to go. They needed to get somewhere safe before those things noticed them.

"We need to get going." Jen scanned the rest of the area, surprised that those things seemed to be completely ignoring them and only going after the she-bitch. "Stay quiet. Let's move."

David was so sure all the things were after him, but as Jen led him to the other side of the parking lot, sticking to the shadows along the edge of the way around, none of them followed.

She reached the other end to where the sidewalk led down one of the side streets that would take them to the church and paused to look back. The fire had completely engulfed the building, bursting out from the windows. She didn't see any signs of the skitterers or the she-bitch. None of the horrors they had just survived. There was no trace of the cop that had saved their life up until now, or Andy, though as annoying as he was, had almost been like her second younger brother. Sure, he'd been older than her, but she'd protected him many times from school bullies, and he'd been around so much while she was dating his sister. She couldn't see any of them...

But as she was about to turn away, she did see back just hidden where the fire's light started to disappear into shadow, the man from the party. She remembered his sickly smile and cold eyes and odd suit. He was still wearing it as he watched them.

Then he reached his hand high above his head and slowly started to wave.

CHAPTER 38

They had gone for three blocks and chills were still racing down her spine. She knew she should be on the lookout for monsters, demons, what have you, but as hard as she tried, she could not get the image of the smiling man waving at her out of her thoughts.

"Jay Jay." David tugged on her arm, and she was pulled from her thoughts to look down at his worried face. He hadn't said much since they'd gotten away from the store, and she had been too lost in her own thoughts to try to console him. He had to be terrified of everything going on. She was being a terrible big sister, and she knew it.

"Hey Davey. How are you doing?" She took a look around at the houses, then back to meet her brother's eyes. The street was dark, unlike when they had been in their own neighborhood. There, people were watching television, curtains open wide, no sense of worry to the world outside. This neighborhood, most the houses were dark, doors had bars on them and there were no large screen televisions plainly visible from the road. This was a neighborhood where the residents were more about keeping to themselves and less about watching the world outside.

Jen briefly thought about the monsters coming after them. If the two of them were attacked in the middle of the street there, would anyone notice? Would anyone care or try to help them?

Jen already knew the answer.

Even with the streetlights that lit the street, it was not that bright. The area was still and quiet, not at all like she expected. There was no loud music playing, no cars driving down the street. The houses could be abandoned as far as she knew.

It made Davey's timid voice that much louder in the unsettling silence.

"How much farther?"

"I'm not sure." And she didn't. She wished she did, but she wasn't too familiar with this part of town. She knew where the crossroads were, roughly for when Andy had mentioned the church, but she'd never been to this area of town before. She had no clue how many more blocks they had to go.

In a city as large as Cronenberg, they were bound to come to a church sooner or later. She was surprised they hadn't already. It was like they had all disappeared on them now that they were looking for them. When her mother used to drive them around, it felt like they were everywhere. Her mother had once made a crack about it, how every street corner had to have two things, a liquor store and a church. It was like you couldn't have one without the other.

"We will find it, though, right?"

"Yeah, of course we will. It's on this street. We just follow it until we're there. We can't miss it. It's a big ol' catholic church, so it's going to have large stained-glass windows and a steeple."

"What's a steeple?"

"Um, well, I guess it's a place where people come together to talk to God."

"You mean pray?"

"Yeah, pray."

"Okay." David said. Jen heard what sounded like something scraping through gravel and spun to look where it was coming from.

She found herself looking at one of the houses across the street, but didn't see anything moving. It was a standard orange brick house, almost identical to all the others on the street. She held her breath, continuing to listen for what's over there.

"Why did we never go to church? Shouldn't mom and dad have taken us?"

"Our parents were not churchgoers. I think dad once joked that going into a church would be like putting on a Packer's jacket. It would be blasphemy and flames. Whatever he meant by that."

"Do you think he would have burst into flames going into the church?"

"No, of course not. He was just being silly. Think the joke had more to do with the Packers than church."

"Okay." David kept walking. Jen was trying to keep up but didn't take her eyes off the house. "I'm not going to burst into flames when we go in, will I?"

"Why would you think something like that?"

"I don't know. Something's not right with me. I feel them. I feel them more now. Am I evil?"

"No," Jen stopped walking and lowered herself down to pull her brother into another tight hug. At first, he seemed resilient to let her hold him, but then he melted into her arms. After a few seconds, she loosened her grip so that she could look him in the eyes. She wiped away his fresh tears.

"You are not evil. Evil doesn't exist. Just bad things out there and good people in here." She pointed to his heart as she did.

"I don't feel good."

"Yeah, well, you've been through a lot. It's hard to feel anything right. It's easy when so many bad things happen for you to go numb. We just can't get lost in it, okay?"

She wasn't the best at inspirational speeches and was surprised at herself for her own words. She knew where they were coming from. She felt numb as well. Her father, her mother, her crazy aunt, her nephews, monsters chasing them. It was all crazy, and emotionally, she felt dead inside, numb to it all. She had to be, as she had to keep going. She had to keep him going. She was saying it as much to herself as she was for him.

"Okay." He said back to her, and she saw it then, just how numb he had become. 'Okay' seemed to be what he said to everything now. Where was her brother? The fearless little kid who snuck downstairs after he was supposed to be in bed to watch horror movies with her. Where was the little shit who used to mess with her, joke around with her?

She wished she had more time to think about it as she saw over his shoulder a large shape walking slowly down the street in their direction. It was still over a block away, and she couldn't make out any details, but she knew what it was.

It was the wolf-goat. She knew it had to be. They hadn't seen him in a while. He must have been keeping his distance, waiting for his turn to get them.

"Davey, we need to hurry. You ready to run?"

Davey nodded. "Yeah, I know. They're here. They're all here."

Jen looked at him briefly and then scanned around them. It was then that she noticed how all the shadows around them seemed to be dancing, the darkness completely alive with motion.

"Go!" She grabbed his hand, and they ran.

CHAPTER 39

Jen could run faster, but David would never have been able to keep up with her. After a block of running, she could already hear him breathing heavily and knew he was trying his best. She had to shorten her stride, and she kept his hand in hers so she could sense when he was slowing down.

Occasionally she would look back to check on David, but every time she did, it made her want to run faster, and that wasn't possible. Not without leaving him to the death that followed them.

More things were chasing them. It wasn't just the skitterers, the she-bitch or the wolf goat. These were things straight out of nightmares, rushing to catch them. There were zombies, ghouls, monstrosities that looked like they had once been dogs but were now partly mummified. It was like an army of fear had taken to the streets to chase them. She saw things were digging themselves out from beneath the street to brush off the cement and dirt and break out into a run.

All of this had to be out of some kind of nightmare. She had to be dreaming it.

Her own burning lungs and the terrified eyes of her brother looking up at her were all the reminder that she needed to know this was all real.

Thankfully, she could see the bright lights up ahead and hoped that it was the church. She could see what looked like a large, open lot that was well lit. It was a block away, and she pushed herself to not slow down and when David started to, she tugged on his arm, not letting him. She could hear him crying, but they had to keep going as they were so close.

She thought for sure the things were going to get them. She refused to look back to know just how close they were. Any minute, she expected to feel her burning lungs get pierced through by one of those long talons of the skitterers. It was going to happen; she could taste the sour taste of copper in her mouth expecting blood to explode from it. It was going to happen. They were going to die on the one-yard line, unable to cross over into safety.

But it never happened.

They made it first to a basketball court that, from a distance, she had thought had been a parking lot. If all the lights had been on, it would have been great for summer night games. As it was, only a quarter of the lights were lit, creating pools of light in the sea of darkness. With the fiction they were running from, it would take them running the full length of the court to get to the front of the church.

They were close to it though, the church she had begun to think of as their salvation, and she started to worry as the place was completely dark. She wasn't sure what she had been expecting, but she'd thought there would at least be some light illumination from within. Movies always showed that churches were open all the time, that they were always places of salvation.

The building was a traditional Catholic Church, but darker somehow. Maybe it was just because of the dimly lit court, but the building walls seemed black, being raised and held high by pillars of dark marble. Long stained-glass windows stood high between each pillar, though the imagery was lost to the night. As they neared the front, she could see how it rose higher than the rest, as a large bell tower stood high above them as though trying to rise into the heavens.

She was still running through the court to get around to the front of the building when she mentally asked herself why she hadn't gone to the back door. She was now equal to both, but they could have gone straight to the back door initially. It would have been closer and faster.

Damn, she was cursing to herself, and realized she needed to get out of her own head. In sports, she didn't have time to second guess. You made a decision; you owned it and committed one hundred percent. She could see the front, or at least the bushes that were the landscaping at the corner of the building. They were going to make it. They were getting closer, though she could hear the skitterers behind them getting louder. She heard popping sounds and saw some of the light casting her shadow forward disappear, and her heart clenched in her chest.

"Faster. Hurry." She said to David and could feel him trying harder.

They made it and she chanced to look back to see just how close the things were and stopped dead in her tracks.

She didn't see any of the monstrosities. They were all gone. Only the smiling man was there, standing in the center of the basketball court. The light nearest them was the only one in the area remaining lit, keeping him at the edge of their pool of light, his face just on the verge of being revealed from the darkness. She didn't have to see him, though, to see that large smile.

Quickly, she scanned the shadows around them. She still heard that loud chewing sound of the skitterers, but it was echoing all around them.

David ran up the stairs to the large, heavy wooden doors. There were four sets of them, and he ran to the closest on the left. The doors themselves looked like they could handle a heavy assault, but the stained-glass windows that stood tall on each side weren't going to hold up to an army from hell. If religion alone didn't keep these things out, they were screwed. Jen rushed to catch up with him, but stopped when she saw him just standing there and not going in.

"What's wrong?"

"I'm afraid. I don't want to burst into flames." She could hear him crying and quickly spun him around to pull him into a hug.

"You're not going to burst into flames. Bad people go into churches all the time and none of them blow up."

"But then, how will it keep out the monsters?"

Jen could hear the skitterers and sensed they were gathering behind them. It was that ever present sound of ripping paper and echoing voices, but it was becoming rhythmic as the things were getting closer. It was reminiscent of locusts and their nightly song that would sometimes drone on for hours. It would rise and fall, then rise again before trailing off for a brief reprieve. Then the cycle started all over again.

Jen didn't look back at the things nearing them. She held David tight and focused on pushing away the terror, the frustration, the loss of hope that was threatening to trap her as they stood there.

They were so close to crossing that threshold, and they didn't have time to talk things through. Not when they were almost to the finish line.

"Davey, we have to get inside. I'll explain once we get in there, but we need to get through those doors before those things get here."

"They're already here."

"I know. We have to get in there to get away from them."

"And I won't burn up?

"No, you're not going to burn up. I'll hold your hand and we'll both be okay.

David wiped the tears from his eyes and pulled back from her, nodding as he did.

She straightened and held her hand out to him. Then they turned to the door and reached to open it.

The door didn't budge. It was locked; the church was locked up. All of this, the fighting the way there, the people dying to get them somewhere safe; it had all been for nothing as they couldn't even get into the building.

It was over, and they were both going to die.

CHAPTER 40

Jen looked closer at the door, making out in the dim light the chain that was wrapped around the large ornate handles. So not only were the doors locked, but they were also chained shut.

"No, no, no no no no no," she screamed, thrusting the chains down in frustration. What was this? Do churches close and why are the doors chained shut? Even if the church was locked at night, chaining up the doors seemed extreme.

Jen didn't have time to think about it. They had to get in there.

She turned around to see if there was something they could use to get the doors open and saw the first of the skitterers coming towards them. It was not alone. Another creature that looked like a large hairless rat running on its hind legs was not far behind the spider-like creature. This new monstrosity had long claws that were half the length of its body, and its teeth extended jaggedly beyond its jaw so the mouth couldn't close properly. Its red eyes gleamed with hunger as it raced towards them.

"This way." Jen grabbed David and rushed to the side of the door, dodging out of the way of the two quickly moving creatures. The things missed them but slammed into the front door. The skitterer bounced back and was disoriented. The ratrocity didn't slow. It immediately turned and was clawing its way after them. Jen was flailing to keep the thing away from them, working to keep its short arms with those large claws from slicing at her. It wasn't working as she saw her arms turning red and felt the cuts mingling with the wounds from earlier.

"Jen!" David yelled, and she knew from his terrified voice that more of them had to be coming. She stopped trying to deal with the claws and grabbed the thing by its body. It thrashed violently in her grip, and she struggled to keep hold. She could see the skitterer coming towards her, and she tossed the ratrocity in its direction. The skitterer grabbed it in midair and immediately started tearing apart its flesh. The ratrocity was howling in pain for only a few seconds as it was torn apart.

Jen didn't even have time to breathe as two more of the ratrocities slammed into her. She was able to spin and throw one to the ground, quickly stomping down her foot to hold the beast in place. The other one was on her back, clawing at her face. She could feel chunks of flesh being ripped away as it was getting closer to her left eye. The thing was a fighter and relentless. It was getting closer to her eyes, and she could feel her balance slipping. She kept reaching back, trying to grab at the thing, but every attempt took her hands away from blocking it from more of her face.

It finally tore into her left eye. She felt the claw rake across the base of it, and upon contact with the soft orb, it pressed in. Pain fired through her temples, a pressure like her head being pinned in a vice clamped down caused her to scream. She could feel the slime of the viscous fluid as it oozed down what was left of her cheek. Then she felt herself falling, but was lost in vertigo, no longer able to see the world around her, and she felt another claw dig into her other eye.

She heard the glass breaking. She felt herself land, and then everything else faded away.

★ ★ ★ ★

David watched as Jen fell through the window next to the door, the rat-like thing that had been clawing at her back, jumping away rather than riding her into the church. He had seen it gouge out her eyes, popping them so the white goo dripped down her cheeks before she fell and realized that his sister was probably dead.

He quickly went through following her into the church, careful not to cut himself on any of the broken glass. He held his breath as he crossed the threshold, expecting that at any moment he would feel the flames across his skin, dying in a fiery inferno. In return, all he felt was the cool stuffy air of some place where the heat had not run for some time and the sun was not able to properly warm on its own.

It smelled wrong in there, not at all what he would have expected. The air was sour like bad eggs, and David covered his nose just from the smell.

His sister was on the floor. She wasn't dead after all, just writhing in pain. Her arms were red with blood and torn flesh. He thought she should be bleeding more with how little skin still covered them. Horror movies always showed people bleeding more. She had bled a lot, still, and her face was just as bad. The rat thing had clawed and tore off much of the flesh of her cheeks so that it hung in strands barely connected to what remained. Her eyes were a mass of red and white goo as squashed eyeball was mixed with the blood flowing down the side of her face.

Jen had always been the strong one in their family. The strongest of them all. She took care of him, watched over him. His father was not around much, always gone for work, and their mother often ignored him, being there for him only when it was convenient for her. Often, he felt like she never noticed him.

It was kinda how he got started watching horror movies. He would come downstairs after he was supposed to be asleep, and his sister would be on the couch watching them. He would sneak down and lie on the floor next to the couch. Their mother would go into her own room or hang out with her own friends. Jen would be down there watching them either by herself or with her friend, and he would hide so he could see them.

It didn't take long for him to be discovered, though. Though it wasn't hard, as he would often scream out when a monster jumped out of the closet or off the rooftop to kill someone.

One time, she caught him when it got to a scene where this girl wearing a school uniform and was speaking some language he didn't understand was grabbed by a large sea monster. Clara had snuck up behind him and the moment the girl was grabbed by the creature, Clara tickled him on his sides. He had rolled over, scared beyond what he thought was imaginable to see she was above him, laughing as she continued to tickle.

He watched as she giggled, then stopped when Jen told her to. Clara did but made a rude gesture with her finger before going back to the couch.

David had never been a fan of Jen's friend, and how much she hung out with Jen. It was less time David got to play with her.

"David?" Jen gasped.

"Hey Jay jay."

"Are we safe?"

David looked at the large hole in the glass window. He could see skitterers were out there as well as the rat things pacing back and forth. He could feel their fear. It was the same fear he had felt just a few minutes ago. However, he also knew, like his own, that it was fading.

They were just waiting for the others.

They were all coming now, and he knew that with him being in there, they were not going to stop. He needed his protector now more than ever.

The rat thing that had mauled Jen wasn't pacing like the others. It stood there at the hole looking in, watching him. Its red eyes locked onto his.

He recognized all the creatures that were chasing them. The rat things he had seen in a book. It was one of Andy's books about some game he played. They were some kind of monster that attacked Andy's party. They looked nasty.

He wasn't happy that this one had hurt his sister. He still needed her. She still had to protect him.

The rat-thing took a step back, but it was too late. The rest of them that had been pacing outside the door started to attack it, smelling the fresh blood on its claws. They tore it apart, feasting on its little flesh.

David smiled and looked back down at his sister.

"Davey-" her voice trailed off and he could see her chest heaving as she tried to breathe.

"Jay jay?" He said, knowing she was dying. He couldn't let that happen. She couldn't go yet.

Then she stopped breathing, and her new life began. He could feel her like the others now, and watched as where her eyes had been, two new eyes formed, black orbs completely void of life. Shark's eyes looked up at him as she turned in his direction.

She smiled, revealing long shark teeth growing in her mouth, forcing out the old regular teeth to point fangs with blood dripping from the gums where they had emerged. Her mouth could no longer close properly, and as it tried, the side of the mouth split open, extending out into the already torn flesh of her cheek.

"Da-vey." it said as it slowly stood.

He wasn't safe. He realized it now. It had taken her sister. He needed her. She needed to be with him, and now he was alone.

More of them were coming. As the thing that was his sister stood, he could hear the wolf one climbing up the stairs outside. He had known they had been waiting for it, and now it was here. He needed to get away.

He ran further into the chapel, out of the entryway into the church.

Behind him, he could hear the front doors being ripped away, the crunch of wood being splintered and broken, iron fittings being forcefully ripped from cement.

In his head, he saw the creature through its own eyes, ripping it away and throwing it down the front steps. From his sister's ears, he heard her calling out to him in that raspy voice, still trying to learn how to speak, "Da-vey."

They were all coming. He knew he had to find somewhere he could hide, but where? It was a church, and he saw lots of possibilities, but none he didn't think he'd eventually be found. He had nowhere to go. He needed to get out of there. The church was supposed to be his sanctuary, but they were inside. How was that possible?

No, he needed somewhere that was safer and where there would be people that protected him. He thought about the police officer. He had tried to help them all. If David went to where there would be more of them, they would try to protect him. He should go there.

David tried to think of where the police station was, but wasn't sure. His mom always drove him everywhere, and he didn't know where things were. How would he find it?

David heard them behind him coming to the chapel and he quickly ducked into one of the pews, laying on the bench. It was the worst place to hide, but the only place he could get to before they were inside.

He had to think of where he could go, but there wasn't any place. The only thing he could think of was getting out of there and finding someone to help him. He could run to one of the neighbor's houses and knock on the door. He had to; he had no other options; they were going to find him in there.

He saw the chapel doors rip away. The wolf thing lowered itself, compressing as small as it could make itself as it stepped through. Those long porcupine-like needles that ran down its back scraped across the frame, leaving deep gouges in the wood.

He could feel them all around him. He could hear the skitterers outside crawling on the walls and imagined those sharp legs tearing into him. The rat things were out back, waiting for him to run out there. He could feel their thoughts of ripping into flesh and devouring it with their oversized teeth. They were everywhere; he had no place to go. He saw through all of their eyes as they were all focused on the hunt for him.

There was a loud crash in front of the chapel, then a crashing sound from the back. David didn't have to look up to see what was happening. He watched through wolf-thing's eyes as it grabbed the back pew and ripped it from the floor. It held it in those large claws, breathing heavily as it scanned the room. Then it threw the large piece of wood to the front and watched as it slammed into the wall. The impact made a large hole after the pew fell to the ground.

Dark vines emerged from the hole made by the pew and started to stretch across the wall. They pulsated in rhythm to his heart, and David tried to control his breathing. He didn't like that it was beating in time with him.

Wolf-thing grabbed the next pew and ripped it from its mount on the floor. This time, he threw it faster. Not waiting to see if anything moved. David tried to guess how many more pews were between it and him, but it was hard to tell. David hadn't been counting himself when he had dashed, but knew it couldn't be far.

Breathing. David could hear it breathing. He had thought he had been hearing it through its ears, but no, those were his own ears. It was getting closer to him. He could smell it. He had never noticed the acrid stench of rotten meat before, but with every breath it exhaled, the smell poured over him.

It ran its claws on the back of one of the pews, the sound like nails on a chalkboard amplified and echoed through the tall building. Then it grabbed and tossed the pew like the others. This time, David could feel it as it was ripped up as it had shifted the floor beneath him, some of the floorboards partially pulling up with it, and with the floorboards the carpet that had been covering them.

David could see the monster holding the pew high over its head, as it was now right behind him. His pew was next, but it didn't matter as the wolf-thing was looking down at him, those burning eyes glaring at him.

Wolf-thing tossed the pew to the side as David was already quickly sliding down to the floor. It was trying to grab him to catch him, but it was too big, and he was too quick. It wasn't easy though, as it was right over the pews. If he'd been smaller, it would have been easier, but there was a support beam and some other padded beam that folded up that made it difficult to climb through

"Dav-ey…"

He made it into the next pew just as he felt the floor rising up behind him. The squeal from the metal holding down the pew screamed, howling as it was ripped apart.

David wasn't going to make it into the next pew. He was barely free from the other one and already heard the crash as the one he'd been in was hurled to the front. He had to go faster.

David rushed to the end of the pew, to where he would be in the center aisle. He tripped over the wooden decoration at the end but still stayed on his feet as he emerged in a run, breaking as fast as he could.

He heard a roar that sounded more like a massive bear coming from behind him. It shook the windows, causing them to rattle in their panes. Glass from the front of the church fell over, shattering to the floor. David almost dropped to the floor as he felt weak in his knees as he ran.

He looked back. He couldn't help it, and as soon as he did, he realized his mistake. He stumbled. It was hard to run as he saw the wolf-thing tear the pew he'd just come from and flung it aside like it was nothing, just so it had nothing to keep it from chasing him down.

He saw the hunger in those eyes and felt the craving emanating from it. It was a devourer, and David was his next meal.

David tried to turn himself back around, but he was transfixed by those eyes. He didn't realize that he had stopped running and the wolf-thing was walking towards him, each step shaking the ground. The thing seemed to grow as it was walking, getting bigger as it loomed over him.

Somewhere in the way it moved towards him had screamed to some part of David's mind as he found himself taking steps back. He wasn't running, but some instinct allowed him to keep away from this creature.

It howled again, breaking him out of whatever daze he had slipped into. He turned and ran, only to come face to face with the thing that had been his sister. She was looking down at him with those large black pupils. The veins around them had darkened, purple webs running beneath her skin. It looked like the vines that continued to grow from the holes in the walls at the front of the chapel. Just like those vines, they pulsed with his own heartbeat.

"Dav-ey," that scratchy voice rasped out at him.

This time he did fall back, right onto the hooves of the wolf-thing. It bent over him, its long tongue licking across its long, uneven teeth.

It lowered down to where its snout was just inches from his nose. Now there was no way to avoid that godawful smell as each breath filled his lungs. He could feel his stomach turning and tasted bile at the back of his throat. His eyes burned.

And the room reverberated with a loud booming laugh. It cascaded through the rafters and shook the glass in the windows more violently that when the wolf-thing howled. David could feel his ears grow wet and his hand came away with blood.

Then, as the laughter eased into echoes, someone in the back of the room slowly started to clap.

CHAPTER 41

"Okay David, time to put away your toys. You've had enough fun, haven't you?"

David could hear the footsteps as someone approached them, continuing to slow clap as they walked.

"Hey wolfie, let the boy breathe, will ya?"

The wolf-thing backed away and continued back until David could see the man approaching. It was a tall man wearing an old dirty suit with a long string tie. He had a black old-style hat and a wide, toothy smile.

The man looked down at himself and then back to David.

"Oh, this will not do. I'll tell you, kid, you've got one hell of a dark imagination. Comes from watching too many movies, that's what I think." The man's appearance and suit changed as he talked and suddenly the man looked normal. He was no longer the old smiling man, but was in what looked like a nice suit, brown hair, and a comforting smile. He brushed off his arms, shaking away the last remnants of the old suit.

"Much better." The man said.

"Dav-ey." The thing that has been his sister said. David quickly moved to the side so that he was no longer standing between the old man and what had been his sister. He was looking around, trying to see where he could escape.

The things that had been chasing him seemed afraid of this old man. Was he a priest? David didn't think so, as he didn't look like any priest David had seen in the movies. His suit was nice but nothing like what a priest would wear and he wasn't wearing any robes or white collar.

"Who are you?" David asked, looking at the man, then looking at the back door. Those rat things were still back there, but David wasn't sure if he could run faster than them.

This guy had to be a priest. He was in a church. The demon monsters were afraid of him. Who else could he be?

David looked back at the man, who continued to stand there smiling at him.

"Trust me, David, you don't want to do that." The old man said. His voice was warm and pleasant. David found it relaxing to hear that smooth baritone.

"Do what?"

"Run out there."

"Why not?"

"Because eventually you're going to lose to your creations. These things you've made are amazing. Even to me, I've never seen anything like this, and I've been around for a long time,"

"I didn't make them."

"Just keep telling yourself that. That's why they're running loose, wiping out a whole neighborhood just a mile from here. That's going to be hell to clean up, by the way."

"I didn't make them." Indignation rose in David's voice.

"Hmmm," the old man made a disbelieving face at David and then walked over to the large wolf-thing. The old man ran a finger along one of the long incisors before stepping around to the large creature's back. He flicked the end of one of the porcupine needles, however the needle was solid and didn't flinch.

"Remarkable creature. Do you know where these creatures come from? Not who is creating them, but where their mass comes from?"

"No, I mean. Aren't they demons? Don't they come from hell?"

"Not entirely. That's what is unique. There's a part hellfire, but part something else. They're part-" the old man's voice trailed off as he looked over at David, "human."

"Is that why they didn't burn up in the church?"

"Church? Church!? Oh boy, I hate to disappoint you, but this isn't a church. Oh no, unsanctified a month ago when the Catholics closed it down. You know, lack of interest in the big man, at least in this neighborhood. No, there's nothing holy about this place. In fact, you know what I love to do in unsanctified churches?"

David shook his head, looking again at the back door.

"As soon it is unsanctified, I like to go in and take a nice healthy shit. Not in the bathroom. Oh boy, oh no, I like to go right up there on those stairs, right up to that altar, and drop a nice big deuce right where they had their golden boy statue. Then I like to piss along where all of them would be hypocrites and be on their knees taking communion. They want the blood of Christ, I'll give the piss and shit of me." The old man said. He had walked up to the front of the church and was pointing his finger at the first step. When he finished, he stopped and looked there for a moment as though relishing a memory.

"You know, he's up there. He doesn't give a shit about these apes down here. They're all ants under his magnifying glass and he's turning up the heat. He doesn't care. I'm the man of the people. I've been down here since day one. I've hugged Adam and I've fucked Eve. She wasn't as good as Lilith, but it was a helluva night."

David winced as the old man looked over at him.

"Guess you're a little young for that yet. You'll get there."

"You're the devil?"

"I've been called worse."

"What's worse than the devil?"

"I can think of a few." The old man said as he sat on the carpeted step leading up to the stage. "Boy, we need to talk."

A wave of sound flowed through the skitterers outside, a crescendo of that chewing locust sound. David was surprised by them as they'd grown quiet, and he'd forget they were out there as the old man had been talking.

"Your creatures here, they are impressive. Out of all my spawn, I've never seen anyone do anything like this. I mean, it's amazing. It makes me think you might be the one. You just might be the end of all creation.

"I mean, you make these things, and they are human, demon hybrids. They're like seedlings of hell. No, wait, demonlings. I like it. I love it. I do a lot with marketing and demonlings, that's a winner. It's a name I can sell."

"Sell to who?"

"You think too much. You get caught up in your own head."

David watch as his dead sister was walking around the front of the church, keeping her eyes locked on the man that called himself the devil.

"You actually get into people's heads and find their worst nightmares, as well as create some of from your own. You just need to control it. To harness it. I mean, these have all been great creations, but you need to learn strategy. You can't just start killing everyone, you need a plan.

"And some of your creations did not work. Well, one of them. That big guy. Size of a room with no way to really move. Brought down your house if I believe. I had to put him out of his misery. But hey, you live, you learn, and you've got a lot to learn. You just need dear old dad to guide you."

"You're not my dad," David said, his anger rising.

"Oh see, that I am. That little starlet of a mother of yours, she sold her soul to me a long time ago, though she needed to be careful what she wished for. When it became too much for her, she came to me to get out of our little arrangement. I gave her a way out. She didn't quite live up to her end, though.

"We're going to change that, though. You show promise. I think it's time for me to get a little more hands on in your development. We have some grand things to do together, but you have a lot to learn."

"You're not my dad." This time the anger rose up in David, burning away much of the frustration that had built up during the last week when things had started changing. As he had been filled with more and more creatures' thoughts and emotions that had confused his own, he'd stumbled through how to talk, how to think, how to feel. That was all being pushed away as the anger took hold and he yelled once again at the old man, "You... Are... Not... My... Dad!"

The windows exploded inward in a shower of glass as the skitterers en masse charged the chapel. David took a step back from the old man, not worried they were coming for him. He knew who they were coming for. Before they could reach him, David's dead sister lurched forward and grabbed the man.

David saw the shock on the old man's face as those sharp, serrated teeth tore into his throat. As much as David wanted to stay and watch, he turned and ran for the door. The wolf-thing had already passed him, and the tentacle girl walked through the front door, walking casually to get in on the kill.

Now was his time to escape. He had to push himself, though the uneven floor made it hard. Much of the floorboards were in awkward directions from the pews that had been attached to them being ripped free.

He almost made it to the door when a familiar voice called out to him.

"Hey buddy?" His father, a voice he hadn't heard in over a week and one he never thought he'd hear again, called out to him.

David stopped and looked back in time to see the skitterers attack his dad, but it couldn't be him. He had seen his dad killed by the wolf-thing. He thought he had seen his dad killed. He struggled to remember what had happened, but as hard as he tried, it was a blank as to what he had seen and could remember.

Tears flowed from his cheek. It was the first time in days he felt something more than anger that he'd have to hide from everyone. He couldn't believe it. His dad was right there...

And his dad was being attacked by all of them.

"Stop!" David called out, and all the monsters around him listened. They withdrew from the man they were attacking, creating a path for David to run to him. He did so, and as the man stood, David wrapped his arms around him.

"It's all about control. I told you, kid. Your demonlings here, they're quite the piece of work."

David pulled back and looked up at the man holding him. It was his father's face, but that smile and dark eyes were not.

"You're not my dad," David said, and the wolf-thing was back, getting ready to attack the man. David stepped back, but this time, he wasn't running away.

"I keep telling you, kid," the man started as the wolf-thing bared its lips in a snarl and lunged to attack. However, instead of devouring the man, the man grabbed the wolf-thing by the nape of the neck. As he did so, the wolf-thing shrunk until it looked like a black-haired puppy trying to nip at the man's arm.

The devil dropped the puppy to the ground.

"I am your dad." The devil looked at the door. "Oh good, you're here."

David turned as the devil passed him to greet the rough-looking woman trying to walk over the uneven floor. It took a few minutes for David to recognize his own mother. She looked lost and confused, looking around as though unsure how she got there.

"Now, my dear, our son doesn't believe that I'm his father. Would you like to tell him?"

David's mom watched her approaching husband, only a vague look of recognition. She seemed out of it, like she looked after she'd taken some of her nighttime pills.

"You, your back. Hey hun, look, it's your dad." She said wistfully.

"That's not Dad," David said, again annoyed. Around him, he could hear the rising rhythm of the skitterers' call.

"Sure, it is. That's him. Who else would it be?"

"I said that's not my dad. He killed dad. He controls these things!"

His mom looked around, seeming to notice the creatures around them for the first time.

"No, he didn't kill Sam. You did that. I knew it was you. You like to create things. You always have. You don't remember that dog you had that we had to rid of? We never bought it for you. You just had it one day, and we could tell it wasn't natural. I could. We had to get rid of it before Sam came home from making one of his movies. He would have seen how unnatural it was. Then when it killed the Reed's baby, we knew. I knew it had to go."

"Mom?" David wasn't sure what to say. She wasn't making any sense. They had gotten him a dog last year, but it had run off. It had never attacked anyone.

"He's your dad. He's your real dad." She said.

"And there you have it. Can we get past this? I'm getting bored and have a side piece in SoHo I want to pound before morning." The devil said, walking over to David, who could feel his anger throbbing to attack the man again. As the devil came closer, David noticed that there were no signs that the wolf-thing, his dead sister or the skitterers had attacked him.

"Yeah, so your drugged out slut actress of a mom sold her soul to me. She wanted out of her deal ten years ago, and I offered her a new deal. Raise you. She already had pretty boy as a husband and another kid. You were the perfect little seed in suburbia. Even better, your dipshit of a dad moved you guys out here. Man, did that suck to be you, little miss actress wannabe. You got stuck in cornfields raising the kids while he was off making movies."

The devil was enjoying relishing in her pain as he circled around David. Then he stopped and was suddenly very serious.

"You haven't been living up to your side of the bargain. You haven't been taking care of our little boy. In fact, you've been popping those pills like candy since long before your little circus stunt tonight. Oh, you've been a very bad mommy, and bad mommy's need to be punished." The devil took a step towards David's mom, and there was a part of David, somewhere deep. Maybe it was his last little bit of humanity, some hidden emotion that had not yet been replaced by anger, that had him want to get in front of the Devil and stop him from hurting her. David felt it and somehow found joy in killing that last little emotion inside him.

He watched as the devil moved towards his mother and felt like he wanted to be the one cutting her open. He wanted to feast on her insides. He wasn't sure where all this newfound explosive anger came from, but it spread through him in a fountain of hate that he wanted to use and lash out.

"See, boy, that's what I'm talking about. You gotta control that. Your tapped into hell now, and there is a lot of fury burning through those fires." The devil said without even turning to look back at him. The devil walked up to his mother and ran his finger in a soft caress down her cheek.

"I hate destroying beautiful things."

"I... I can do better." David's mom whimpered, and he could feel the fear emanating from her. Behind him, he could feel the demonlings hunger. They sensed it as well, and they craved to devour it. They hungered for it... at first.

As they continued to feel her fear, they realized how wrong it smelled. It was as though the fear was tainted.

David suddenly had a sense of inspiration that the fear was tainted because the soul was tainted, or the lack thereof.

The demonlings were shuffling away from her, and he could sense their sudden disgust with the foulness of it.

"What do you say, Davey?" The devil asked, and David's stomach churned with his use of David's nickname.

"I say you're not my dad."

"Are you really still harping on that?" The devil turned from his mom, clearly frustrated. "I'm beginning to not give a shit if you are the destroyer. You're beginning to piss me off."

The devil backed away from his mom and, as he did, swiped back, his nails extending into claws and slicing through her throat. As he continued towards David, he continued to change, his skin turning a purplish black color and growing until he was eight feet tall. Long horns sprouted from his forehead. His feet turned into goat hooves and the suit was gone now to show his developed body. His eyes became fire, burning red hot as he now glared down at the boy.

"I'm done with this 'you thinking you have a choice' shit." The devil boomed, his voice now a deep, booming thunderclap in David's ears.

The devil was not the only one who had been changing. Wolf-thing stepped out from behind David, emerging as the large beast it had been before. It snarled at the Devil then leapt over David to get to him. The Devil showed his teeth in a large grin as it was moving towards him, but as it was about to grab it as it had done before, purple tentacles wrapped around him.

The Devil howled in frustration and as he fought against the tentacles, the wolf-thing beat down using his large claws like hammers driving down a nail. Behind David, he heard wood splintering and shattering inward. He didn't have to see that the rat things had broken through the back door and were now racing towards the action, joining the skitterers as they swarmed over the massive eight-foot frame.

They were all thrashing at him, but they were getting stronger. David could feel more control over them, how they worked in sync because he coordinated their attack, and they grew stronger because he poured more into them. Claws were now penetrating that near indestructible black skin.

The only one not fighting him was his sister, who stood between David and the devil. She was staying true to what she always did. She was standing there to protect him. She was guiding him, taking steps back, working him towards the back door.

There was a tremendous roar, and David saw as Wolf-thing ripped off one of the arms and tossed it aside.

Then his sister had him back to the door. He turned to leave, and the old man was standing there, his arm draped around the shoulder of his mom, no signs of her throat being cut. The man was no longer the eight-foot monster, but back to wearing the expensive suit.

"Smoke and mirrors all part of the game. You've got a lot to learn. The anger's good, kid, and I get it your pissed at me. Well, get past it. Get past it, kid, or I'll make sure this night never ends, and you'll see your mother and sister killed over and over. Or I can give them both back to you." The devil snapped his fingers, and his sister was no longer the dead monster standing next to him, but back to her old self. She turned to him, smiling like she used to.

"Davey!" she said as she bent down and gave him a hug.

"Jay jay?" David tried to hug her back, but as he did, he realized he could still feel her, that he was still connected to her. She may have looked alive, but when she pulled back and he looked her in the eye, he could see that this was just for show. It was still his dead sister holding him.

"Yeah, not the real thing, but as close as you're going to get. And hey, look here, you get your dad back." The devil pointed and David turned in time to see wolf-thing getting transformed into his dad, walking towards them with his unforgettable warm smile.

"You can hate all you want. Be angry all you want. Use it, channel it. Just don't let it control you. Now let's see how else we're going to salvage tonight. Got your sister. Your dad's body was never found so we'll say he was just out of town. I have pull with the police so the case will disappear. Who else do we need?"

David watched as tentacle girl was transformed into Clara.

"We don't have that annoying kid, so the story will be he ran away. These things can go." The devil snapped his finger. The rat-things and skitterers exploded in a pop of pink goo, erupting from their bodies.

"Okay. The story goes that daddy came home, and you guys went out and got lucky as a massive gas leak blew up your neighborhood. Your aunt and her kids weren't so lucky as they blew up in your house. Most the houses in your neighborhood are fine but the gas killed everyone.

"Now Davey," David was glaring at the devil, focusing on that smiling face and how he wanted to have wolf-thing tear that smile off it. "There is that anger you need to control. We'll work on that. I'll stop by every now and again. Your family is going to be moving to Washington D.C., so I'll have plenty of people to visit. They love me there. It's a great place. You'll need to be somewhere with a larger body count as your family. Well, they have a special appetite now, and we'll have to keep them well fed."

"You're not my dad."

"Now Davey," His sister said, smiling down at him, those devil burning eyes suddenly glaring at him from her face.

"There's no need to go over that again," his mother said, now her eyes glowing with those burning eyes.

"Everything's going to be fine, bud. We'll get moved out east, I'll stop making horror movies. Maybe I'll even start making those political videos. Plenty of money to be made off politics. The devil is in the details." Wolf-thing, who now looked like his dad, said, his eyes also burning as the face smiled at him.

"The devil is in the details." All of them said in unison.

"Don't worry, my boy. We have big plans for you. Everything is going to be just fine. We're going to have a lot of fun, lots of fun together.

EPILOGUE

It had been a week since what David had start to think of as "devil's night" and he still had a hard time grasping just how much they had fallen back into what on the surface seemed like normality. Seemed, because while it looked and sounded like they were a normal happy family, David knew that underneath, none of it was real. He was trapped in a new reality, one that he was slowly learning. One where, beyond all reason, he was still there in his childhood home, even with the kitchen destroyed, had somehow survived the chaos that destroyed the rest of the neighborhood.

In this new world, he found that the devil was his true father, and demons were scattered throughout the world.

Yes, the devil was his father. It was something he still could not believe. It was harder to understand when there was a copy of his dad living there now, every day when David got home from school.

But that had never been his dad. Each time David saw that face, there was a moment when something twisted inside of him. It was a second for which he missed everything that had been. The man who raised him who would no longer be there.

It was only a brief glimpse into his past before it would be gone. Since David had gained control over the demonlings, something had shifted in him. Rage was always just under the service of his calm exterior, but grief and loss, those emotions were mostly gone. Even when he tried to mourn his parents and his sister, the feelings were not there. Like his family, he felt his own kind of death inside, leaving him a shell of what he was.

He was changing. Each day, things were different. He felt like he was getting older, faster. He was becoming more mature.

The thing that was his sister still tried to talk to him as though she was alive and sometimes, when he was tired, he slipped into believing it. When he did, he would sometimes ask her questions like he would have asked Jen. Most times she stays silent, but sometimes she answers.

He had asked her about what was happening to him. She had told him now that his other parts had been awakened, his growth was accelerated. At first, he hadn't understood what that meant, but a day later it had made perfect sense. Like overnight, he thought differently and was able to grasp what she had told him.

Because the changes weren't just in his mind, the thing that had been his mom had pulled him out of school. This way, strangers wouldn't see him growing taller every day. He was already up to wearing Jen's old clothes and they didn't buy him new as they said his growing wasn't done.

The thing that was not his dad told David yesterday that they would be moving soon. People would notice that David was growing up faster than he should. They needed to get away from people they knew. That means they had to get away from their family.

David thought that it was also because his father's family would realize something was up with his dad. They would figure it out, realize that the imposter was not him.

It's not your dad. It was never your dad. Your dad is the devil.

David never wanted to accept it. It was easier not to accept it. No matter if it was true, he didn't want it to be true. He wanted his family back, but he already learned what happened when you wished for something too hard. He had his family back, even if they were only just for show.

David looked around his room. Last week, everything in there felt like his and that it belonged. Now he didn't care for any of it and seemed to belong to a baby. He was supposed to be packing as they were going on a vacation out east, but couldn't find anything he cared about enough to put in his suitcase. He was not that kid anymore, no matter how much he wanted it all back. They would go on vacation, but David knew they were never coming back. He would never return to sleeping in this room.

Maybe that was for the better. This was the room where all the nightmares happened.

His not-father came into the room, walking much like his dad used to when he wanted to talk. The not-father was always somehow able to mimic David's dad so well that if not for the wrongness and connection David felt to him, he would never have known it wasn't the man who raised him. It was unsettling, and David watched it with apprehension as it sat at the end of his bed. It looked at the open suitcase.

In the week that everything had changed, this was the first time not-father had ever entered into his room like this and something inside David tried to pull at those emotional strings of remembering, but nothing happened. Instead, David sat there waiting for not-father to talk. Through David's connection with him, David could sense the words would be coming from his real father and not the creature on his bed.

"Come on, bud, you need to pack," it said. Not-father smiled a warm smile at him, but David turned away, looking back at his room, his thoughts still lost in how everything had changed in the last week.

It would be easy to lose himself in the illusion of his "new" family. His not-father channeled what David remembered of him and acted like a father should. His sister was as she had always been. Clara, who for some reason David didn't understand, would be going with them and had been living at their house now. While he knew it had to do with him, how it made sense for Clara's parents allowed her to, he didn't understand. They lost both of their children and acted like they had never had kids.

The devil must have done something, but what David was not sure. The one thing David realized over the last week was he had much to learn. The devil had made that night seem like a surreal nightmare, as it had all been covered up to not have happened. The implausible was accepted as truth and no one questioned it.

And in return, David's own nightmares were gone, to be replaced by waking monsters that lived around him.

"You'll like starting a new life."

"Sure." David said, still trying to cope with everything.

"We'll get out there and it'll get easier." Not-father said.

"Okay."

"And once we get there, we'll get a bit to eat. It's been a week, and I'm starving."

David cringed. There it was. The reminder that his not-father wasn't real or was there to guide him and raise him anymore. David was growing up too fast anyway, but they didn't control him, teach him, or nurture him. He controlled them. He wished he were more comfortable with that. If he still felt emotions, he was sure he'd be more scared of it.

The memories of what happened still burned fresh.

His not-father met his eyes, the smile on his face twisting to a smirk. David nodded in response. Not-father was hungry and fixated on food. That's what it saw when it looked at anyone, just a fleshie to be devoured. All of David's children were getting hungry.

They'd get out east, get situated and then he'd let them feed. He hadn't let them for the last week, but their hunger was clouding his thoughts.

They would get to a city, and then he would let them feed. David had a plan, something his father had told him to do. Cities were large and full of so much corruption, so much sin to feed from. Sinners don't taste the best, but they were the easiest to replace. The devil taught him that and reminded him; it was all about the long game.

The devil knew that all too well. It's had spawn before, little demon seeds that had infected the earth. According to the Devil, David was the first with true promise. David just needed to learn and wait.

The devil was in the details, the preparation and planning the long game. David just needed to learn to wait.

"Come on, bud, let's hurry up. We have a plane to catch."

WORD FROM THE AUTHOR

Hey everyone. Thank you for reading my latest book. I hope you enjoyed reading it even half as much as I did writing it.

I had the idea for this book years ago, and the initial concept was to create a prequel book for a later villain in my Invisible Spiders series, and David may still be just that. Maybe, maybe not... who knows what the future will bring?

What I can say is that it was a blast for me to write this book. Creating a character, especially a young one with an active imagination whose every fear would uncontrollably become a monster out to kill him... because he believes they are out to get him, was such an open canvas of things to work with.

It was fun...

And then pulling some of my history, such as before I started writing books, I was trying to be a filmmaker and make movies. I could pull some of that for this book. I was able to pull in some of my own personal trauma; I was able to in a sense, pull in some of my knowledge of working with a child that is currently not speaking. There was so much I could pull from my life and put it into this book that, in a way, this is the most personal book I've ever written.

Because I created that the boy grew up in a household surround by horror movies, something I know plenty about, it also opened the door for little horror movie Easter eggs. I loved having those sprinkled into this book that as I started doing it; I started doing with character names just as much as certain lines and call backs.

For me, it was a lot of fun.

This book took me less than two months to write. I've never had a book fall together so easily. This book was so much fun, and I hope it comes through in the writing.

271

Thank you so much for all your support.
And remember – Stay Spooky everyone!

www.ingramcontent.com/pod-product-compliance
Ingram Content Group UK Ltd.
Pitfield, Milton Keynes, MK11 3LW, UK
UKHW041843280225
455729UK00014B/124/J